Loyalty Is Everything

Lock Down Publications and Ca$h
Presents
Loyalty Is Everything
A Novel by *Molotti*

Loyalty is Everything

Lock Down Publications
Po Box 944
Stockbridge, Ga 30281

Visit our website @
www.lockdownpublications.com

Copyright 2022 by Molotti
Loyalty is Everything

First Edition November 2022
Printed in the United States of America

This is a work of fiction. Names, characters, places, and incidents either are products of the author's imagination or are used fictitiously. Any similarity to actual events or locales or persons, living or dead, is entirely coincidental.

Lock Down Publications
Like our page on Facebook: Lock Down Publications @
www.facebook.com/lockdownpublications.ldp
Book interior design by: **Shawn Walker**
Edited by: **Kiera Northington**

Molotti

Stay Connected with Us!

Text **LOCKDOWN** to 22828 to stay up-to-date with new releases,
sneak peaks, contests and more…
Thank you.

Submission Guideline.

Submit the first three chapters of your completed manuscript to ldpsubmissions@gmail.com, subject line: Your book's title. The manuscript must be in a .doc file and sent as an attachment. Document should be in Times New Roman, double spaced and in size 12 font. Also, provide your synopsis and full contact information. If sending multiple submissions, they must each be in a separate email.

Have a story but no way to send it electronically? You can still submit to LDP/Ca$h Presents. Send in the first three chapters, written or typed, of your completed manuscript to:

LDP: Submissions Dept
Po Box 944
Stockbridge, Ga 30281

DO NOT send original manuscript. Must be a duplicate.

Provide your synopsis and a cover letter containing your full contact information.

Thanks for considering LDP and Ca$h Presents.

Molotti

Prologue

March 31

Lil Ced stood in his bedroom, looking at the body-length mirror hanging on the back of the door. He ran a brush over his freshly cut, deeply waved head, and then fixed the collar on the black suit jacket he wore. Behind him, Shana was sitting on their bed in a beautiful, white wedding gown. "You look amazing," Lil Ced complimented Shana, turning to face her with a small smile on his face. His smile hid his nervousness.

"Thanks. And you look as handsome as I always imagined you'd look on our wedding day," Shana said, forcing herself to smile. The two had been in love since before they knew what love truly was. Lil Ced had never met a woman as perfect as Shana, and Shana had never met a man that could compare to Lil Ced. They were each other's first and only loves. They were best friends and soulmates, with a bond most people never got to experience.

"Girl, I'm in love with you, but this ain't the honeymoon. We're past the infatuation phase, we're riding the thick of love, at times we get sick of love. It seems like we argue every day," Lil Ced sang along with John Legend, staring deep into Shana's big, brown eyes

Shana smiled, showing her perfect white teeth. She knew that was one of Lil Ced's favorite songs, whenever they weren't seeing eye-to-eye, he would put that song on repeat.

They were in an apartment Lil Ced had recently rented, on the northside of Chicago. Nobody knew about the apartment besides them, and that's how they wanted it. Nobody could know where they were, at least not until after tonight.

"What if we went to Idaho or Wyoming? We should be good there, I never hear about anybody getting killed in Wyoming," Shana said.

Lil Ced locked eyes with her and saw a sign of hope, a glimmer of faith and he hated the fact that he had to be the one to ruin that.

"Just because you don't hear about it, don't mean it's not happening, and no matter where we go, they always gone come searching. And even if they don't...the police will," he said, before leaving the room.

Lil Ced returned, holding a white bottle of Bel Air and two plastic cups. "Why won't they just leave us alone and let us be happy?" Shana asked sadly.

That was a good question, one Lil Ced wished he had the answer to. "Because they don't understand how deep this love is, and I'm tired of tryna force them to understand. I'm tired of runnin too, I'm tired of all this shit," Lil Ced gruffed. He could feel himself getting angry, just thinking about everything he and Shana endured over the course of their twenty-two years on earth.

Shana stood up directly in front of Lil Ced. She was five-nine, but the heels she wore added to her height and made her look way taller than Lil Ced, who stood five-eight. Shana was the color of honey straight from the honeycomb, whereas Lil Ced was as dark as a freshly brewed cup of coffee.

"Will you dance with me?" Shana asked as Ed Sheeran and Beyoncé's "Perfect" duet started playing on the Blue-tooth speaker.

"Of course. But take off those heels so we don't look funny," Lil Ced said, but it wasn't like anyone could see them anyway. Shana slid out of her heels and the two lovers danced in each other's arms. "Cause we were just kids when we fell in love, not knowing what it was. I will not give you up this time. Darling, just kiss me slow, your heart is all I own, and in your eyes you're holding mine," Lil Ced sang to Shana. Shana always loved how Lil Ced loved to sing, even though he couldn't sing.

"We are still kids but we're so in love, fighting against all odds, I know we'll be alright this time. Darling, just hold my hand, I'll be your girl, you'll be my man, and I see my future in your eyes. Well baby, I'm dancing in the dark, with you between my arms, barefoot on the grass, while listening to our favorite song." Shana sang Beyoncé's verse while they danced and stared deeply into each other's eyes

This was indeed Shana's favorite song and Lil Ced knew that. "When I saw you in that dress, looking so beautiful, I don't deserve this, Darling, you look perfect tonight," Lil Ced sang. He had tears in his eyes.

"I love you," Lil Ced whispered to Shana.

"I love you more, ugly" she replied. After their dance, they sat on the soft gray carpet and poured cups of champagne. "Do you remember Valentine's Day 2012? You bought me this necklace," Shana asked, touching the gold necklace she wore. Lil Ced took a gulp from his cup before answering.

"How could I forget? I convinced you to ditch school so we could go to the movies."

"And when my daddy caught us, he chased you from 87th to 103rd. He was so mad because he couldn't catch you. I never saw him run so fast!" They shared a laugh together.

"I'm not gonna lie, he had me a lil scared that day," Lil Ced admitted, laughing even louder. Lil Ced dug into his pocket and pulled out a glass vial containing a yellowish liquid. "You ready?" he asked Shana, waving the vial at her.

"As ready as I'll ever be," she replied sadly, the tears she'd been fighting were now dripping down her cheeks.

"Head up, gangsta, what I tell you about all that soft shit?" Lil Ced asked with a fake smile. He tried his best not to show Shana he was just as scared as she was

"You was just crying, so shut up, punk!" Shana teased. Lil Ced twisted the cap off the vial and split its contents between the two cups of champagne.

"I love you, my beautiful wife," Lil Ced told Shana, making her smile.

"And I love you more, my handsome husband." They were both crying now. Lil Ced picked up his cup first and sniffed it. They then wrapped their arms around each other and lifted their cups to each other's mouths.

"Til death do us part," they said in unison before gulping down the cups. Shana's eyes grew as big as two full moons when

Lil Ced started convulsing wildly. Before she could do anything, Shana started convulsing just like Lil Ced. The two lovers laid wrapped together convulsing in a sad ball of love and pain, until everything went black, and all their pain faded away.

Chapter 1

January 1998

Cordale sat in the lobby of Little Mother of Mary's Hospital, toying with the zipper on his leather Avirex jacket. His best friend, Willis, sat to his right with a huge smile spread across his face. "You look nervous as hell, G," he told Cordale. The truth was, Cordale was indeed nervous. He had butterflies flying around his stomach. His girlfriend TayTay was in labor giving birth to their first child.

She begged for him to stay in the room by her side, but he had a weak stomach and knew the sight of her pushing out their son might've made him throw up. "I'm just anxious to see my lil mans, that's all," Cordale said. Willis already had a son and his girlfriend had just given birth to their daughter two weeks ago, so he knew exactly what Cordale was going through.

Willis patted him on the back. "Congratulations G, and welcome to the daddy club," he said as a middle-aged white nurse opened the door to the room where TayTay was delivering.

"He's here!" the nurse smiled, showing all of her teeth. Cordale rushed to the room to see TayTay holding their newborn son. Cordale's older brother, Ladale, stood in the corner of the room with what looked like a smile on his face.

"Look, Cedric, there go yo daddy!" TayTay told their son, smiling from ear to ear. Cordale reached out and grabbed the chocolate baby boy. It surprised him that his son wasn't crying like most newborns did.

"What's up, Lil Ced?" Cordale asked, holding him in the air. He had a Kool-Aid smile on his face. "Here go yo uncles," Cordale said before passing his son to Willis first.

Willis cradled him for a minute before handing him to Ladale. Once he was in Ladale's arms, Lil Ced started crying loudly.

"I see you scared of me, just like yo daddy," Ladale joked, rocking his nephew in his arms.

"You got both of us fucked up!" Cordale mumbled just as his

pager went off. The sound of his pager beeping knocked the smile right off TayTay's face. "You hungry, bae?" he asked her after looking at his pager.

"No," she replied quickly. She knew he was looking for a reason to leave. "Can't it wait, baby? We just had our first child. Please don't let the streets ruin this special moment," TayTay pleaded, already knowing that his pager going off meant he had business to attend to.

"I'll be right back, baby. I promise," Cordale assured her.

"Can't Ladale or Willis go for you?"

"You know it don't work like that," he replied, causing TayTay to smack her lips.

She wasn't worried about him leaving her to go cheat. In the four years they'd been together, she'd never caught him cheating so she didn't question his loyalty. She knew Cordale was a hustler, and if he didn't hustle, they didn't eat. He wasn't just selling bags anymore. He had weight and was building an empire, so he spent a lot of time in the streets. For the most part, TayTay was extremely understanding, but today she had every reason to feel some type of way. "You only been here for a few minutes and yo father leaving you already. Welcome to the world, Cedric," TayTay bitterly told her son, watching his father leave the room.

"You sure you don't wanna stay, bruh?" Ladale asked Cordale once they were in Cordale's Monte Carlo.

"You know how Shaw be actin when I send other people to handle my business," Cordale said.

"Fuck all that shit, mane!" Ladale snapped. "We not 'other people,' we yo business partners and we spending our money too! Why the fuck I gotta sit in the car, like I'm a little ass kid?" he asked. It went like this every time they traveled to the hundreds to grab pounds of weed from a BD named Shaw.

Cordale met Shaw through TayTay, who was Shaw's younger cousin. She introduced the two when Cordale was still grabbing ounces and now, he was buying ten pounds at a time. Not all ten pounds were his, five belonged to Willis, and Ladale only had enough money for one, but they always re-upped together.

Shaw was a BD from 109th and Wabash, and he made it clear to Cordale that he trusted him and him only. No one else, especially none of the GD's from the Low End that he ran with.

Cordale wasn't originally from the Low End. He wasn't even from Chicago. He and Ladale were from South Memphis and had moved to Chicago in 1992, when their father died. They moved on 47th Place with their grandmother, right off of Cottage Grove.

Cordale stayed to himself. Ladale was the one that always wanted to go out and try to make friends. One day the guys that hung out on their block decided to try Ladale, who ran and went to get Cordale, who was younger but more aggressive. Not to mention, he owned a snub nose .357. When Cordale came out to address the guys that chased Ladale, he didn't come aggressive, he simply asked what happened and what was the problem. One guy thought it would be cool to disrespect Cordale, which he found out was a mistake.

Cordale passed his gun to his brother and beat the guy bloody. After the fight, he found out the guys who hung on his block were GD's.

He let them know he and Ladale were GD's from South Memphis and after that, they started to treat the brothers like they were their own. Willis was one of those guys. He and Cordale click instantly and went on to become the best of friends

"You say the same shit every time we come out here to re-up. I'm tired of hearing that shit, bruh," Cordale told his brother calmly.

"If it ain't broke, don't fix it. Business been good," Willis said from the back seat. He too was tired of hearing Ladale complaining.

"And it could be better if we all played our parts better, instead of doing all that partying and spending. We supposed to be stackin all our paper up," Cordale said, not taking his eyes off the road.

"Nigga, you party too," Ladale shot back defensively.

He felt as if his brother's words were directed towards him. "I never said I didn't, bruh. Why do you always point out what the next nigga doin?" Cordale asked, looking at Ladale through the rearview mirror.

"Fuck all that shit, G, you just had yo first child, tonight is a fuckin celebration!" Willis said, trying to diffuse the situation.

"You right folks, pass me that bottle of Hen," Cordale told Willis, who passed him a fifth of Hennessy. Cordale lifted the bottle and took a big gulp before passing it to Ladale.

When they pulled up to Shaw's house, they counted their money, put it together and Cordale got out the car. Cordale knocked twice before Shaw swung the door open and stretched his long frame in the doorway. Then he invited him inside.

Shaw was tall about six foot six, with shoulder-length braids and dark skin. "I had nodded off in this bitch." Shaw yawned, leading him into the kitchen. The kitchen smelled like nothing but weed. Shaw had a scale on the table and a garbage bag full of weed, waiting to get bagged up.

"TayTay had y'all son today, didn't she?" Shaw asked, taking a seat at the table.

"Yeah, we named him Cedric." Cordale smiled.

"Congratulations. I'ma give you a lil something extra to celebrate becoming a father," Shaw told Cordale while pulling pounds out of the garbage bag and putting them on the scale.

"You know you ain't gotta do that, skud, you ain't never came short."

"I know, but I prefer keeping business, business. I'm not gone conduct business with you as if we were family or friends, because that's where niggas fuck up at. Friends and family members get comfortable and think if they fuck up yo money, it'll be cool. I don't never want us to mix business with friendship, you feel me?" Shaw asked and Cordale nodded in agreement. "How many you grabbin?" Shaw asked.

"Ten," Cordale replied, passing him a wad of money. After counting the money, Shaw said, "I'ma give you twenty-five pounds, the ten you paying for, five for becoming a father, and ten on consignment. How that sound?"

"That sound good, but I hate getting shit on consignment

because anything could happen and then I'll be owing you. Naw bruh, I'm good with just the extra five you blessing me with." Shaw liked Cordale. He felt he was a stand-up guy with morals and a money-making mentality. They spoke sports while Shaw weighed every pound. When he was done, Cordale put the pounds in a garbage bag and carried them to the car.

Cordale decided to let Willis and Ladale take over for the night and had them drop him off back at the hospital. When he entered the room TayTay was sound asleep. "I'm back, baby." He woke her up with a kiss on the the forehead.

"Hey baby," TayTay said sleepily. She looked at the clock that hung on the wall and saw he was only gone for a little over an hour and a half. She wasn't mad anymore. She knew he had to handle business to provide. Despite all the long nights in the streets, dodging bullets and ducking the police, Cordale made sure he took care of home, and always treated TayTay good and she appreciated that.

"How you feel, baby?" Cordale asked, taking a seat in the chair next to TayTay's bed.

"My coochie still sore, but I'm ok," she said, making Cordale laugh. "You think you ready to be a mother?"

"I think it's too late for me not to be ready. How about you?" Cordale thought for a moment before answering.

"I hope I'm ready. I pray every night that I can give my son a better life than the one I lived. I want him to be a better man than I am, in every way possible. I don't want to fail as a father," he admitted.

"You won't fail him," TayTay assured him. He thanked her with a kiss.

"I hope he like sports and grow up wantin to be like Mike," Cordale said, thinking of his son's future.

The two spoke about Lil Ced's future until TayTay nodded off. Cordale planned on sleeping in the chair right by her side, but he got a page from Willis. He knew it was concerning money, so he called him from the hospital's phone and had him come pick him up.

Cordale climbed into Willis' Impala and flamed up a Newport. "What the fuck is you doin, G?" Willis asked, screwing his face up. He knew Cordale hated cigarettes.

"I got a son now, G. That shit finally hitting me," Cordale replied, before hitting the cigarette too hard. He started coughing violently. Willis laughed and snatched the cigarette from his hand and put it in his mouth.

"Congratu-fuckin-lations, my nigga. Now let's get this fuckin money so you can feed him," Willis said. He drove to their trap house on 47th Place and parked in front. "I see you got more weed than we had money for. You been stacking forreal, huh?" Willis asked as they entered the trap.

"Naw, he threw me an extra five for becoming a father," Cordale explained, taking a seat on the raggedy brown couch that sat in front of a small TV in the trap's living room.

"I'm taking everything back to the store. It's time to stop playing, mane, we got kids to raise," Cordale said, grabbing the garbage bag containing the pounds. He had already given Ladale two, he passed Willis six and kept seven for himself.

"Who you telling, G? We on the same page. It's Ladale we need to be talking to."

"I know and trust me, bruh, I'ma sit that nigga down and put a bug in his ear." Just as Cordale was finishing his sentence, Ladale walked in the trap, along with two grimy looking niggas.

"What y'all up to?" Ladale asked. His eyes were bloodshot red. It was obvious he was sky high.

"Shit, who the fuck is these niggas?" Willis asked the question Cordale was about to ask.

"Who the fuck is you?" one of the guys gruffed, causing Ladale to chuckle.

"These are a couple of the guys from the ickies," he said.

"Stop bringing niggas in the spot, like we don't hustle outta here," Cordale mugged, tying the garbage bag up. He didn't trust most of the people his brother hung out with.

"They cool, bruh," Ladale said.

"They cool with you. I don't know them niggas. Where my car

keys at? I got shit to do," Cordale said with a slight attitude.

Ladale wanted to take it there because he felt like Cordale was playin him out in front of his boys. He pulled the car keys from his pocket and threw them on the couch.

"I hope you put some gas in my shit," Cordale muttered, picking up his keys. He grabbed the bag of weed. "Aye Will, I'm outta here, G. I'll holla at you in the morning."

Willis got up and grabbed his bag of weed. "I'm bout to call it one too. I'll holla at both of y'all tomorrow," Willis said, following Cordale out the trap.

Molotti

Chapter 2

April 2008

"Yeah, boy! Can't nobody beat me in Madden!" Lil Ced told Blue boastfully, after destroying him in their third game of Madden '08.

"My daddy can beat you," Shana told him intently.

"But yo daddy can't beat me," Lil Ced's father Cordale said. Shana, who was Willis' oldest daughter was born seventeen days before Lil Ced and she loved to throw that in his face whenever they debated.

"Pick the Bears and you gone win," Shana told Blue, who was her younger brother by a year and also her favorite sibling. Over the years, Willis continued to extend his family, while Cordale decided one was enough.

He loved Lil Ced and didn't want any more kids. Lil Ced was the perfect child. He was smart, had manners, was funny, respectful and stayed in a child's place.

Both Cordale and Willis came a long way over the years, constantly expanding their business and now they were the plugs. They had dudes from out of town coming to cop from them. Cordale was able to give his son the best of everything, and he took pride in that. He was also humbled by his success. He knew many men would kill to be in his position, so he never let it get to his head.

"Come with me to check on the chicken," Cordale told Lil Ced, who hopped right up. They were barbecuing at Cordale's house on 47th Place. He had the money to move into a bigger home, in a better neighborhood, but he felt more secure on 47th.

Everybody knew him and he knew everybody. He showed the whole hood love and the hood returned that love, so once his money really started stacking, he didn't feel like he needed to leave the hood. He wasn't worried about getting robbed or someone breaking in his crib. "That chicken look good, don't it, mane?" Cordale asked as he flipped the chicken wings that were cooking on the large grill.

"Yup and I'm ready to taste one." Lil Ced smiled showing his big, half-grown front teeth.

"They not ready yet," Cordale said as Willis and his oldest son, Meechie, entered the backyard. Meechie was carrying two pairs of black boxing gloves.

"I bet you can't beat me in these," Meechie told Lil Ced, dropping a pair of the gloves at his feet. Lil Ced hated Meechie due to the fact that Meechie was nothing but a bully. He was bigger, stronger, and faster than Lil Ced, and he loved to prove it every chance he got.

"I'm bout to play Madden with Blue," Lil Ced replied quickly. In fact, he had spoken too quickly because Blue and Shana were already on their way out the house and into the backyard.

"Lil Ced, I know you ain't scared, is you?" Willis instigated, taking a seat on one of the lawn chairs in the backyard. Lil Ced peeked over at Shana before responding.

"I'm not scared of nobody! I just feel like playing the game," Lil Ced lied. He didn't want to fight Meechie and get beat up, especially not in front of Shana.

"Shana, how yo boyfriend gone protect you and he a punk?" Meechie asked his younger sister, trying to embarass her and Lil Ced.

"Hey! Shana doesn't have a boyfriend," Willis stated sternly, causing Shana to lower her eyes.

"I'm not no punk, dude," Lil Ced mumbled, not taking his eyes off the chicken cooking on the grill. Cordale pretended to be wrapped up in flipping wings. He wanted to see how his son reacted to Meechie's bullying. He didn't raise a coward and it would be a problem if Lil Ced backed down.

"Fight me then," Meechie growled, kicking the gloves at Lil Ced.

Lil Ced looked up at his father, who kept his own eyes on the food. He knew his father would scold him for being a punk, so he reluctantly picked up the gloves and began to put them on.

"I got fifty dollars on Meechie," Willis, who was an avid gambler, told Cordale, before stuffing a handful of hot popcorn into his mouth.

"Bet," Cordale said quickly. Even if he didn't think Lil Ced could win, he didn't show it and he wouldn't. He always showed Lil Ced he believed in him and had his back, no matter what.

The two boys squared up and Meechie attacked first, throwing two wild hooks. One connected with Lil Ced's ear, making him stumble. Lil Ced put his guard up higher and when Meechie came close, he threw a flurry of wild punches that missed, giving Meechie the opportunity to hit him in the nose with a jab. Lil Ced wanted to quit right then and there, but he caught Shana's eyes and saw the worry in her expression and that made him want to fight. He had to prove to her he wasn't a punk.

The two danced around each other, trying to catch their breath. Meechie threw another wild hook that missed and left his face wide open. Lil Ced threw a quick three-punch combo that snapped Meechie's head back. Meechie grew enraged and rushed Lil Ced, throwing haymakers. One connected, putting Lil Ced on his ass. Lil Ced bounced right back up and angrily rushed Meechie, throwing a combination of punches. Only two of the punches hit Meechie before he hit Lil Ced in the mouth with a stiff jab.

"Time out!" Cordale called from where he was eating a hot piece of chicken fresh off the grill. Lil Ced approached his father sheepishly, unsure whether he was doing well enough. He was so mad he was ready to cry, but he couldn't, not in front of his father or Shana. Those were the two he always wanted to impress. "Pick yo head up, mane, you doin good," Cordale told Lil Ced who looked at him in disbelief.

"For real?" Lil Ced asked, surprised.

"Yeah. You lettin him do all that swingin and he tiring his self out. Now all you gotta do is finish him. Swing a lil more."

"And duck," Ladale said, walking up from behind him. "Stop fightin like you scared and stop letting him go on you, use his aggressiveness against him," he added.

Lil Ced looked at his father, who nodded in agreement. "He ain't lyin," Cordale said

"So, swing more and duck?" Lil Ced asked, wiping sweat

away from his forehead with his forearm.

"Basically," Ladale said dryly before pushing Lil Ced back towards the middle of the yard.

Lil Ced moved towards Meechie, who was smiling confidently, like he was enjoying every moment of embarrassing Lil Ced. To Meechie's surprise, Lil Ced swung first, catching him in the lip, drawing blood. Meechie countered with two jabs, forcing Lil Ced to take a step back. Meechie threw a punch Lil Ced weaved and countered with a shot to the eye.

The punch dazed Meechie, Lil Ced saw that, and tried to end the fight with a haymaker that Meechie side-stepped. Meechie then threw two punches that landed on Lil Ced's jaw and forehead. Lil Ced was able to duck the third punch and come up and connect a jaw shattering uppercut that dropped Meechie to the ground with a thud.

"Damn!" Willis chuckled before getting up and going to check on Meechie, who was stretched out over the grass. Lil Ced caught Shana and Blue laughing at their brother's loss. Seeing Shana cheer for him filled Lil Ced with pride.

"I told you!" Cordale told Lil Ced, throwing playful jabs at his stomach.

"That lucky ass punch," Willis said, passing Cordale a crisp, fifty-dollar bill. Cordale handed that fifty and another one to Lil Ced.

"Thanks, Daddy." Lil Ced smiled.

"Don't thank me. You won it," Cordale told Lil Ced.

Lil Ced rushed over to where Shana and Blue were standing sharing a plate of chicken. "Here," Lil Ced, handing Shana both of the fifty-dollar bills.

"What's this for?" Shana asked.

"For being my best friend," Lil Ced answered with a smile on his face. If he wasn't so dark, he might've been blushing. "Well here, take one back," Shana said, confusing Lil Ced.

"Why?" he asked.

"Because you're my best friend, so I want you to have half of it, plus you earned it," Shana explained. Lil Ced examined the fifty before stuffing it back into his pocket. "Here come Uncle Ugly," Shana whispered to Lil Ced, who looked to see his Uncle Ladale approaching.

"Where my cut at, lil nigga?" Ladale asked, holding his hand out. Lil Ced looked at Shana, who was still holding her fifty-dollar bill in her hand. "Don't tell me you gave her all yo money," Ladale said, twisting his face up.

"Nope, we split it," Shana told Ladale, sticking her tongue out at him.

Ladale ignored Shana and mean-mugged his nephew. "Stop bein a sucka. You supposed to make her give you all her money, and when she don't got no more to give you, you leave her alone until she get some more."

After Ladale said this, Lil Ced began to chuckle. "You sound crazy, Uncle."

"You a learn one day," Ladale said before walking off.

"I hate him," Shana said, once Ladale was out of earshot. Ladale was always mean to the kids. Every time he came around, he found a way to harass them. The only times that they were safe was when their fathers were around to make him leave them alone.

"Don't worry about him. We all know he crazy., Lil Ced said, making a funny face, causing Shana and Blue to start laughing.

Back inside the house, Ladale sat at the kitchen table rolling a blunt of weed. "Where Cord go?" he asked TayTay when she entered the kitchen and began making a plate.

"I don't know." She shrugged. "You was just in the back with him, why didn't you ask where he was going?"

"I didn't know he was leavin," Ladale responded dryly. "What's up doe?" he added.

"What you mean, 'what's up?'" TayTay asked, sitting her plate in the microwave.

"See, there you go with that funky ass attitude. I'm just askin what's up and you actin like that's a problem," Ladale snapped.

"Nigga, did you forget this is my house? I can speak however I feel like speaking in my house," TayTay said, rolling her neck. She didn't hate Ladale, but she didn't like him either. She felt like he was a lazy bum that leeched off of Cordale and Willis. Ladale gave her a weird vibe whenever they were alone, she could feel him staring at her in lust and he always said lil slick shit.

"Fuck you too then, stuck-up ass bitch," Ladale spat, getting up from his seat. He hated how TayTay acted so bougie like she was the rawest woman on earth.

TayTay sneered at his disrespect. "I bet you won't call me a bitch while Cordale here!" she shot back.

"Why wouldn't I?"

"Because you know he a beat yo scary ass. You only talk shit when he not around. I been peeped that."

"Bitch please, ain't nobody gone do shit to Ladale," Ladale said, making his way towards the front door. He knew Cordale would have a problem with him disrespecting TayTay, so he was leaving now and would deal with Cordale after his anger settled. This wasn't the first time he and TayTay had had words.

"We gone see!" TayTay yelled, following Ladale to the front porch. She had her cordless house phone in her hand, dialing Cordale's number. Ladale stuck up his middle finger, before climbing into his Grand Prix and speeding off.

Ladale rode through Low End, selling bags of weed to different regulars he knew always needed weed. He had enough weed to sell weight, but he preferred selling bags. In his mind, a stick-up kid would target the weight man, before the guy who was selling bags. Little did he know in Chicago any come up was a good come up.

A crowd of women walking up 61st and Evans caught Ladale's attention. He turned up the radio, which was playing Shawty Lo's "Dunn Dunn," and pulled next to the crowd. "What y'all on?" he asked, rolling down the passenger's side window. The thickest woman in the crowd stopped first.

"Going to get some weed," she said.

"I got some weed. What y'all tryna get?" Ladale asked, putting his car in park. He wanted to get out, but he knew the area was run by the Black Stones, so he stayed in the car.

"We tryna get a seven and we don't want no huff," the thick

woman said, approaching his window.

"Hop in so I can show you what I got," he replied, unlocking his doors. The thick woman got in and he passed her a dub sack of weed. She opened the baggie and took a whiff, before examining the weed through squinted eyes.

"It look goood, how much you want for a quarter?" she asked.

"It's free if you kickin it with me," Ladale replied with a sly grin. This was how he got most of his women, offering them a good time. The woman sitting next to him wasn't pretty at all, but she was thick as hell.

"I can't leave my friends," she said with a smile.

"They can come with us. I got somewhere we can all go and get high."

"Let me ask them," the woman said and climbed out of the car.

She spoke to her friends for a moment before a short, pretty, pigeon-toed woman approached Ladale's window. "You Cordale's brother, ain't you?" she asked.

"I'm Ladale and yeah, Cordale my lil brother," he stated. If it was one thing he hated, it was being known as Cordale's brother and not as his own man. Everybody looked at Cordale as some kind of king and Ladale was just his brother. After talking it over for a few seconds, the women piled into Ladale's car. "Y'all drink?" he asked, pulling off.

"Yeah, we do." the thick one answered, just as Ladale's phone started vibrating. When he saw it was Cordale calling, he turned up the radio so the women in the car couldn't hear his conversation.

"What's up, bruh?" Ladale answered cooly.

"Where you at?" Cordale asked. He could hear in his voice that he was mad.

"I'm ridin, bruh. What's up?"

"You know what's up, nigga, you disrespected TayTay. Now come apologize!" Cordale demanded, causing Ladale to frown up.

"Bruh, she got a funky ass attitude and she snapped on me for no reason, saying all type of shit."

"Bruh, I'm not tryna hear none of that shit. You was man enough to call her out her name, now be man enough to come apologize," Cordale growled, raising his voice.

Ladale could picture TayTay standing next to Cordale smiling, while he called himself checking him. That made him even madder. "That shit dead, G. She not the fuckin Queen of England and I'm not no kid. You trippin, bruh," Ladale said before hanging up in Cordale's face. Cordale called back twice but Ladale rejected both calls

"You ok?" the thick woman asked.

"Yeah, I'm good. What's yo name, by the way?" Ladale asked.

"Eboni with a I."

"Ok, Eboni with a I, roll up. I need to get high," Ladale told her, pulling up to the liquor store on 55th and State.

He knew he would have to see Cordale sooner or later, but it most definitely wouldn't be tonight. He had his mind set on getting high and drunk, before fucking the shit out of Eboni with a I all night long. Almighty Cordale wouldn't be raining on his parade tonight. That thought put a broad smile on his face. He bought a fifth of Svedka and strolled back to his car. He drove around drinking and smoking with the ladies, before settling on a destination. He ended up taking the women to one of their traps on 46th and Ellis. They smoked and drank until Ladale passed out, and the women left him snoring on the couch with his pockets empty.

***

"I'm so Hollygrove, New Orleans, Lilweezyana. Home sweet Home Depot, you will need a hammer!" Lil Ced rapped along with Lil Wayne, while looking out of the window. He was in the car with his father on his way to Willis' house. He was always happy to go over Willis' house because he knew he would see Shana.

"Turn that radio down for a second," Cordale told Lil Ced when his phone started ringing loudly. "Yeah?" he answered. He was quiet for a while before speaking again. "I'm on my way right now," he said before dropping his phone onto his lap. "We gotta make a quick stop," he told Lil Ced who nodded in response. "Do you know what loyalty means?" Cordale asked Lil Ced after riding in silence for a few minutes.

"Yeah," Lil Ced lied.

"What it mean then, smart guy?" Cordale asked, knowing his son wasn't being honest.

Lil Ced looked at the roof of the car like he was thinking about how to best word his response. "How about you just tell me?" he said, making Cordale laugh.

"Loyalty means staying down with someone through thick and thin, right or wrong. When you find out who your real friends are, you stay loyal to them. When you find a good woman and you fall in love, you remain loyal to her. Loyalty is the best characteristic anybody can have. Loyalty is everything," Cordale told Lil Ced, who nodded like he understood everything being explained.

"I'm loyal to Shana and Blue," he said smiling. He always had a smile on his face, even when nothing was worth smiling for.

"That's good and make sure you always remain loyal to them. Everybody won't deserve yo loyalty and everybody won't be loyal to you, remember that."

"Ok, Daddy," Lil Ced replied as Cordale pulled up on 47th and Lake Park.

"Stay right here," he told Lil Ced, before jumping out of the car and approaching a group of men.

The only person in the crowd that Lil Ced recognized was Willis. He watched his father argue with one of the men, before Willis blindsided the guy, knocking him on his ass. Cordale, Willis and two other men proceeded to beat the guy until he was bloody. Lil Ced never saw his father so angry. He was scared to even speak when his father climbed into the car, breathing heavily.

"That's what happens when you're disloyal. If you ever catch a nigga doin some disloyal shit, you fuck him up and cut him off. You should never cross someone you consider your friend, and you only get one chance at loyalty. Once you cross the line, it'll never be the same," Cordale explained as they drove off.

The rest of the ride was silent. Cordale was thinking about his operation and how he could eliminate the ones holding him back. Lil Ced kept repeating the word, *Loyalty*, in his head. He didn't want to end up like the guy who had just got beat up, so he was trying to burn the meaning of loyalty into his memory. Little did they both know, Lil Ced's future would revolve around that motto, "Loyalty is Everything."

Chapter 3

May 2009

Che Che peeked out of the window for the tenth time in the last five minutes. He was in one of Willis' traps on 51st and Calumet, waiting on his replacement to show up. Willis was big on timing, and he did the most whenever somebody was late, so all of his workers made it their duty to show up early. But here it was fifteen minutes after his shift was over, and Che Che's relief still hadn't shown up.

The doorbell to the apartment building rang and Che Che buzzed the door. Seconds later, someone knocked on the door. Che Che swung the door open in a rush to leave and what he saw made his stomach flip. His replacement, a young guy named Lil Charles was stretched out across the hallway floor. In front of him were two men masked up, holding guns.

You know what time it is, nigga," the shorter of the two men barked, aiming his gun at Che Che's face. Che Che tried slamming the door shut, but the taller of the two caught it with his foot and kicked it back open, before storming inside. "Lay yo ass down and don't move," the shorter guy yelled. Che Che complied, all while mentally kicking himself for not checking the peephole before opening the door.

The taller guy ransacked the crib, going to all the right spots, as if he already knew where everything was at. It looked like an inside job and since Lil Charles was beaten half to death, it would look as if Che Che was the one that set it up. The thought alone scared Che Che. He knew Willis would have him killed. The taller guy had a garbage bag full of weed and all the money Che Che made during his shift. He whispered something in the shorter guy's ear before making his way out of the apartment. The shorter guy made the mistake of taking his eyes off Che Che for a split second. That gave Che Che the opportunity to reach under the couch and grab the chrome Smith and Wesson .357 revolver with the black rubber grip.

Che Che fired a round from the floor that made the short guy flinch out of surprise. He fired again and hit the guy in his shoulder, knocking the gun out of his hand. The taller guy was already halfway down the stairs. He never even turned around to see what was going on behind him. The shorter guy took off running down the stairs, but Che Che was up on his feet, not too far behind him. Once he was in the doorway of the apartment, he lined the short guy up and shot him twice in the back.

The impact of the bullets hitting his back, caused the short guy to crash into the front door of the apartment building, knocking it open. When he fell to the ground, the hot concrete burned his face. He looked for his car to see his accomplice had already left him. It didn't matter because he could feel the life draining from his body. He heard the door open and the last thing he saw was a pair of white Air Ones running away from the building.

When Willis picked Che Che up from his grandmother's house, he could feel the anger radiating from Willis like heat. "So, tell me one more time, how did they get in?" Willis asked, not taking his eyes off the road.

"I was in the spot waiting on Lil Charles to get there. He was fifteen minutes late, so when the doorbell rung, I assumed it was him. So, I opened the door, and he was stretched out on the floor with two niggas standing over him, masked up with they pipes out. They had the ups on me," Che Che explained for the fourth time.

"And then what?" Willis asked for the fourth time. He was tryna make sure he didn't miss anything. and he'd been able to grab that Che Che's story didn't change.

"They laid me down in the living room, shorter nigga stood there, while the taller guy went through the spot. Once he bagged everything up, he left out and I grabbed the seven from under the couch and hit the shorter nigga in his arm. Then he tried to take off and I hit him all in his back," Che Che said, before rolling down his window and flaming a Newport.

"I'm glad you was able to clap one of them hoe ass niggas," Willis chuckled, lightening the mood. Willis navigated through the city streets, before pulling into the parking lot of the Checkers on 55th and State. He parked next to a black Hummer H2.

Cordale got out of the Hummer and into Willis' back seat. "You know who it was that got killed?" Willis asked him once the door was closed.

"Naw," Cordale replied.

"It was that BD nigga Devonta that be with Ladale," Willis said, and Cordale started shaking his head.

"Bum ass nigga," he gruffed, before reaching for the Newport Che Che was smoking.

"He was with another nigga that went through the crib like he been there before."

Cordale asked, "And you think that was Ladale?"

It got silent for a while. Then Willis looked at him through the rearview mirror. "I'm not accusing Ladale of nothing. I'm just sayin that shit look suspect."

"If it was Ladale, you would've known immediately by the way he talk."

We both country as hell," Cordale said.

Che Che spoke for the first time since he got in the car. "The taller nigga never spoke out loud. He was silent during the whole robbery until the end, when he whispered something in the other nigga's ear and left out."

Cordale sat silent while digesting the information he'd just received. He knew Ladale was a slimeball and he wouldn't put robbing Che Che past Ladale, but he couldn't see Ladale robbing Willis. They were like brothers. Ladale knew how they felt about loyalty, and he knew the consequence of being disloyal, so Cordale just couldn't see it.

"I'm about to call him now," Cordale said, pulling out his phone and calling Ladale. He put the phone on speaker once Ladale answered the phone.

"What's up, bruh?" Ladale asked.

"Shit, what's up with you?" Cordale answered.

"Shit, I'm chillin with my lil bitch in the hundreds."

"You heard what happened at Willis spot on Calumet?"

Cordale asked.

It got silent for a pause and Ladale asked, "Naw, what happened?"

"Two niggas ran in there masked up and took everything."

"Get the fuck outta here Mane." Ladale said, smacking his lips in disbelief.

"One of the niggas got killed on the way out."

"Fuck him," Ladale said dryly

"It was yo boy Devonta," Cordale said and Ladale got quiet.

"Fuck, dude. Me and him had fell out over some paper he owed me." Cordale saw Willis glance at him through the mirror

"When this happen?" Cordale asked.

"A couple days ago. He owed me for a QP and when I drove him about my money, the bitch ass nigga started talking greasy. I'm glad he dead, his pussy ass got what he deserved," Ladale spat.

"Aight bruh, I was just callin to put you up on game. Hit me up when you in the hood."

"Bet," Ladale said, disconnecting the call.

Willis turned around in his seat and glared at Cordale. "You believe that shit, G?" he asked.

"I don't think Ladale would rob you," Cordale stated firmly.

"Them niggas was just together the day before yesterday, now all of a sudden they fell out? I don't believe that shit at all!" Willis said. He was mad and he didn't hide it.

Cordale opened the door and got out of the car and stretched. "What's done in the darkness always comes to the light, so sooner or later we gone find out," he told Willis before closing the door and jumping into his truck.

***

"I bet you can't do this," Lil Ced challenged Blue before taking off and doing a round off then a backflip, landing sloppily on his feet. He smiled with pride when he saw Shana was watching. Blue took off and tried to do the same, only his roundoff was off and he did an awkward twist instead of a backflip.

Blue got up laughing at his failed attempt. "Let's go in the field and have an apple war," he suggested.

Blue was short and chubby and wasn't much athletic, whereas Lil Ced was short and slender and full of energy. He could run and play all day

One thing Blue was better at than Lil Ced was throwing apples. He could hit you from a mile away. Blue had dark skin with ice blue eyes, that's why they called him Blue. Shana and Willis' youngest child, a little girl named Millie also ran to the crabapple tree.

Shana, unlike Millie, loved rough housing with the boys. She liked to throw apples, play fight, and get dirty. Millie was more of a girly-girl who liked to play with Barbie dolls.

"Shana, do you wanna be on my team?" Lil Ced asked while they snatched the hard crabapples from the tree branches

"No way, not today, y'all always on the same team and Millie always quits on me," Blue complained, stuffing his pockets with apples.

"But you can throw better than both of us, so it's an even match," Shana argued.

Blue looked around the playground and pointed at a tall, light-skinned kid. "Hey you!" Blue yelled, waving the kid over. They always saw the kid at the park and sometimes, he would be with a younger boy and watch Lil Ced and the gang throw apples at each other.

"What's up?" the kid asked Blue.

"We bout to have an apple war, do you wanna be on my team?" Blue asked.

"Who we goin against?" the kid asked.

"My sister Shana, and her boyfriend, Lil Ced." Blue pointed at the two who were filling Lil Ced's White Sox cap up with apples.

"Yeah, I'll play."

"Hey! I got a partner!" Blue yelled to Lil Ced and Shana. Lil Ced trotted over to where they were. He was walking due to all his pockets being stuffed with apples.

"What's your name?" he asked the tall kid.

"Dameian, but they call me Blake."

"Ok Blake, the only rule is don't hurt Shana," Lil Ced told him, pointing a finger in Blake's face. Blake was way taller than Lil Ced, so he had to look down at him.

Shana was standing behind Lil Ced and blushed. "I can take a hit," she said. "So don't hold back."

The war started and lasted an hour before Blue threw a perfect curve ball that hit Lil Ced in his throat, dropping him on contact. Shana rushed to where Lil Ced laid in the grass holding his neck. "Blue, you do this every time," Shana snapped. She was as protective over Lil Ced as he was over her.

"I'm good," Lil Ced rasped, sitting up. He hated getting embarrassed in front of Shana. Blake stood over Lil Ced and offered his hand.

"Thanks," Lil Ced told him when he got up. "You did good today, so next time you can be on Blue's team again," Lil Ced told Blake, dusting himself off while walking to the water fountain. It was starting to get dark, and Cordale would be pulling up any minute. Blake went home, leaving Lil Ced, Shana, Blue and Millie sitting at the basketball court waiting on their ride.

"I got a gift for you," Lil Ced told Shana, digging into his drawstring Nike backpack. He came out holding a jewelry box. "I hope you like it," he told Shana, passing her the box. She opened it and pulled out a gold bracelet with a heart shaped pendant on it.

"It's beautiful," Shana said, smiling from ear to ear. Lil Ced helped her put it on her wrist.

"You don't never buy me shit," Blue complained, kicking a rock across the court.

"Shut up," Shana told him while still admiring her gift. "Thank you, Cedric."

"Don't call me that, I always tell you that."

"I know, but I like your name and I'm special, so I don't wanna call you the same thing everybody else calls you," Shana said just as Cordale pulled up and honked the horn. The kids all piled in the back seat.

"Y'all hungry?" Cordale asked, looking at the kids through the rearview mirror.

"Yes!" they all said in unison.

"Y'all want some Mickey D's?" he asked. He knew they all loved McDonald's.

"Yes!" they all said together. Cordale took the kids through the McDonald's drive thru. After getting their food, Cordale dropped Willis' kids off and Lil Ced climbed into the front seat and snapped on his seatbelt.

"How was your day today?" Cordale asked his son as he navigated through the traffic.

"I had fun. We had a big apple war and Blue won, as usual."

"Let me guess. Shana was on your team?"

"Yup," Lil Ced said shyly.

"You love you some Shana, don't you?" Cordale asked, also smiling, seeing Lil Ced nervously fumbling with the string on his shorts while thinking.

"Yeah, I do, she's my best friend."

"Is she your best friend or your girlfriend?" Cordale looked over to him an answer.

"Both," he finally said before asking, "how was your day?"

"It was good. I made some money, and I was able to take yo mom out, we had a good time."

"That's what's up, lil nigga," Lil Ced said, reaching up and rubbing his father's head.

"What's the most important thing in the world?" Cordale quizzed out of the blue.

"Loyalty," Lil Ced answered quickly.

"What's a man with no loyalty?"

"A man with no loyalty is a man lost, and you shouldn't have a man like that around you."

"How many chances you get with loyalty?"

"One chance," Lil Ced replied. Cordale had been asking his son the questions since he was eight years old and now Lil Ced could answer in his sleep.

"So, what about trust?" Cordale asked Lil Ced.

"What about it?"

"What does it mean?"

"Trusting someone means you have faith in that person. If you trust someone, you must feel like they're dependable."

"Can you trust everybody?"

"No. Trust should be earned."

"How important is trust?" Cordale asked.

"Being trustworthy is an honorable label and it's important to surround yourself with people you can trust," Lil Ced said and Cordale swelled up with pride. He took pride in raising a thoroughbred. He always had these types of conversations with Lil Ced and taught him things he felt like he needed to know as a man.

When they pulled up to their home, Ladale was sitting on the front porch. "What's up, bruh?" he asked after taking a drag off his Newport.

"What's wrong?" Cordale asked, after seeing the look on Ladale's face.

"Yo boy Willis pulled up on me asking questions about the nigga Devonta."

"Devonta got smoked hittin his spot and the nigga was known for bein with you. That shit look suspect, so you can't blame him for wantin answers," Cordale said, reaching for the cigarette

"You right, bruh, but I don't like the way he was comin at me."

"Well, let that shit go, bruh. If you know you didn't have shit to do with that shit, then you ain't got nothing to worry about." Cordale paused to hit the Newport. "But if you know anything about that shit, then I'ma be the first to tell you how wrong you are, and you know the consequences behind doin some snake shit like that." Cordale flicked the cigarette and led Lil Ced into the house, leaving Ladale on the porch.

***

As the weeks went by, both Cordale and Willis kept their ears to the streets in hopes of hearing who was with the BD Devonta when he ran in Willis' spot. It was as if nobody knew anything about the situation. Willis was real determined to find out who it was, he didn't care about the money or the weed. He wanted to kill whoever it was to prove a point. Don't cross Willis!

TayTay entered their bedroom, holding two Oreo milkshakes. She handed Cordale one and climbed into bed next to him. They were in the middle of watching *Belly* on DVD. That was Cordale's favorite movie. "My boy Ox let that bitch take him out the game. Couldn't be me," Cordale scoffed, more to himself than to TayTay.

"You say that same shit every time we watch this movie."

Cause that shit be blowin me," Cordale snapped when the doorbell rang. "Get the door, Lil Ced!" he yelled. Lil Ced, who was in his room playing his Xbox 360, ran to the front door and swung it open to see Ladale, along with a rough looking guy he had never seen before.

"What's up, punk?" Ladale asked Lil Ced, pushing past him, almost knocking him down to the ground. Ladale reeked of alcohol and weed.

"Who is this nigga?" Lil Ced asked, still holding the front door open. He knew his father was strict on having strangers inside his home.

"Stop asking folks questions and go get me something to drink," Ladale told Lil Ced, plopping down on Cordale's black leather sofa.

Instead of going to the kitchen, Lil Ced ran to his parents' bedroom. "Daddy, Uncle Dale here with some bum I never seen before," he said frantically.

"What?" Cordale frowned, getting up and storming to his living room. "Who the fuck is this nigga you got in my muthafuckin crib?" Cordale snapped, standing over Ladale.

"That's my boy, Baby Clarence. He good," Ladale said dryly. He had the remote in his hand, flipping through channels on Cordale's seventy-two-inch flatscreen TV.

"I don't know this nigga. He good with you, not me!" Cordale growled. When Ladale didn't respond, he snatched the remote from his hand and threw it on the floor. "You don't hear me talking?" he growled. Ladale looked up with his face twisted into a mug.

"What the fuck is wrong with you, bruh?" he asked, slowly standing up. He was a few inches taller than Cordale, so he had to look down at him when they were standing face-to-face.

Lil Ced sat on the stairs leading to the second story of the house, watching everything unfold from a distance.

"Nigga, you know my rules and you disrespecting me by bringing a stranger into my house, where me and my family lay our heads at," Cordale said, growing impatient.

Bruh, I'm not Lil Ced. I don't have to follow yo rules. I'm a grown ass man!" Ladale shouted. His eyes were bloodshot red and glossy. He looked like he was off more than just weed and liquor. Cordale and Ladale fought a lot as kids, but by the time Cordale turned fourteen, he was more of a skilled fighter than Ladale. Ladale had found that out the hard way. Eventually, their fights slowed down. It had been a few years since the two had gotten physical.

Cordale grabbed Ladale's neck and shoved him down onto the couch. Ladale tried to bounce right up, but Cordale was all over him, connecting hard punches to his face and head. TayTay flew past Lil Ced down the stairs, screaming for the brothers to stop fighting.

Baby Clarence stood there looking high and stuck. Ladale tried to lift Cordale up and body slam him, but Cordale was able to put him in a chokehold. "Disrespectful ass nigga," he gruffed, choking Ladale tighter.

Ladale twisted his body and made gurgling noises, trying to break free.

"Let him go, bae," TayTay told Cordale, attempting to break the hold he had on Ladale's neck. When Ladale went limp, Cordale let him go. He then dragged Ladale to the front door and sat him on the front porch.

"Get the fuck out my house before I beat yo ass too," Cordale told Baby Clarence, who quickly exited the house. Cordale slammed the door and sat on the stairs next to Lil Ced.

"You okay, Pops?" Lil Ced asked Cordale, who was breathing heavy.

"Yeah, I'm good, mane. I just let that nigga take me out my element," Cordale replied.

"He disrespected you doe." Lil Ced's response made Cordale smile.

Sometimes, he could talk to Lil Ced and forget he was only an eleven-year-old boy. Lil Ced was mature and advanced, way beyond his years. He was a thinker and very observant. "And disrespect is unacceptable. You can never let a nigga slide with disrespecting you, because if he get away with it one time, he'll continue to try you," Cordale was saying when Ladale started pounding on the door.

"Just ignore him," Cordale told Lil Ced before getting up and going to the kitchen.

Lil Ced went to his room and called Shana from his cell phone

"Hey Cedric," Shana sang. She sounded happy to hear from him. The two always spent hours on the phone, talking about nothing. Some nights they would fall asleep still on the phone.

"Guess what happened?" Lil Ced giggled.

"What?"

"My daddy just beat up my uncle Dale," Lil Ced said and Shana burst out in laughter.

"Why?" she asked, and Lil Ced explained what led his father to beat up his uncle. "I'm glad Dale got beat up. That s what he get for always being so mean to us."

I wish you could've saw it. After the fight, my daddy threw him on the porch and locked the door." The two spoke for an hour, until Willis made Shana get off the phone to get ready for school in the morning.

When Lil Ced got off the phone, he played Grand Theft Auto IV for a while, before cutting the game off. He laid in his bed, thinking about his father and how cool he was. Lil Ced admired everything about his pops and wanted to be just like him when he grew up. He watched the way his father walked and talked and tried to emulate his every move. In his mind, his pops was way cooler than all the rappers and guys he saw in movies.

Lil Ced knew when he got older, he would be successful, and he planned on taking care of Shana the same way his father took care of his mother.

Cordale was Lil Ced's inspiration, but Shana was his motivation. He tried to impress her with everything he did. Shana loved to read, so Lil Ced made reading one of his hobbies. Shana's favorite subject was history, and even though he hated history, Lil Ced made sure he paid attention, just so he could talk to Shana about what he learned. Lil Ced was way too young to know what love was, but he knew one thing: His loyalty belonged to Shana.

The next morning, Lil Ced was awakened by his father. "Go get yoself together, I want you to take a ride with me," Cordale told Lil Ced.

It was early, around eight in the morning. Lil Ced groggily climbed out of bed and went to brush his teeth and wash his face. After twenty minutes, the father and son were in Cordale's Dodge Charger, dropping off pounds and picking up money. Cordale was serving pounds of Mid and Kush all over the city. You couldn't mention weed and not think of Cordale. He had started off selling bags of Mid with Willis on the corner of 47th Place.

Now he had an empire. He and Willis were both established in their own right, but they considered themselves as partners. Next to Willis, Cordale's closest friend was a guy named Ed. Ed was a stone-cold killer who knew how to hustle and make some money. But he preferred to put in work. He was Cordale's enforcer, when somebody crossed Cordale, Ed paid them a visit. Ed was the definition of 'loyal" and Cordale trusted him with his life.

When Cordale pulled up to Ed's house on 105th and Corliss. Ed was in the front, playing with his two pit bulls. Cordale parked but didn't get out of the car. He rolled down the passenger's window. "Put them crazy as ass dogs up so we can get out," he yelled to Ed.

Ed led both of the pits into his home and returned with a

White Castle bag in hand. Ed, muscular and brown-skinned, sported a bald head and full beard combo. Cordale and Lil Ced got out of the car and met Ed on his porch. "This that paper Big Mike owed you," Ed told Cordale, passing him the White Castle bag. "What's up, lil nigga?" Ed asked, turning his attention to Lil Ced.

Lil Ced nodded sheepishly in return. He was low-key scared of Ed. Not because he rode around all day with a pair of crazy ass dogs, but because Ed had a look in his eyes that sent chills through Lil Ced's body. Ed reminded him of DMX.

"Did you ever holla at that Vice Lord nigga with them crates?" Cordale asked, flaming up a Newport. Ed was supposed to be buying a crate of handguns from a Vice Lord over east.

"Yeah, I already made that shit happen, G. You know I don't fuck around," Ed replied, smiling

"The nigga Ladale came to the crib off that shit last night. I had to put my hands on that nigga."

"You lyin," Ed chuckled in disbelief.

"Man, I choked that nigga out and threw his ass on the porch."

"He didn't even get a punch off," Lil Ced added, making everyone laugh.

"That's yo brother," Ed stated.

"He better get his shit together before I cut his water off," Cordale replied.

"Lil Ced, go hop in the car and let me holla at yo pops real quick," Ed told Lil Ced, who did as he was told. "On some real shit, yo brother gettin out of control," Ed told Cordale seriously.

"Why you say that?" Cordale asked Ed, passing him the cigarette.

Ed took a drag on the cigarette before answering. "He been fucking with the wrong type of niggas. Stick-up kids and shiesty-ass niggas that would use him in order to get close to you. And not to mention, the nigga been playin with his nose." There was a rumor going around that Ladale used cocaine, but Cordale had never witnessed him using the drug.

"Yeah, the nigga who got smoked robbin Willis' spot was one of his homies."

"Yeah, and a few people claim they saw them together that morning," Ed said.

This was news to Cordale. He hoped Willis hadn't heard the rumor, it would add to his suspicion. "Be honest, G, do you think Ladale had something to do with that shit?" Cordale asked.

Ed went silent for a moment before saying, "Yo brother soft as hell, G." They both laughed. Ed continued, "But he also a master manipulator. Whenever he high, drunk, and trying to impress a mufucka, he liable to do anything."

Cordale hated to admit it, but Ed was right. Ladale was impulsive and moved liike he had something to prove. Cordale tried every way possible to put his brother in a position where he could win, but Ladale was a natural fuck-up. Cordale and Ed chopped it up for a few more minutes before Cordale left to continue running errands.

Chapter 4

October 2009

When the new school year started, Lil Ced was happy to find out he and Shana were in the same class. Since Willis lived a few blocks away from the school they went to, Lil Ced walked home with his kids and got picked up from there. Lil Ced liked school. His grades weren't the best, but he dressed nice. He had all the newest Jordan's and kept all of the latest games, so everybody thought his family was rich. Lil Ced didn't look at it that way. He never looked down at the kids whose families were less fortunate.

Meechie, who was two grades above Lil Ced, hung out with a few kids who had already started gangbanging and trying to sell drugs. Blue, on the other hand, loved school also. He was a troublemaker and had all the jokes, so everybody liked him. Shana was a bookworm, all the teachers loved her. TayTay loved her also, because she motivated Lil Ced to be smart and do better in school.

One day while walking home, Blue noticed a group of kids making fun of Blake and his younger brother. Blake's face was red with embarrassment. He looked as though he wanted to fight, but he recognized he was outnumbered.

"Aye! Leave him alone with yo Lil Bill lookin ass!" Blue told a rough-looking, dark-skinned kid wearing an oversized white tee, a pair of pants that looked two sizes too big, and a pair of white Air Ones. All the other kids started laughing at the would-be bully. "Them fat ass Ones you got on, them bitches fake!" Blue added, making the crowd of kids laugh even harder. The laughter fueled Blue to go harder. "Yo Momma a stripper! Yo whole house smell like booty!" Blue joked.

The kid was so embarrassed, he stepped in Blue's face. "You better shut yo fat bitch ass up before I knock you out!" the kid threatened. Everybody fell silent, waiting to see how Blue would respond.

Blue chuckled nervously. He wasn't a fighter at all and

avoided confrontation at all costs.

"Yeah, I thought so!" the kid snarled. He had treated Blue and punked him in front of everybody. That was way better than any joke.

"You ain't gone do shit to him," Lil Ced said loudly. He didn't like bullies and he wouldn't let anyone bully his friend.

The kid stepped in Lil Ced's face. "Who gone stop me?" the kid asked, putting his forehead against Lil Ced's forehead.

"Get out my face, boy!" Lil Ced roared, giving the kid a shove, only to be shoved in return by one of the kid's friends.

"Stay out of that!" Blake said, shoving the kid to the floor.

The dark-skinned kid took his shirt off and walked towards Lil Ced.

"Why you hit me?" he asked. Before Lil Ced could respond, the kid took off on him. Lil Ced stood his ground and the two kids duked it out, until an old man walking down the street broke the fight up.

Lil Ced wanted more. He stood there, chest heaving, waiting for the second round. "Anybody who think they gone mess with one of my friends, gone have to fight me!" Lil Ced shouted to all the kids who were right there. Thanks for having my back," Lil Ced said, turning to Blake.

"They always tryna jump on somebody. I'm glad y'all was around or they would've jumped on me," Blake replied.

"Friends stick together. They ain't gone ever jump on you if I'm around," Lil Ced promised, and he meant every word. That was the beginning of a new friendship. After that day, Blake became one of Lil Ced's best friends. His younger brother, Cragg, happened to be in Blue's classroom.

They all became inseparable and did everything together. After school they would meet up and ride their bikes together searching for any type of trouble to get into.

"What do you want to be when you grow up?" Shana asked Lil Ced. They were sitting on top of the monkey bars at the park, watching Millie chase Cragg and Blue with a water gun. Shana always asked Lil Ced questions about his future, and he always had the same answer. "I'ma be just like my pops," he always said with pride.

"Your father is a drug dealer," would always be Shana's response.

"So what?" Lil Ced hunched his shoulders.

"Why don't you want to be a firefighter or a lawyer?"

"That's boring stuff."

"You could play sports, you're real good at baseball," Shana said.

"Naw, I'm too small," Lil Ced countered. "Plus, you gone be my wife and you gone be a lawyer, so if I get in trouble, you gone get me right out of it." Lil Ced thought he had it all figured out.

He thought being a big-time drug dealer was all pros and no cons. He didn't know about all the long nights on the block dodging the police and ducking the stick-up kids. He didn't know how having money changed the people close to you. The only thing he knew for sure was that his pops drove the nicest cars, wore the nicest clothes and was able to provide the best for his family and that was enough for him.

Shana thought differently. She dreamed of becoming a lawyer, owning her own house, starting a big family, and having a enormous wedding. she wasn't amazed by the street life at all. Not only that but Willis stayed in her ear about never settling for a guy that was in the streets. He told her that a nigga in the streets wouldn't know how to treat her. He made sure he taught his princess to know her worth.

"You do know a lot of drug dealers never get rich, and they end up dying in the streets, right?" Shana asked Lil Ced, who smacked his lips before answering.

"Yeah, all the niggas that don't know what they doin."

"You don't know the first thing about selling drugs," Shana giggled. Lil Ced would never admit it, but she was right. "I know that loyalty—"

"Is everything," Shana cut him off and finished his sentence, she knew exactly what he was going to say. "Its more to selling drugs than surrounding yourself with loyal people," she added.

"My pops gone teach me everything I need to know about selling drugs as I get older," Lil Ced said with confidence.

"Well, my daddy told me to never deal with a guy that's in the streets," Shana said, knowing exactly what to say to make Lil Ced speak with some sense.

"Well, when you get older, yo daddy won't be able to tell you who you can or can't marry," Lil Ced shot back but before Shana could respond he got hit in the head with what felt like a rock. he almost fell off the monkey bars. He looked around the playground and saw Blue winding up to throw at him again. He quickly jumped from the monkey bars and took cover behind the jungle gym."Shana, it's wartime!" he yelled. Shana jumped down and took off sprinting to the crabapple tree. The kids broke into teams of three and had an epic apple war. This time, even Millie played until the last man was standing. Before it got too dark, the kids got on their bikes and rode home together laughing about all the big hits of the war.

***

For the past few months, Ladale tried to maintain a big bankroll without fucking it off on partying and women. He wanted a lane of his own, so he started to sell weight as well as bags. He still hung around a group of shiesty ass niggas but that was mainly for protection. His right-hand man Trell was a GD, originally from the Robert Taylor Housing Projects, but migrated to the hundreds under his uncle, Wild Bill. Wild Bill was a crazy ass GD from 108th and Wabash, a block they called the 8Ball. He was a savage that didn't have to hustle, he simply extorted the niggas that did hustle.

Ladale hung under Trell and Wild Bill, mainly because he knew nobody would fuck with them. He gave Wild Bill a few pounds and Bill gave him the green light to open up shop on the 8Ball. Another nigga Ladale hung with a lot was Kenny Mac, who was also from the 8Ball. Kenny Mac robbed any and everybody he caught flexin. It wasn't hard for him to get Ladale drunk and gas him up to accompany him on a hit or a robbery.

Ladale loved the sense of power he felt after committing a robbery or doing a hit. When people saw him with Kenny Mac or Wild Bill, they figured he was just as gangsta as they were, and they feared him. He loved the fact that he wasn't living in Cordale's shadow. On the 8Ball, Dale was one of them guys.

"I'm pulling in right now, bruh," Ladale told Cordale over the phone as he pulled into the Wendy's parking lot on 87th and Wentworth. This was the first time Cordale saw Ladale's burgundy Dodge Magnum with twenty-two-inch rims. Ladale eased next to Cordale's Lincoln Navigator and rolled down his window. "What's up, folks?" he asked. His eyes were so low they appeared to be closed. He had Kenny Mac in his passenger seat and they both had their fitted caps cocked hard to the right.

"I see who really gettin money. I'm tryna be like you when I grow up," Cordale joked, admiring his brother's whip. He was happy his brother had finally found his way. He grabbed a duffle bag from the back seat of his truck and climbed into the back seat of Ladale's Magnum. His diamond cross swung freely from his neck with every step he took. When he got settled in his seat he shook up with his brother.

"What's up, gangsta?" Kenny Mac asked, extending his hand for a shake.

This was the first time the two had actually met, but Ladale had told him plenty stories about his brother getting money.

"What's up, fam?" Cordale asked dryly, shaking Kenny Mac's hand. "It's ten in the bag, bruh," he told Ladale. He didn't want to mingle with them for too long, it was no telling what type of bullshit they were into.

"I got a mufucka tryna grab twenty pounds of mid, of course I put my tax on it. And he went for it," Ladale said, flaming up a Newport.

"Tomorrow," Cordale replied, not really wanting to talk business in front of Kenny Mac.

"You don't got it now?" Ladale asked, not catching his vibe.

"Everything I got now is counted for, bruh. I'll be back good in the morning," Cordale said, opening his door.

"Ok cool," Ladale said as his brother got out the car.

"Be safe, bruh," Cordale said, looking him in the eyes. He had a look of deep concern written on his face. The truth was, he was always worried about his brother's wellbeing. Ladale loved attention and he didn't know that when you were getting money, attention was your worst enemy. he always let it be known he had some paper and he put himself in positions where his back door was wide open.

"You too, bruh," Ladale said, before speeding off. Cordale got in his truck and drove to Mellow Yellow, a restaurant in the Hyde Park area. Every Wednesday while the kids were at school, he would meet up with Ed, Willis, and Winky, Willis' younger brother at Mellow Yellow and they would discuss business over lunch. It was a tradition each of the men enjoyed because they were all the best of friends, and they valued the time they got to spend together.

When Cordale arrived, Ed, Willis and Winky were already seated. "Finally," Willis smiled, taking a sip of Sprite.

"First things first, I want to let everybody know I handled that rat problem we had in the hood," Ed said, speaking on one of the folks that had told on somebody from the hood. The paperwork had come back, and Ed waited outside his grandmother's house and shot him three times in his face.

"That's good. What y'all think about grabbing some X pills? One of my cousins back in Memphis got a boyfriend that'll let em go for a dollar a pill," Cordale said while texting someone on his phone.

"How would we get them?" Willis asked.

"We would probably have to send somebody there and back," Cordale replied.

"That's too much," Winky frowned, shaking his head in disapproval.

"Now if you could talk them into delivering the pills to us for a fee, then I'd be willing to fuck with it," Willis said, throwing a few French fries in his mouth.

"Whatever happened with that lil beef between the lil folks and the moes of 45th?" Willis asked Ed.

"I popped one of they asses," Ed replied nonchalantly as the waitress brought their food to the table. After everybody got their food and the waitress walked off, Winky spoke.

"You shot one?" he asked in a hushed tone. That caused Cordale and Willis to burst out laughing.

"Yeah, I went to holla at Nard and one of his shorties said, 'It ain't shit to talk to the bricks about,' so I left his ass right there," Ed explained with a small smile on his face.

"So, it's on with moe nem?" Cordale asked. He wasn't doing too much sliding, but he did need to know who they were warring with. He actually hated warring, it was bad for business, but it was also a part of the game. Cordale stood by his boys through whatever, right or wrong. Ed, being the gangsta he was, would handle every aspect of the war so Cordale would never have to get his hands dirty.

After he confirmed the war was on, Cordale went on to the next topic. "I got fifty comin in tomorrow. Ladale say he got a serve for twenty of em," he told the table. It seemed like mentioning Ladale threw off everybody's vibe.

"He look like he been doing good, he pulled up on me in a Magnum on some rims." Cordale smiled, he felt good being able to speak highly of his brother.

"Was it a steamer?" Winky joked, causing everybody to laugh.

"Could've been," Cordale admitted.

"Him and his boy Kenny Mac robbed Bob-O," Ed informed the table over a mouthful of burger.

"Which Bob-O?" Cordale asked. Ed told the table how Ladale, along with Kenny Mac, stuck up Bob-O from Welch World. He told them Ladale had actually robbed more than a few people, including a BD from Front Street that Cordale did plenty business with. Cordale was mad that Ladale had robbed someone he introduced him to, and he didn't even say shit about it. He didn't know Ladale had been running around town like a bandit. Ladale's actions could've gotten him hurt.

He was glad Ed kept his ears to the streets, and he kicked himself for being so out of the loop. He made a mental note to speak to Ladale before he robbed the wrong person and got himself killed.

The friends chopped it up while they finished their food and then for another half an hour after their food was gone. They planned on watching the game together later that night. Winky paid for the meal and then they all left and went their separate ways.

***

It was a sunny, cloudless day and Lil Reggie only had another half-hour of driving left, before he could collect his cash and go buy himself a bottle of Remy. He always needed a drink after completing a pick-up. He thought of the liquor as a reward to himself. He'd been doing pick-ups for Cordale for two years now and the police had never stopped him, so at this point he was very confident about the trips.

"My bitch say every time she look up, I'm about to do a cook up. I told her if she knew what I know she would shut the fuck up!" Lil Reggie rapped the lyrics to Gucci Mane's "Heavy." He had the song blasting, riding the Value City truck through downtown Chicago. He usually dropped the pounds off to Ed, but today he was dropping them off straight to Cordale.

When Lil Reggie navigated off the highway on 47th Street, he relaxed a little more. He knew he was only minutes away from collecting his cash.

When he stopped at the red light on 47th and Michigan, a gray minivan swerved in front of him and two masked men hopped out of the already open side doors with AK-47s aimed at the truck. Lil Reggie stomped the gas and rammed the minivan, which made one of the masked men fire into the truck. A bullet hit Lil Reggie in his abdomen, and he put the truck in park. He thought about it, and he wasn't ready to die over another man's drugs. He pushed the door open and fell out of the truck.

One of the masked men ran past him, with his AK aimed at his face. Lil Reggie closed his eyes, he wanted to pray but he was so scared he couldn't get the words out. He didn't open his eyes again until he heard the doors to the truck open and close. When he did open his eyes, it was just in time to see the minivan and the Value City truck speeding off.

"Fuck!" Cordale yelled when he'd gotten the call that Lil Reggie had gotten hijacked and was in critical condition after being shot. He was in his truck with TayTay, in the middle of a shopping spree.

"What happened?" TayTay asked him after he startled her. He explained what he had just found out and by the time he was done, his stomach was hurting. Nobody liked to take a loss and fifty pounds wasn't a small "L." Cordale called Ed and told him to meet him at his house ASAP. When he made it home, Ed was sitting in his driveway in his red Mustang, he got out to meet them at the front door.

"G, what the fuck happened?" Cordale asked Ed as soon as the door was closed.

"They say a minivan pulled up in front of the truck and two niggas jumped out with K's. Lil Reggie tried to pull off on they ass, but they started dumping, he got hit and crashed," Ed explained.

"Did he see any faces?" Cordale asked.

"I haven't spoken to him personally, he was in surgery when I got the call," Ed was saying when someone knocked at the front door. TayTay opened it and Ladale barged in without speaking.

"What's going on? You good, bruh?" he asked Cordale, who was pacing the floor, which was what he did whenever he had a lot on his mind.

"Somebody hijacked my load!" Cordale shouted. He was mad and nobody could blame him.

"It had to be some inside shit, because you switch trucks every time and only a few people know about the pick-ups, so it shouldn't be hard to figure out," Ladale said, and he was right. Only a few people knew how Cordale handled his pick-ups, and nobody but Lil Reggie knew where he had to go to pick up the load, and even he only found out the morning of the pick-up. Cordale took a moment to think and quickly scratched Lil Reggie off his list of suspects for the simple fact that he didn't get robbed picking the drugs up, he got robbed before he could drop the load off.

"Do you think Willis could've had something to do with that shit?" Ladale asked, flaming up a Newport.

Cordale got even madder, due to the fact that he would ask a question so stupid. "That don't even sound right," he gruffed, still pacing.

"How come it don't?" Ladale asked and paused to hit his cigarette before continuing. "He thought I had something to do with his trap getting hit. He been actin real funny ever since that shit happened. And now yo load get hijacked, where he at? If the shoe was on the other foot, you would've been by his side the minute you heard the news."

"I can't see folks pullin no shit like that," Ed said, shaking his head.

Cordale finally sat down and tried to digest what Ladale had just said he immediately dismissed his accusations. He and Willis were too tight for him to entertain those thoughts. The two friends started off with nothing and had built an empire together, from the ground up. They always had each other's backs. Willis was Lil Ced's godfather.

"Bruh, you be having too much faith in these niggas. You know like I know that you can't put shit past nobody," Ladale said, getting up from where he was seated on the couch. "I'ma put my ear to the streets and I'ma let you know right now, if I find out that nigga had something to do with that shit, I'ma kill him," he added, before walking out the house.

***

As the days went past, Cordale and Ed kept their ears plastered to the streets, in hopes of hearing who hijacked his truck.

Cordale asked Willis if he'd heard anything, but he hadn't. He also had people searching the streets for any amount of information. It was as if a ghost had robbed Cordale, because nobody seemed to know a thing. Chicago was a big city, but everybody knew everybody.

If you were getting money, then you were rubbing shoulders with other guys that were getting money and everyone would know of you. If you were a savage, everyone would hear stories about you shooting or robbing, and your name would ring bells in the city. That's just how Chicago was, if people didn't know you personally, then they most definitely knew of you. Cordale's name rang bells on the south and east sides of the city, but no one knew who had robbed him. That alone let him know that whoever did it made sure they covered their tracks well.

Cordale eased his truck in the parking lot of the Harold's Chicken on 103rd and Halsted. Ladale was sitting on the hood of his Magnum with his Chicago White sox cap slammed to the right side of his head. He was surrounded by a few guys Cordale had never seen before. Cordale put his 9mm on his hip before jumping out of his truck.

"What's up, bruh?" Ladale asked, giving him a brotherly hug. Cordale could smell the liquor coming from his pores.

"What y'all on out here?" Cordale replied, leaning on Ladale's car. He didn't want any of Ladale's friends standing behind him.

"Man… bruh, I got some Hennessy in the car I been sippin on. Now all I need is a bussa to take to this room I got on stony," Ladale said, making himself laugh.

"You most definitely gone find one out here, the hundreds got all the bussa's," Cordale replied.

"Bruh, you know I love the fuck outta you right?" Ladale asked loudly, making everybody look at him.

Cordale didn't like the attention he was putting on them. "Yeah, I know mane, and I love yo crazy ass too." He smiled.

Ladale smiled too, but his smile quickly faded, and his face got serious. He leaned closer to Cordale and lowered his voice. "I think I found out who got down on you," he said. This caught

Cordale's attention.

"Who?" he asked quickly. Ladale fumbled through his pockets for a while, before pulling out his cell phone. He played with the phone for a few seconds, before showing Cordale a picture of a guy, sitting on top of a black Monte Carlo SS sitting on twenty-two-inch rims. The guy held a wad of money in each hand.

"Who the fuck is he? He look familiar," Cordale asked, trying to figure out why the guy looked so familiar to him.

"That's Willis' cousin, Sharod," Ladale replied and recognition instantly kicked in for Cordale. "I think Willis had him hijack yo truck," Ladale said and Cordale screwed his face up.

"And why would you think that, bruh?" he asked, tired of Ladale putting that same bullshit in the air.

"Cause the lil nigga was just fucked up, now all of a sudden he got a new car, some money to show off and he selling weed."

At first, Cordale thought maybe Willis or Winky could've put Sharod on, but then he remembered Willis telling him how Sharod didn't have a hustler bone in his body. But Cordale still wasn't convinced that Willis would have Sharod rob him.

"I'm telling you, bruh, I got a funny feeling about that nigga. You the one that taught me to never put shit past nobody. You better start practicing what you preach," Ladale said.

It got quiet for a brief second, before Cordale said, "I'ma holla at him but I just don't see it," he admitted. Willis had no reason to commit treason.

"I should take Sharod ass down, shouldn't I?" Ladale asked, hoping Cordale would give him the green light.

"No, you shouldn't," Cordale said firmly. "You know we live and die by that loyalty shit, and since we don't know for sure, we not gone do shit. Just keep yo eyes and ears open and see if you can find out something, with some proof to back it up," he told Ladale, who nodded in response. Cordale was tired of standing with Ladale and his crew, so he lied and said he had something to do.

"Don't let loyalty blind you to what's going on right under yo nose," Ladale warned Cordale, who climbed in his truck and sped off.

After leaving the hundreds, Cordale went to Willis' house where he knew the kids were just getting in from school. As soon as he stepped in, Lil Ced ran up and gave him a hug. "What's up, lil dude?" Cordale asked. His son was his best friend and it made him feel good when Lil Ced showed him affection.

"What's up, Pops? We just made it in, and me and Blue was just about to play Madden," Lil Ced said, hoping he didn't have to leave.

"Gone head, I came to holla at Willis," Cordale told Lil Ced, who ran off to play the game with Blue.

Cordale found Willis in the kitchen, standing over the stove, making himself a grilled cheese sandwich. "What's up, G?" Willis asked Cordale, who took a seat at the kitchen table.

"Shit. Tired than a muthafucka, mane," Cordale replied, making Willis chuckle at his country-ness. They had been friends for over ten years and Willis still found the way he spoke to be funny.

"You still ain't heard shit worth looking into?" Willis asked, flipping his sandwich over.

Cordale didn't answer immediately, because he didn't know the right way to word what he wanted to say. "What Sharod been on?" he asked.

"Shit. Fucking up as usual," Willis replied with a shrug. "What made you ask about him?"

"Somebody threw his name out there," Cordale replied.

Willis put his sandwich on a paper plate and sat at the table across from Cordale. "Why the fuck did his name come up?" he asked, before taking a bite from his sandwich.

"That's the same shit I was wondering. They say he got a new whip and he all of a sudden selling weed now. When I heard that shit, I was thinking maybe you put him on."

"Naw, I haven't given him shit, but I'm sure he didn't have nothing to do with yo load gettin took. How would he even know about the load?"

"You tell me," Cordale shot back and he regretted the words as soon as they left his mouth. He didn't mean to say it the way he said it.

"Fuck that supposed to mean?" Willis asked, looking up from his plate.

"I didn't mean it like that, bruh. I'm just saying it was only a few people that knew about that load."

"Since some stupid muthafucka mentioned my lil cousin's name, you assuming I let him know about the load?" Willis asked, offended to the utmost. No matter how Cordale tried to put it, if the roles were reversed, he would've never assumed what Cordale was assuming.

"I didn't say that," Cordale replied.

"In so many words, you did."

"You asked if I heard any news and I told you what I heard. You acting like I came in here saying you set that shit up!" Cordale snapped.

The two friends stared at each other intensely for a second before Willis said, "You might as well have said that shit, instead of beating around the bush." He was more hurt than mad. Just like Cordale, Willis' motto was "Loyalty is Everything." They both had it tatted across their forearms and he felt like loyalty should never have to be questioned. If someone's loyalty had to be questioned, then there was a problem.

"Why you so defensive doe, G? When you was accusing Ladale of having something to do with yo spot getting hit, I handled that shit like a brother," Cordale said, screwing his face up. Tension was starting to build in the room. The two were like blood brothers, so this wasn't the first time they had a disagreement, but this time it was more personal than any other time. They had never fucked with each other's money.

Cordale decided it was best he left before he or Willis said something they couldn't take back. He stormed into the living room where the kids were huddled in front of the TV, playing the PlayStation 3. "Come on, Ced," he said, not hiding the anger he was feeling. Lil Ced said his goodbyes and they left.

Chapter 5

March 2010

Cordale was starting to sweat under his spring Pelle, so he took it off and threw it on the back of the Ashley's furniture truck that he was standing in front of. He, along with Ed, were hauling boxes stuffed with pounds of Kush off the truck and into one of his traps. He had to grind extra hard through the winter to make up for the fifty-pound loss he took. His grind paid off, he expanded his operation and was now selling X pills, as well as Kush. The pills were bringing in good money and his cousin's boyfriend was delivering them, so he didn't have to risk somebody driving back and forth from Chicago to Memphis.

Things were never the same with him and Willis after they had words, not because of the words, but because a week after they argued, Sharod had gotten shot four times. Willis asked Cordale was he behind the hit, which Cordale denied, but Willis didn't believe him. They still spoke and did some business together, but the trust had been damaged.

The kids were still inseparable and seemingly oblivious to the tension between their fathers. It didn't take long for Lil Ced to notice that he went from seeing Shana every day, to seeing her every few days. Whenever he mentioned it to Cordale, he brushed it off, claiming that everybody had been busy lately. It was a sorry excuse.

Ladale surprisingly was still doing good for himself. It had been a long, long time since he'd called Cordale, begging for a front or asking to borrow some money he would never pay back. His name was still commonly associated with bullshit, whether it was a robbery or a shooting, he was always involved in something. Despite that, Cordale was proud of him even though he hadn't gotten the chance to let him know it.

A horn honked, grabbing Cordale's attention. It was TayTay, smiling at him sitting in her Nissan Sentra. "What's up, my love?" Cordale asked, approaching her car. He leaned in the window and gave her a quick peck on the lips.

"Hey bae, I was running a few errands and I just happened to ride past, seeing you lifting boxes looking all strong and sexy. I had to stop," TayTay replied, making Cordale smile.

"Is my waves on point?" he asked, running a hand over his head.

"Yes, sir. I wouldn't mind taking you home with me right now," she flirted.

"I'll be there soon and we gone see if you got this same energy." Cordale leaned in and kissed TayTay again, this time more passionately. "I can't wait to make you my wife," he said, staring into her slanted, brown eyes. They had been together for almost fifteen years now and TayTay was ready to become his wife.

Cordale didn't have a problem with getting married, he actually wanted to marry TayTay. He just wanted to be able to give her the perfect wedding and that took a lot of time, money and planning.

"And I can't wait to make you my husband. I hope I don't have to wait forever," TayTay said, causing Cordale to playfully pull her hair.

"Don't do that, TayTay, not right here and not right now."

"Ed!" TayTay shouted, trying to get Ed's attention. He was still busy moving boxes. "He don't want to marry me, Ed!" she yelled when he looked her way.

"Yes, he do!" Ed shouted back with a smile.

"Stop doing that, baby, we'll talk about it later," Cordale said.

"You promise?" TayTay asked, pouting.

"I promise," Cordale said, giving her another kiss. That made TayTay's day.

"Ok baby, I'll see you later, be safe." TayTay pulled off. Cordale watched her drive away and made a mental note to start preparing for their wedding. TayTay was a good woman, and she deserved a big wedding. She deserved a lifetime commitment, and he was going to give her that.

"You better stop playin with that lady," Ed told Cordale,

snapping him out of his thoughts.

"I am, G," Cordale replied, grabbing a box and taking it in the trap.

***

"Hello?" Lil Ced answered his phone sleepily. It was a little after one in the morning and he had school the next day.

"I can't sleep," Shana said in a hushed tone. She always called Lil Ced whenever she couldn't sleep, or when she woke up in the middle of the night after a bad dream, and they would sit on the phone until they fell asleep.

"What's wrong?" Lil Ced asked.

"I keep having that same nightmare that my daddy gets killed."

"It's just a dream, you know that."

"I do, but my grandma told me whenever you keep having the same dream, that's your soul trying to tell you something," Shana explained and she believed that. "And in every dream, you be the one that kill him," she added. She couldn't see him, but Lil Ced was smirking.

"Now why would I kill my godfather?" he asked jokingly.

"I ask myself that same question every time I have that nightmare."

"Maybe we be fighting for yo heart, and I win every time," Lil Ced said and even though he was joking, Shana took that and ran with it.

"Maybe that's why my daddy always tell me not to deal with a guy that's in the streets."

"Stop overthinking it, Shana, it's just a stupid dream. You must've watched a scary before you went to sleep," Lil Ced said, and Shana blushed on the other side of the phone. She did watch *The Texas Chainsaw Massacre* before she went to sleep. Nobody knew Shana as well as Lil Ced did.

"I got a question for you," she said after a brief silence.

"Ask it."

"Do you love me?" Shana asked. Lil Ced was only twelve years old, and he knew the word love, but he didn't fully comprehend what love truly was. He wasn't old enough to know love came with pain. He didn't know how love could drive you crazy, and you do things you wouldn't usually do. He didn't know about the sacrifices that came with love and neither did Shana, but they did know they loved each other.

"Yeah, do you love me?" Lil Ced asked.

"Yes, with my whole heart," Shana replied, making him smile from ear to ear

Every kid they went to school with knew Shana was Lil Ced's girlfriend. Plenty of times, they had gotten caught kissing or holding hands. Lil Ced was notorious for writing "C & S" all over the walls of the school's bathrooms and on the desks in the classrooms. If Lil Ced caught one of the boys flirting with Shana, he would start a fight, and if Shana caught one of the other girls looking too hard, she would grab Lil Ced's hand to show he was hers and she was his.

TayTay called it puppy love and she would always have long talks with him about how to treat a lady. She told him a loyal woman was priceless and if he ever wanted a woman to truly be loyal to him, he would have to be loyal to her. She taught him that any fool could treat a woman wrong, but it took a special kind of man to treat a woman right

"I love you more than anybody in this world," Lil Ced stated. He always knew just the right words to say to make Shana feel good. "Always and forever," he added, putting icing on the cake. They both turned on their TVs, turned to *Disney Channel* and watched TV together, until they both fell asleep on the phone

The next afternoon, Ladale picked Lil Ced up from school. "Come on, lil nigga!" he gruffed at Lil Ced, who was busy saying his goodbyes to Shana. "I can see it now, you gone be a straight tender-dick ass nigga when you get older," he chuckled when Lil Ced climbed into the car.

"Shut up," Lil Ced shot back, not understanding what his uncle meant by *tender dick*.

"You need to hang around me, so you can see how you supposed to fuck these hoes, then duck these hoes," Ladale said, causing him to frown up. He couldn't imagine hanging around his uncle longer than he had to. He hated being around him.

"I know how to treat a lady," Lil Ced told him, looking out of the window. He was a little down because he really wanted to go over Willis' house.

"Have you ever seen that movie, *'Paid In Full?'*" Ladale asked, flaming up a Newport.

"Yeah, with Money Makin Mitch."

"Sometimes I look at you and start feeling like Uncle Ice," Ladale said and erupted in laughter but Lil Ced didn't get the joke.

"Where we goin?" he asked, once he noticed that they weren't headed to his house.

"I got a few moves to buss before I drop you off. Just sit back and chill," Ladale told him, turning up the radio to tune him out.

The first stop Ladale made was at the gas station on 63rd and state. He sold a pound of Kush to some fat nigga who was so musty, Lil Ced had to roll his window down after he got in the car. After that, Ladale pulled on 87th and Wabash. A tall, brown-skinned guy with shoulder-length dreads approached his window.

Before he made it to the car, Ladale took off his Boston Red Sox hat he had slammed to the right. He knew the Stones off 87th were into it with the GD's. That had nothing to do with him personally, but he would rather be safe than sorry. He served his Stone homie three pounds of sour diesel and sped off as soon as the money was in his hand.

After that, Ladale stopped on 108th and Wabash. "I'll be right back," he told Lil Ced, before climbing out of the car and approaching a group of men who were standing on the corner of the block. Lil Ced sat in the car, texting Shana. He was tired and ready to go home and take a nap. After thirty minutes of texting, he started to nod off.

The sound of a gun going off woke Lil Ced up with a startle. Another gun went off, then tires screeched, and a car zoomed past where he was sitting in Ladale's car. Lil Ced was on the floor covering his head. This was the closest he'd ever been to gunshots, and he was scared as hell. He flinched hard when Ladale opened the car door.

"You straight?" he asked Lil Ced. He looked like he was just as scared as Lil Ced was.

"Yeah," Lil Ced replied with a nod.

Ladale got in the car and started it up. Lil Ced looked out the back windshield and saw a small crowd gathered together, around a man who was stretched out a few feet away from the stop sign. "Is he ok?" he asked Ladale, unable to take his eyes off the guy as they pulled off.

"I hope so," Ladale mumbled, fumbling to pull a Newport from the box.

Lil Ced was quiet the whole ride home. He was so happy to get away from Ladale, he ran into his home when they made it. Cordale wasn't home and Lil Ced didn't want to let his mother know what had happened, so he went into his room, closed his door and called Shana. He told her what happened and answered every question she had for him. "Were you scared?" Shana asked.

"Yeah, a little," Lil Ced admitted.

"That's exactly why I want you to be something other than a drug dealer. I don't want you dying in the streets," Shana said seriously.

"I won't, I promise," Lil Ced vowed. He would do anything to please Shana, even if it meant living until he was a hundred years old.

"I know you won't because I'ma make sure of it," she replied. When Lil Ced heard the front door open and close, he told Shana he would call her back. He ran downstairs, hoping to meet his father in the living room, but he and Ed were headed for the kitchen and they both looked angry. Lil Ced stayed in the living room and eavesdropped on their conversation.

"So, this dumb ass nigga Ladale been braggin about doin that shit?" he heard his father ask Ed.

"Hell yeah, man. They say once he get drunk, that's his favorite story to tell," Ed replied.

Loyalty is Everything

"It's gone be some bullshit behind that if the wrong people catch wind of it. I told that stupid ass nigga not to do that shit in the first place. As soon as I heard the news, I knew it was his work," Cordale was saying when Lil Ced decided to enter the kitchen. He was small for his age and looked almost identical to Cordale when he was that age.

"What's up, lil man?" Ed greeted Lil Ced, who pounded his big, rough fist.

"What's goin on, mane?" Cordale asked, rubbing his son's head.

"Nothin, I just wanted to know if I could ride my bike to Blake's house?" Lil Ced asked, taking a seat at the kitchen table.

"Dude, yo homie live too far for you to be riding yo bike to his house at this time of day."

"I wanted to go over there earlier, but Uncle Dale had me with him for a long time."

"Where he take you?"

"We rode around meeting different dudes, and then he took me somewhere and some dude got shot."

"What?" Cordale asked. He figured Ladale had bussed a few serves with Lil Ced in the car. That itself was a problem, but for him to put Lil Ced in harm's way had Cordale steaming mad.

"I was sitting in his car and another car did a drive-by and left some dude stretched out," Lil Ced explained, making Cordale even madder. Ladale was a pain in the ass already, but this was a new level of fuckery.

"Go upstairs and let me holla at Ed. We'll talk about this later," Cordale said and Lil Ced ran off to his room. Cordale wanted to call Ladale over and beat his ass all over the house. That's how mad he was. Ladale was careless and messy. Not only was he the one that hit Sharod up, but he was going around town bragging on it, letting everybody know his business.

Cordale knew, as usual, he would have to be the one to clean up Ladale's mess. He was tired of that shit. It came to a point where a man had to be held accountable for his actions. Their mother had taught them that, but it seemed as if Ladale missed that

63

lesson

It had been almost a week since Cordale had heard from Willis and he wondered if he'd heard the rumor about Ladale being the one to shoot his cousin. Cordale and Willis were speaking less and less nowadays and even though Ed was a good, thorough nigga. It wasn't a friend on earth like Willis. He thugged it out with Cordale through some of his darkest days. In many ways, Willis was more of a brother to him than Ladale was. Cordale decided to go pay him a visit, just to talk and see where his head was.

Cordale, along with Lil Ced, arrived at Willis' house twenty minutes later. As soon as the door opened, Lil Ced zoomed past Willis, straight to Shana's room.

"What's up, G?" Cordale asked, stepping into the house, closing and locking the door behind him. Willis had an NBA game playing on the huge flatscreen that hung on the living room's wall.

"Nothing much. You good? You look tired as hell," Willis said, noticing how worn-out Cordale looked. You could look at him and tell he had a lot on his mind.

"I'm good, I'm just tired as hell. I was up all night, fucking with Ed. We went to this reggae club up north."

"Was it crackin?"

"Hell yeah," Cordale replied, pulling out a pack of Newports and taking one out. "What's going on with you? Business been good?" he asked after lighting up his cigarette.

"I can't complain, a few minor losses but nothing major. How about you?"

"Everything been good on my end," Cordale said.

Both he and Willis watched Lebron James dominate the basketball court, before Willis said, "Ladale was the one that ran in my trap with that BD nigga." His words caught Cordale off guard.

"And how you know that?" he asked with a chuckle.

"Yo brother talk too much. He one of them niggas that crave attention, so he brag on certain shit and you know how much the streets talk. Niggas couldn't wait to run back and tell me the shit he been saying," Willis replied. He studied Cordale's face, trying to gauge his reaction.

"Do you got facts to go with that shit, or is this just 'he say—she say?'" Cordale asked.

"How do you think he paid for that Magnum?" Willis paused to let him respond but when he didn't speak, Willis continued. "And it was him and them niggas from the hundreds that shot my lil cousin Sharod up."

Cordale's eyes grew a size bigger. He had hoped Willis hadn't heard that rumor. "If you heard all this, why haven't you said shit to me about it?" he asked.

Willis shrugged before saying, "When I found out that it was him who ran in my spot, I chalked it up as a loss only out of the love I got for you. Then when I found out he shot my lil cousin and he around here braggin on it, like we pussies and he some gangsta, that fucked my head up. I been losing sleep behind that shit."

Cordale took a deep pull off his Newport. He never took his eyes off Willis, who was focused on the game while speaking. "I been tryna figure out the best way to handle the situation without everything we built falling apart," Willis said.

Cordale didn't know how to respond. He couldn't tell Willis to ignore the shit that Ladale did to him and his people, but he also wouldn't give him the green light to harm his brother. That was out of the question. "We can fix this shit without it getting out of control," was all he could think to say.

"How?" Willis asked, turning his attention from the game to Cordale.

"I can't do nothing about what happened to Sharod, but for the money and weed they took out yo spot, I can give you thirty bands." Money wasn't an issue he could give Willis thirty thousand and make it back within a month. He wasn't trying to pay Willis off on some scary shit, he was simply trying to right his brother's wrongs and keep peace with his best friend.

He was torn between love and loyalty. The love he had for his only brother and the loyalty he had to his best friend. If thirty thousand could avoid an unnecessary beef, then he was willing to pay it.

"What I look like taking thirty racks out yo pockets, when you ain't did shit to me? I'm one hundred percent sure you didn't know nothing about the shit that nigga had going on," Willis said, screwing his face up.

"You right, but both of y'all my brothers, what I'ma do if y'all were to get into it?"

"Stay out the way," Willis said sternly, but his words also had a faint hint of a threat behind them

"I can't do that, bruh," Cordale replied firmly. It seemed as if the two were at a stalemate. "In so many words, you telling me you got yo mind made up on dealing with my brother," he said and Willis just stared at him, so he kept speaking. "Thirty bands and I'ma have a talk with my brother and make sure he don't fuck with you or none of yo peoples."

Still no response from Willis, so Cordale stood up and looked his best friend square in the eyes. "Just think about it, bruh," he told him before shouting for Lil Ced, who ran down the stairs, followed by Shana and Blue.

"See you later uncle Cordale." Shana waved as Cordale and Lil Ced left out

***

The next day, Cordale had Ladale and Ed meet him at his home for a sit-down.

It was a lot of things they needed to discuss, most importantly, the situation with Willis. When Ladale pulled up, Cordale and Ed were already on the porch, sipping Patrón from plastic cups. Cordale wasn't a drinker at all, so when Ladale saw him sipping, he cracked a smile. "Everything ok, bruh?" he asked.

"Actually, it's not, bruh," Cordale replied, not returning his smile. "Why you have to go and do all that snake shit, bruh?" he asked Ladale.

"Bruh, what the fuck is you talking about?" Ladale shot back, caught off guard.

"I'm talkin about you runnin in Willis' trap and you having something to do with Sharod getting shot up."

Ladale's face twisted into a sly grin. He picked up the bottle of Patrón and took a big gulp before answering. "Man, fuck them niggas!" he spat, wiping his mouth with the back of his hand.

Cordale bit the inside of his jaw. It took every ounce of willpower he had for him not to swing on Ladale. Ed shook his head in disgust. Cordale was his main mans, but he didn't really care for Ladale. He knew what type of nigga he was from the jump.

"How you gone say that, bruh, when we built this shit from the ground up together?" Cordale asked.

"That's yo friend, not mine." Ladale hunched his shoulders, taking another gulp from the bottle.

"I'm giving him thirty bands to throw that shit out the window," Cordale stated and Ladale erupted in laughter. He was pushing Cordale's buttons with his blatant disrespect.

"Well, I hope you got the whole thirty grand, cause I'm not giving dude shit. Fuck that nigga!" Ladale said defiantly. He wasn't worried about Willis. He knew if Willis sent somebody through the 8Ball shooting, Wild Bill would respond. He felt invincible hiding behind men that had no real love for him.

Cordale and Ed both knew Ladale wasn't as half as gangsta as he was pretending to be, so they were both fed up with this tough guy act., "Look bruh I'm not about to let everything I built fall apart because of you," Cordale said, pointing a finger in Ladale's face. "I'm the same nigga that gave you a million chances! Every time you fucked up... I was there to put yo back on yo feet. Anytime you needed money, I'm the one that hit yo hand and this the thanks I get?" he asked, screwing his face up. The few cups of liquor he'd consumed had him drunk.

"And to you I'm forever grateful, but as far as me coming out of my pockets to pay him off," Ladale blew out air before continuing, "that shit dead and whatever dude wanna do, we can do it," he gruffed, taking another gulp from the bottle.

Ed stood there biting his tongue. He wanted to give Ladale a piece of his mind, but he decided to let Cordale handle him on his own. He wasn't as nice as Cordale was and he could see himself knocking Ladale out. "I'ma pay him the thirty bands, just come with me and let him know it ain't no smoke," Cordale told his brother, causing Ed to shoot him a look of disdain. He felt like Cordale should've made Ladale pay his own tab, or at least pay some of it. It made Ed sick how Cordale babied Ladale. Thirty thousand wasn't chump change and word on the street was that Ladale was up, always flashing money and bragging on how much money he had. Ed planned on telling Cordale about himself once they were alone.

"Ok," Ladale said quickly. He was cool with his brother paying his tab and he wanted to be there to smile in Willis' face. He was guilty of everything he was being accused of and he was getting off easy. He was in a win-win situation. If he knew it would've gone this way, he would've robbed Willis much earlier.

"Winky birthday party Saturday. It's at Mr. Ricky's, we can do it there," Cordale said.

"Bet," Ladale replied and left, still holding Cordale's bottle of Patrón.

As soon as Ladale pulled off, Ed went in. "What the fuck is yo problem, dude?" he asked Cordale before knocking back his cup of Patrón.

"What you mean, bruh?" Cordale slurred.

"You supposed to make that bum ass nigga pay his own debt. He the one that fucked up, not you," Ed growled, poking him in the chest with his index finger.

"I can't have my brothers out here beefin," Cordale replied sadly, looking down at the ground. "I love Willis like a brother and Ladale is my brother. I can't go against neither one of them, and I can't just sit back and let them kill each other. If i can pay 30 racks to squash that shit then it is what it is," he said, sticking a Newport into his mouth. He fished through his pockets drunkenly until he found his Bic lighter.

Ed wanted to argue, but he wasn't in Cordale's shoes, and he couldn't fully empathize with his dilemma. He could see it in

Cordale's body language that he was really hurting, and as a friend, he hated to see his boy down and out. "If you feel like that's the best move to make to resolve the situation, then I'm behind you all the way," he told Cordale, who nodded before downing his cup and throwing it on the ground.

He was slapped and it was so much on his mind, it felt like his head would explode at any minute. He couldn't understand how his brother was so nonchalant about all the snake shit he was involved in. He hated a disloyal nigga and for the first time in his life, he was really looking at his brother sideways. He could only imagine what other folly Ladale had committed that he didn't know about. "I need some more liquor," he said, looking around for the bottle that Ladale had left with.

"Naw, you had enough, G. It's time for you to go in the crib and lay it down," Ed told Cordale, who grinned.

"You right, bruh," he slurred.

Ed helped him inside and told him he'd be back in the morning to check on him. Cordale fucked with Ed the long way. Ed was a true friend. Ed was loyal.

Loyalty is everything.

***

Saturday night came quick, too quick, if you asked Cordale. But as planned, he, along with Ed and Ladale, strolled into Mr. Ricky's nightclub on Dixie Highway. The big security guard nodded at them and gave them a quick pat down before letting them inside the club. Willis had already paid security for all of his people to get in with their weapons, so the search was just a front. The security didn't even look inside Cordale's Gucci backpack, which was stuffed with the thirty thousand, the money was in fifty- and hundred-dollar bills.

The club was packed from wall to wall, everybody who was somebody was there. Cordale saw Banks from Madville with a few of his guys. They were mingling with a group of women. Cordale and Banks shook up GD as he passed by. Then he saw

Teflon from Moe Town. They knew each other from doing time together in the county.

Cordale nodded at one of the Black Souls named B.K., who he knew from both of them always being at the same club. B.K. nodded back and lifted a bottle of Remy in the air. Cordale caught a glimpse of his gold Rolex.

It was a vast variety of women in the club, and they came in all shapes, colors and sizes. Everybody was mingling having a good time. Even the professional ball player, Tony Allen, was in the building. In the corner of the club, he peeped the young niggas, Mo Money and Nutso, lurking in the shadows. They were getting money selling drugs, but they made their names by robbing any and everybody they knew were getting money. Cordale was relieved he had his gun on him. He wished they would try him.

Cordale found Willis and Winky by the bar. "Happy birthday, boy," he greeted Winky, with a handshake and then a half-hug. "Let me get a bottle of Patrón for the birthday boy," he told the bartender, passing him two hundred-dollar bills.

Willis and Winky were both dressed in all-white AKOO outfits, with white low-top Air Ones. Winky wore a white Sox cap pulled low over his head.

"This for you, my nigga," Cordale told Willis, passing him the backpack. Willis trusted him, so he didn't have to count the money, he knew it was all there. "So that shit dead, right?" he asked Willis, whose eyes were locked on Ladale.

"Yeah, as long as that nigga stay in his lane and stay out my way," Willis said, not taking his eyes off Ladale, who was standing there with a smirk on his face.

"What's funny?" Winky asked. He was feistier than Willis and known for knocking niggas out.

"Yo brother mugging me and shit. I just can't take him serious." Ladale chuckled.

"Aye, chill the fuck out, bruh!" Cordale snapped, pointing a finger in Ladale's face. Ladale mugged his brother, but his frown faded quickly, and he walked off without a word. "I don't know what's wrong with that nigga, but I promise you, bruh, he not gone get out his body no more," Cordale told Willis before downing a shot of Patrón.

"I'm not tryna talk about that shit, it's my brother birthday. Let's have some fun," Willis said, grabbing a thick, light-skinned woman by her wrist.

Cordale moved through the crowded club until he bumped into a tall, caramel-colored woman with big round eyes, and a smile that lit the club up. She was slim, with a small ass, and she couldn't have been older than eighteen or nineteen.

"Check it out," Cordale told her, tapping her on her shoulder. The woman smiled but shook her head no. "Damn, a nigga can't get a few minutes of yo time?" he asked. He followed the woman's eyes and looked to his left to see Mo Money watching him with a sneer on his face. "What's up?" Cordale asked him. He knew of Mo Money, but he didn't really know him personally. His name was ringing, and he was known for putting in work. You probably wouldn't have guessed that at first glance, because he was short, around five foot five, and all he did was smile.

"She bad as hell, ain't she?" Mo Money asked Cordale. He had dark skin and his hair was braided into two big braids.

"She aight," Cordale replied dryly. The woman he was trying to holla at must've been Mo Money's girl.

"What's up with them pounds? I heard you got some Lemon Sour Diesel. I ain't never even heard of that shit," Mo Money said with a sneaky smile on his face, switching the subject. His smile did not show his fangs, but he was a known snake.

"Yeah, I got that and some granddaddy Kush in right now. I want thirty-four hundred a pound."

"Twenty-eight hundred if I'm buying more than ten," Mo Money said. It sounded like he was demanding *that* price instead of asking for it.

"I can go an even three bucks for you," Cordale replied as Ed and Willie walked up.

"What up, DMX?" Mo Money asked Ed with a smile. Ed lived in his hood, and he would see him with those big, crazy ass pit bulls, so he called him DMX.

Molotti

"What up, homie, you cool?" Ed asked Mo Money just as the woman Cordale tried to holla at walked up to Mo Money and whispered in his ear. His eyes darted to the other side of the club and his lips spread into a sly grin.

"You know I'm always cool. I got a lil business to handle, y'all be smooth in this bitch," Mo Money said, before quickly walking off. You could tell he was up to no good.

"That lil nigga in here on some hot shit." Cordale frowned. He hated niggas that didn't know how to have a good time, without starting some bullshit and ruining everybody else's night.

On the other side of the club, Ladale was making it rain dollar bills on a few women who were shaking their ass to a Waka Flocka Flame song. The line of coke he'd just snorted in the bathroom had him feeling himself. He was holding a wad of money in the air with one hand and throwing up the rakes with the other hand. When Gucci Mane's "Long Money" came on, the club went crazy. Women were pushing each other trying to get next to Ladale.

Some way, somehow, Ladale ended up where Winky was rapping along to Gucci's song. Ladale started throwing money towards Winky. "Pistol in my coupe, try my troops you get blown away!" he rapped, making it rain on Winky's head. Winky cleared the space between them with three steps.

"Stop playing with me, you bitch ass nigga!" With each word, he snarled, spitting in Ladale's face. Ladale smiled before turning his back on Winky and throwing a handful of bills in the air over his shoulder. Winky took off and knocked Ladale on his ass with a vicious right hook. The punch put him to sleep, he didn't know what had happened when he woke up. Ed was holding Winky, while Cordale was trying to help him off the floor. On the way up, he stumbled and almost fell again, but his brother caught him.

"Come outside, you bitch ass nigga!" he roared at Winky, before trying to spit on him.

Winky broke out of Ed's grasp and rushed Ladale, throwing a flurry of punches Ladale couldn't dodge. The club's security broke the fight up and threw both men out of the club. "What's up, hoe

72

ass nigga?" Winky asked, taking off his shirt and throwing it on the ground. Before Cordale, Willis or Ed could intervene, Ladale pulled a .380 from his waistline and started shooting Winky. Even after Winky fell to the ground, Ladale continued to pump shot after shot into his body.

Willis ran towards Winky's body screaming, only for Ladale to aim his gun at him and pull the trigger. Luckily for Willis, he had run out of bullets.

"What the fuck, bruh?" Cordale yelled, shoving his brother, who had a blank and emotionless look on his face. Ladale took another look at Winky before running away from the scene.

Cordale ran to Willis' side to check on Winky. As soon as he looked at Winky, he knew he was dead. Willis was crying his eyes out. He reached on Winky's waist and grabbed his .9mm. "Get the fuck back!" he yelled, pointing the gun at Cordale, who threw his hands in the air.

"Whoa!" Cordale yelped.

"Calm down, G," Ed told Willis, while aiming his .40 at him.

Willis tried to speak, but he was crying so hard, the words wouldn't come out. "I'm sorry, bruh. I'm sorry, bruh," Cordale said, crying too. Winky was his brother too. He felt the same pain as Willis. It hurt him even worse that Ladale was the one who killed him.

"I'ma kill that nigga," was all Willis could say. Ed tucked his .40 and watched without a word. He knew Cordale wouldn't be able to fix this one. Ladale was going to have to deal with the consequences of his actions. When the paramedics arrived, Cordale tried to get in the ambulance, along with Willis and Winky, but Willis denied him. "Go be with yo brother and let me be with mine," he told him with a mug on his face.

Cordale couldn't believe it, but he didn't argue with him. What could he say? He was the one that forced Ladale to come to the party, and asked Willis to let him handle the situation. He was only trying to make everything right, but he only made things worse. Watching the ambulance leave, he knew things between him and Willis would never be the same.

Molotti

Chapter 6

4 years later

Lil Ced sat on the hood of his father's BMW 745, rolling up a Backwood full of exotic weed. Blake and his younger brother Cragg, who now went by the name of Six, stood right there with him, entertaining a few young ladies they went to school with. It had been four years since Winky died, and Cordale and Willis still hadn't made up. Cordale went to the funeral but was turned around at the door. Even after that, he reached out to Willis a million times, only for his words to fall on deaf ears. Willis simply wasn't trying to hear it. Cordale eventually fell into a deep depression after a few of Willis' peoples tried to kill him. That let him know it was on.

He had cut Ladale off and had stopped talking to him for a long time. He simply couldn't understand why he had to kill Winky. Why couldn't he have taken his ass whooping like a man? After the incident, it convinced him to move his family. He didn't believe Willis would retaliate against him but just to be on the safe side, he moved his family into a house on 83rd and Vernon.

Lil Ced didn't know Ladale killed Winky, but when his father told him he couldn't see Shana anymore, he was crushed. When he told Shana, she informed him her father told her the same thing. Neither parent gave a reason for why they couldn't see each other, and that just made them more curious.

Lil Ced was sixteen now and he was feeling himself, growing more and more rebellious by the day. After he started high school, he started sneaking around to see Shana. They would lie to their parents about where they were going and meet up with each other. Shana was crazy about Lil Ced and nobody couldn't tell her their love wasn't real. He went to school at Harlan, and she went to Kenwood.

Sometimes Lil Ced would leave school early, just to be at Kenwood to see Shana before she went home.

He still considered Blue to be one of his best friends, even though they couldn't hang out anymore. Meechie was a different story, due to him being a few years older than Lil Ced, he was deeper involved in the streets. He ran a crew of young GD's that were getting money, trying to make a name for themselves. He was known to be a shooter that got money too.

"Aye, let's go bowling or something," Blake suggested, passing Lil Ced a lighter. They were selling weed now, so they kept money, and Lil Ced even had his own car now since he had his permit to drive.

"Where?" Lil Ced asked, flaming up the wood. He had grown to five-four, short for his age but his father wasn't tall, so he didn't expect to be that tall. He wore his hair cut low and he had no facial hair at all, looking like a younger version of his father.

"Burr Oaks 127th," Blake said. They all piled into Lil Ced's Impala and went to the bowling alley. It wasn't late in the day, so the bowling alley was packed with families with young kids.

Over the years, Lil Ced and Blake built a bond and became best friends. They enjoyed going out and doing stuff like bowling, mini golfing and go kart riding. They liked going anywhere where they could meet young women and have fun. Lil Ced paid for a lane and bought everyone their bowling shoes. He didn't know how to bowl as well as Blake did, but he was a heavy gambler, so he liked to bet both Blake and Six that he would have the highest score. He rarely won, but that never deterred him from making the bet.

On his first roll, Lil Ced rolled a strike. He took that as a sign of good luck and raised his bet with Six. He didn't trust luck enough to raise his bet with Blake, he was too good.

The young woman with Lil Ced was a skinny, but pretty girl named Ladeja. She was one of the baddest girls in the school. She was a year older than he was and a grade higher, and they had been dating since his freshman year. Ladeja was one of them females that grew up privileged. She had a silver spoon in her mouth since a shorty. Her mother was a CTA bus driver, and her father was the owner of a small lounge in Dolton, IL. She wasn't one of them ratchet block bitches, but she was fascinated with the trenches and the niggas from there.

Lil Ced grew up close to the streets, but he was always blessed. He never had to struggle or go through hard times. He only claimed GD because of his father.

Blake and Six were GD because they lived on 79th and Evans, a hood called Evans Mob, which was full of GD's. They were products of their environment.

Lil Ced didn't sell drugs because he needed money to provide for himself or his family, he sold drugs to buy himself extra clothes, shoes and video games. He watched his father run it up off the drug game and he wanted to do the same thing. Halfway through the bowling game Lil Ced was trailing Blake by eight points. His turn was next, he was sitting down waiting, until he felt a presence behind him.

He turned around to see Meechie, along with a few other guys, standing behind him.

"What's up?" he asked, frowning at Meechie.

"Where yo daddy at?" Meechie asked with a grin on his face. He was taller than Lil Ced, around five foot ten, with big hands and long feet. He was still a bully and he used fear to control his friends.

"Somewhere minding his business," Lil Ced replied. It was his turn to bowl, so he got up and grabbed his ball, only for Meechie to smack it out of his hand. "Stop playin with me, boy!" he snapped, watching his ball roll away.

"Shut the fuck up, lil nigga, before I beat yo ass," Meechie told him, stepping in his face.

Butterflies erupted in Lil Ced's stomach. Meechie had beat him up more times than he could remember, but that was when he was younger. He wasn't a kid anymore and he was far from a pussy. He wasn't scared of Meechie or anyone else.

"You not gone beat shit over here," he told Meechie, looking up at him. Cordale always taught him to stand up for himself. Being a punk was unacceptable.

"Stop actin hard, lil nigga, I know the real you," Meechie said, causing a few of his boys to chuckle. He fed off other people's energy.

"I know the real you too, fuck you talkin about."

"So, you know I'm the same nigga that used to beat that ass."

"Well, ain't nobody gone beat my ass now," Lil Ced stated confidently. He wasn't prepared for the jab Meechie threw, and it knocked him on his back pockets. He bounced right back up and tried to rush Meechie. Blake was right behind him, and it went up from there. It was Lil Ced, Blake and Six against Meechie and his whole crew. They were outnumbered, but the boys fought their hearts out. They ultimately got overwhelmed, but the police arrived before they got beat up too bad.

Cordale was pissed off when he picked the boys up from the police station. "What happened?" he asked when they got in the car.

"Meechie came in there and started tweaking with me and then he snaked me," Lil Ced explained. His lip had gotten busted and was slightly swollen. Blake had a black eye, and Six wasn't bruised up at all, he just had a bad headache from getting stomped out.

"Meechie didn't say anything else?" Cordale asked, wondering if Meechie mentioned Ladale killing Winky. Word on the street was he was seeking to avenge his uncle's death.

"He asked where you was," Lil Ced told him.

Cordale lit a Newport and drove in silence for a while before asking, "Do you know why you had to stop seeing Shana and Blue?"

"No," Lil Ced replied quickly, anxious to find out.

"Willis blamed me for Winky getting killed," Cordale said and Lil Ced looked at him with a shocked expression. He never heard of his pops being a killer and he couldn't imagine him killing Winky, even if he was a killer.

"Why would he think that?" he couldn't help asking.

Cordale didn't baby Lil Ced. He always kept it real with him. He figured since Meechie targeted Lil Ced, it was only right that he informed him of everything that was going on. "Ladale killed him," Cordale admitted, causing Lil Ced's jaw to drop.

Cordale went on to explain everything that happened over the years. He let Lil Ced know that Willis and Ladale were beefing hard, and it had spilled over to him. He had never personally shot at Willis, or even spoken a bad word on his name. He said he still had love and respect for Willis, but blood had been spilled. "So, all that shit that mattered once upon a time didn't matter anymore," Cordale explained.

By the time they pulled on 83rd and Vernon, he had told Lil Ced everything he needed to know. 83rd and Vernon was where Lil Ced and Blake hung out. They went to KD's house, KD was a couple of years older than them, and he was a known shooter. He was one of Cordale's go-to shooters whenever there was a problem. KD stood on a lot of business for his block, and for that he was respected by many.

"What the fuck happened to y'all?" KD asked the trio after letting them inside the house he shared with his grandmother. KD was a chunky, brown-skinned kid with a low cut.

He didn't look like the type that would chase you down and shoot you all in yo shit, but that was him. He was always tryna catch a body.

"We sent up the bowling alley," Lil Ced said, flopping down on his full-sized bed.

"With who, Brain Dead nem?" KD asked. The Brain Deads were a hood of BD's they were into it with.

"Shana big brother Meechie and his homies," Lil Ced told KD, who picked up his Xbox controller and resumed the game of NBA 2K he was playing.

"They beat y'all ass!" he laughed loudly. That pissed Lil Ced off.

"Take me to pop one of they ass," he told KD. He wasn't a shooter. He didn't even own a gun and had never shot at anyone. The only time he had ever shot a gun was on New Year's, when his father let him shoot in the air. He hung out with KD a lot and he always had guns around. Lil Ced was even known to tote one of KD's guns every now and then.

Molotti

One time he was in the car with KD and Blake, and they had gotten into a shootout, but he was just the passenger. Blake wasn't as wild or aggressive as KD, but he'd been the shooter on a few occasions.

"You know where they might be at?" KD asked. He wasn't the type to pass up having a good time.

"Yeah, on 47th Place right off of Cottage Grove," Lil Ced replied. KD got up and reached under his mattress and pulled out two guns, a chrome Colt .45 with a lemon squeeze on it, and a seven-shot black Taurus .38 with no hammer on the back.

You tryna slide forreal?" KD asked Lil Ced, passing him one of the guns. Lil Ced nodded, and they left out.

Thirty minutes later, Blake was driving KD's grandmother's Dodge Neon. KD was in the passenger's seat and Lil Ced sat in the back, along with Six. Lil Ced was nervous as hell the whole ride but tried his best to play it cool. When Blake turned on 47th Place and Lil Ced saw a crowd of people, he felt like he would throw up.

"Roll yo window down, Lil Ced," KD told him. He was sitting right behind KD.

A large crowd of men was on their side of the street, mingling close to the curb. When they were just a few feet away from the crowd, KD stuck his arm out the window throwing wild shots before Blake started shooting. Lil Ced froze momentarily, then quickly stuck his arm out the window and applied pressure to his trigger. He sent seven, still pulling the trigger after his gun was empty.

They made it to the end of the block, and somebody returned fire. Lil Ced ducked down and was almost laid out on the floor of the car. "Go! Go!" he and Six yelled in unison. Blake was a good driver and he managed not to panic as he sped away.

Lil Ced didn't get up until they were safely away from the crime scene. He still had butterflies in his stomach, but he was happy he got to shoot at whoever them guys were standing on Willis' block. If it was a war going on, he planned on being involved.

The next morning, Lil Ced skipped school and somehow convinced Shana to do the same. They met at their favorite spot, Giordano's in Hyde Park. They would sit in the restaurant for hours, vibing and eating pizza without worrying about the police bothering them for not being in school.

Shana's body was developing fast She was thick with nice breasts and due to the fact that she was tall, she was considered a young Amazon. She looked way older than her age

Lil Ced told her everything his father had told him, while they ate slices of pepperoni and cheese pizza. She was just as surprised as he was when he had heard what was going on. It was almost too much for her to digest. She never really liked Ladale in the past, but now she really hated him. Not only was he to blame for her uncle's death, but he was also the reason why her and Lil Ced couldn't see each other.

When Lil Ced told her about the brawl at the bowling alley, she found herself mad at Meechie. He needed to mind his own business and let their fathers figure their own mess out.

"I been missin the fuck outta you. I tried to call you last night, but you was probably sleep," Lil Ced said after taking a sip from his cup of Pepsi. Shana didn't stay up late like he did. She was a straight-A student who took honor classes, and she took school very serious.

"I miss you too. How have you been doing in school?" Lil Ced cringed. He hated when she asked him about school. He hung on 83rd more than he went to school and when he did go, he didn't do any classwork or homework. The only thing he liked about school was the girls and the attention he got. He only pretended to be interested in school because he knew how much it meant to Shana. "I been doin alright," he lied quickly.

"That's good." Shana smiled. She looked down at her plate for a while before saying, "I don't want you to get involved in whatever our fathers got going on."

"Yo brother already put me in it," Lil Ced replied and it got awkwardly silent. He dumped crushed red peppers and parmesan cheese on a slice of pizza before speaking again. "Let's go to my uncle Lucky crib," he suggested. Lucky was an older guy who watched both Lil Ced and his father grow up. He was cool as hell and always let Lil Ced bring girls to his house.

It took a little under an hour for them to make it to Lucky's house on the bus. He ended up leaving out shortly after they arrived. Lil Ced had his own room in the house and had it decked out. He had Chris Brown's "Like a Virgin" playing on his phone, while he and Shana laid in the bed talking. That quickly led to kissing, and he was able to get Shana out of her clothes. All she had on now was her bra and panties.

They had never had sex before due to the fact that Shana wasn't ready. Lil Ced never forced himself on her, or pressured her to have sex, because he loved her enough to wait for her to be ready to give up her body. He started moving his kisses lower down Shana's body until he made it to her pussy. He moved her panties to the side before sticking his tongue inside of her. He'd never eaten pussy before and was surprised that she actually tasted just as good as he imagined she would.

Shana trembled with pleasure, unable to do anything but moan, while he explored her pussy with his tongue. The feel of his tongue had her in another world as she moaned and twisted her body, trying to run from him. After ten minutes, she had the first orgasm of her life. Her legs shook uncontrollably and for a minute she forgot how to breathe.

Lil Ced stopped licking and climbed on top of her. He had already slid out of his clothes. He slid his already hard dick inside of Shana's tight, wet pussy and took his time going in and out of her. Her pussy was the best he'd ever experienced. He picked up his pace and ignored the pain from her digging her nails in his back.

"Slow down," Shana whispered and Lil Ced did as she instructed.

"I love you," he whispered before passionately kissing her. The love they made seemed like it lasted for hours, but in reality, it only lasted for fifteen minutes, before Lil Ced came and collapsed on top of Shana breathing heavily.

"I love you so much," Shana told Lil Ced. She was crying now.

"What's wrong?" he asked, rolling off of her.

"I just can't believe what's going on between our families," she cried, wiping her eyes. Lil Ced was upset that she was ruining this special moment worrying about their families' problems. When they were together, he forgot about all of his problems. All of his worries were erased. He felt nothing but peace and happiness when they were together. "Everything's gonna be ok, baby. It's nothing that can keep me away from you," he assured her, wiping tears from her face.

"I don't want anybody else getting hurt," she cried. She was so innocent and pure.

Lil Ced could tell she was really hurt and frustrated by what was going on.

"It's too late for that," he replied. His words came out harsher than intended, but he didn't mean it like that. "The only thing we can do is remain loyal to each other, and not let them come between us," he said, giving her a kiss on the forehead.

His phone vibrated, he found it and saw that it was his father calling. He rejected the call, only for his father to call right back. Lil Ced texted him, telling him he was in class. Cordale texted right back, telling him to pick up and he called again.

"Yeah?" Lil Ced answered.

"I'm at yo school so I know you not here, where you at?" Cordale asked.

Lil Ced wasn't sure, but it sounded like his father was crying. "What's wrong, Pops?" he asked.

"Where the fuck you at, mane?" Cordale yelled. That threw Lil Ced off because his father never yelled at him, so that told him something was wrong.

"I'm at Lucky crib," he mumbled before his father disconnected the call. He made it there in twenty minutes, he walked right in and his eyes were red and puffy from crying. "What's wrong, Pops?" Lil Ced asked, his stomach was turning over. He'd never seen his father in the condition he was in at the moment. Cordale approached Lil Ced and wrapped his arms around him. He cried while holding him.

"Talk to me, Pops," Lil Ced urged.

"She gone, bruh," Cordale cried.

"Who?"

"Your mother. She's gone," Cordale said and Lil Ced's skin began to crawl.

"What you mean, she's gone? Where she go?" he asked.

"She's dead," Cordale said. Those two words shattered Lil Ced's heart into a million pieces. He felt like he was about to pass out. Cordale tightened his grip on him as he broke down and started crying his eyes out.

"What happened?" he asked.

"Somebody came in the crib and strangled her," Cordale said and that made Lil Ced cry even harder. Who would enter their home and kill his mother? Why? He had so many questions that he knew only God could answer.

Shana entered the living room with tears in her eyes, she had overheard everything and was crushed by the news. Cordale looked up and wasn't surprised to see her. He knew they were still seeing each other, he just never said anything about it. "I'ma drop you off at school. We gotta go," he told her.

The ride to Kenwood was silent the only sounds were of Cordale and Lil Ced crying and sniffling. Shana cried too, but not as hard as them. When Cordale pulled up in front of her school, she got out and headed into school without a word.

Neither Cordale nor Lil Ced spoke until they made it home. There were still detectives on the scene, looking around the home. Cordale fought to hold back tears, he wanted to be strong, but he couldn't believe TayTay was gone. She still had so much life to live, so many goals to accomplish and a son to help him raise. He couldn't believe she was murdered inside their own home, the one place where she was supposed to be safe. Just thinking about it felt like a punch in the gut.

Lil Ced was still crying his eyes out. His mother was his heart. Had he known earlier that morning would be the last time he saw her alive, he would've never left her side. After sitting in the car crying for another ten minutes, Cordale opened his door. "Let's go in," he told Lil Ced. On their way inside, they were stopped by several detectives and paramedics who gave them their condolences. A brown-skinned, bald head detective with a full beard stood in their living room, listening to a forensic scientist speak. He excused himself upon seeing Cordale.

"Hello, Mr. Marshall. I'm Detective Pendarves. I need to ask you a few questions," the detective said, offering his hand to Cordale, who didn't shake it. Detective Pendarves sighed before saying, "I'm sorry for your loss."

"Come on with the questions, so y'all can get the fuck up outta my house," Cordale said rudely. He needed to be alone. He wanted to mourn in his own way. On his own time.

"What time did you leave this morning?" Detective Pendarves asked.

"Around seven this morning I dropped my son off at school."

"What was Taylor doing?"

"She was still in bed sleeping."

"And what time did you make it back in?"

"I had to run a few errands and I made it back in around 11:45."

"Do you know anyone who would've wanted to hurt Taylor?" Detective Pendarves asked, studying his body language.

Cordale took a second to think. He had a handful of enemies, but TayTay had none. He couldn't think of anyone who disliked him enough to target his family.

And then Willis came to mind. Was this Willis' revenge for Ladale murdering Winky? Cordale tried to push the thought out of his head, but he couldn't. Willis was the only person that made sense.

"Anybody come to mind?" Detective Pendarves asked, snapping Cordale out of his thoughts.

"No," he answered, shaking his head.

"Anybody you could think of that would've hurt her, because they couldn't get to you?" Detective Pendarves asked and again,

Cordale was silent.

"No not that I can think of," he said finally. Detective Pendarves stared at him, looking for signs of him lying. He could tell Cordale was involved in the streets, just off his vibe and his demeanor. Someone had just entered his home and murdered his partner, but yet and still, he didn't want to talk to authorities. He drove a nice car and lived in a nice home but had no job. Pendarves knew a drug dealer when he saw one and he was willing to bet his badge that Cordale was involved in the drug game.

"There weren't any signs of forced entry, so whoever it was, had to be someone she knew and trusted enough to let inside like a family member or a friend of the family," he explained. His theory made perfect sense to Cordale. In fact, it made so much sense, it made him start to feel sick. Willis was someone TayTay would've let in if he rang the doorbell. She knew they weren't seeing eye to eye at the moment, but she also knew how close they once were, and she also knew how bad Cordale wanted to repair their friendship, so she would've let him in in hopes of helping them come to a understanding.

Before Cordale could respond, Ladale entered the kitchen and embraced him with a brotherly hug. "I'm here for you, bruh," he stated, rubbing Cordale's back. That hug meant the world to Cordale. He needed the comfort at the moment.

"Any more questions?" Cordale asked the detective.

"No, sir. I'll be in touch with you and keep you updated on the case," he said, almost offering his hand to Cordale for a second time, but he remembered how he left him hanging the first time, so he simply turned and left the home.

Ladale left to go to the liquor store and returned with a liter of Remy.

All the detectives were gone, and the family was finally alone. "We gone find out who did this and kill they whole fuckin family!" Ladale told Cordale, pouring both of them plastic cups full of Remy.

Cordale killed his cup in three gulps before speaking. "They said it had to be somebody she knew and trusted," he said, his voice cracking more and more with every word. He poured himself another cup and downed it before he broke down and started crying again.

"If it was somebody she knew, then we both know who it was," Ladale said. Cordale closed his eyes and tried to envision Willis choking TayTay, but he couldn't. Just the thought alone made his tears flow harder. He killed another cup. He was wishing that somehow, the burning sensation from the alcohol would take away from the burning in his heart. He wanted to call Willis, but for what? It wasn't like he would admit to having anything to do with TayTay's murder.

He was sure Willis had heard the news by now and he halfway expected for him to reach out, and considering that he hadn't, he was starting to believe he was somehow involved. If the shoe was on the other foot, Cordale would've sent his condolences. He poured himself another cup and knocked it back. "What the fuck I'ma do now, bruh?" he asked Ladale with tears running uncontrollably down his cheeks.

"You gotta find a way to weather this storm and be there for yo son." Ladale paused to kill his cup, then continued. "I know it's not nothing that I can tell you that's gone make you feel better, but you gotta be strong for Lil Ced," he said and he was absolutely right. Cordale had to be strong for Lil Ced. He poured himself another cup before staggering to Lil Ced's bedroom.

Lil Ced was in the dark, laying on his bed crying. He hadn't stopped crying since he heard the news. "I'm sorry, mane," Cordale mumbled, taking a seat on his bed.

He didn't know what more to say, so he rubbed his son's back in attempt to comfort him. "Yo mom was a good woman, the best I ever met. We were planning a wedding. She stayed down with me for all these years. I promised her a big ass wedding. She deserved that," he was saying but his words got caught in his throat as he choked up and started crying. "We gone get through this shit, mane, I promise," he vowed.

Lil Ced got up and threw an arm over his father's shoulder. He

Molotti

was hurt more than words could express and the pain was unbearable. He wanted to say something, but he couldn't so he just held him, and they cried together

The next day, Cordale met Ladale and Ed at Red Lobster. That was TayTay's favorite place to eat, so he wanted to eat there in her memory. He also ordered her favorite meal, a Cajun seafood boil with extra potatoes and corn on the cob.

Ladale was the last to arrive, as usual. "How you feeling, bruh?" he asked Cordale, who looked bad. His eyes were red and had heavy bags underneath them.

His usually wavy hair was nappy and unbrushed, like he had gone to bed without putting on his du-rag. His clothes were wrinkled and his whole vibe was gloomy, but who could blame him?

"I'm fucked up, bruh," he said as a matter of fact. "I'm fucked up and I want somebody to feel how I'm feelin," he added.

"Anyone specific in mind?" Ed asked. "Man, you know Willis the only mufucka that would pull some shit like that," Ladale snapped.

"So, you wanna push on Willis nem?" Ed asked Cordale, ignoring Ladale.

"I want him and everybody he fuck with, dead," Cordale said solemnly. It was a tough call to make, but it had to be done.

"Say no more," Ed said, throwing a popcorn shrimp in his mouth.

Ladale had a small smirk on his face, he had been waiting on this moment for years now. It was *fuck Willis*, if you asked him. Cordale had contemplated on that all night and Willis was the only person he could see murdering TayTay. He had to respond with violence after Ladale killed Winky. It wasn't anybody he could use to hurt Ladale besides Cordale, and since he couldn't catch him, he settled for TayTay. Besides Lil Ced, TayTay was the closest thing to Cordale's heart. If crushing him was Willis' goal, then Willis had succeeded and now it was on Cordale to make the next move. "I want him dead," he told Ed and Ladale and he meant it. Killing Willis was his new purpose of being alive.

Chapter 7

July 4, 2015

Lil Ced honked the horn of his Jeep Grand Cherokee. He was sitting in front of Blake's apartment building, waiting for him and Six to come out. It was the Fourth and they had a day full of activities planned. It had been a little over a year since his moms had died and Lil Ced had changed a lot. He was more mature, more calculated and colder. He was also more active in the streets. He was selling weed and pills and was making a name for himself as a hustler. He was also more into putting in work. His name was starting to be involved in more and more shootings as of late.

He hadn't seen or spoken to Shana since the day his mother got murdered. That was the day he started to hate her family, because he blamed Willis for being the reason why his mother was dead. He thought about Shana often, but his father let him know he had to cut her off completely, because he didn't know if somebody from Willis' side would harm him in order to hurt him. He knew it would be hard for Lil Ced, but he told him his love for Shana would get him hurt.

Cordale was right. It was hard for Lil Ced, but he fought through every temptation to call Shana, or answer one of her calls. Most nights he found himself missing Shana, but her father took his mother from him, and that wound was still fresh. "I was just about to pull off on y'all ass," Lil Ced told Blake and Six as they climbed into his Jeep.

"You know that be this nigga, taking all day to get dressed," Blake said about his brother. The three were inseparable. Some people called them Ed, Edd and Eddy. They watched each other's backs and held each other down.

Cordale was the plug, so Lil Ced had an endless supply of drugs. He knew how to hustle, but neither him nor Blake was as good a hustler as Six was. That lil nigga hustled his ass off and stacked more than he spent. Blake hustled to stay fresh and have fun. He was the older brother, but Six was more mature. He helped their mother with rent and bills, but he also made sure he was dripped in the latest designer fashion.

Blake was more into putting in work than he was in hustling. He had inherited Cordale's beef and was frontline.

"You brought that pound out for me?" Six asked Lil Ced from the back seat. He was a little shorter than Lil Ced was, with brown skin and shoulder-length dreads.

"Yes, sir. It's in the armrest," Lil Ced replied. Six counted out twenty-seven hundred and reached up front, putting the wad of money in the cupholder, before Blake opened the armrest and passed him the pound of exotic in a Ziploc bag.

They pulled up on 83rd and Vernon and got out the Jeep. Lil Ced felt his waistline to make sure he had his Glock 19, he knew it could go down at any moment. "Where my pops at?" he asked one of his father's workers, who pointed at Cordale's Infiniti Q7. Lil Ced walked to the truck and hopped in the passenger's seat. "What's up, old folks?" he asked his father, picking up a half-smoked wood and flaming it up.

"Shit, just got back from Indiana buying some fireworks. What you up to?" Cordale asked. He had his facial hair cut into a well-groomed goatee, whereas Lil Ced only had a few hairs above his lip and none on his chin.

Cordale was still a couple of inches taller than Lil Ced and those were the only two ways to tell the two apart. Cordale was grooming his son to become a boss. They were best friends and had a bond that would make other fathers jealous. Ever since he lost TayTay, Cordale had become more violent. He stepped on anybody that got in his lane and Ed was by his side, every step of the way.

The war with Willis had spiraled out of control and was way beyond being able to get squashed. A lot of people had lost their lives behind the war. He wouldn't be able to sleep peacefully until Willis was dead. It was still days where he found himself reminiscing on times when everything was all good, when Willis was still his right-hand man. It was hard hating a nigga you once had a unmeasurable amount of love for. A nigga you would've killed for or died for. It was hard hating a brother, but being without TayTay was even harder, so for that Willis had to die. No ifs, ands or buts about it. Fuck how he once felt.

"I'm not on shit. I just popped out," Lil Ced replied, passing him the wood.

One thing Cordale tried his best to teach Lil Ced was responsibility. Once he decided to be in the streets, Cordale started to carry him as a man. He made him pay his own phone bill, he bought his own clothes and shoes, and even though he was grabbing a hundred pounds at a time, he made him pay for his own weed and pills. He knew he could get killed or catch a case any day, and he wanted Lil Ced to be able to take care of himself, if or when that moment came.

"I heard y'all slid through 47th shooting, and y'all ain't hit shit but a few hypes," Cordale said with a chuckle.

"I had that big boy. We fucked them hypes up," Lil Ced replied, joining his father in laughter

"The Draco?"

"Naw, the automatic pump," Lil Ced said, causing his father to laugh even harder.

"Six scary ass started blowing before we even got up on they ass. I was mad as hell on folks nem grave."

"Y'all gotta stop takin Six on hits when y'all know he not on that typa time," Cordale said seriously. He knew Six was a solid nigga, but he didn't know what he would do if them peoples snatched him up for a body. He liked Six and and never wanted to see him in that position.

"He was supposed to be behind the wheel, but once we parked, he wanted to hop out with us," Lil Ced explained.

"Ok, but you need to learn how to be a leader. You know if a nigga with the shit or not. If you know a nigga a hustler, don't force him to be a shooter. And if a nigga a shooter, don't expect for him to get out there and hustle his ass off, it's just not what he does. Everybody can't shoot, somebody gotta be willing to make the assist. As a leader, you gotta influence niggas to play their positions," Cordale explained, before taking a long drag off the

wood.

"I hear you, Pops," Ced replied dryly. "Damn, look at that thick ass bitch walking up the block." He pointed excitedly, jumping out of the truck and hastily making his way towards the thick, dark-skinned woman walking up the block. "I been waiting on yo bald head ass all day," Lil Ced told the woman, who looked confused.

She was pretty, with a beautiful smile, and she couldn't be no older than twenty-one. "I don't even know you," she replied, showing her pretty smile. She looked Lil Ced up and down. He had on a pair of light blue Robin jeans, a fitted white tee, and a pair of white low-top Air Ones. He had a fresh haircut, and his waves were spinning. All the women considered him to be a handsome young man.

"Stop playin, everybody know me," he told her, checking out her juicy thighs.

The sound of a speeding car caught Lil Ced's attention. He looked up to see a smoke gray Acura coming up the one-way. A guy, wearing a black tee around his face, leaned out the window and opened fire. The first shot hit the woman Lil Ced was talking to in the back of her head, bursting it open. Blood and brain matter splashed all over Lil Ced's face and neck. He was caught off guard, but quickly recovered and upped his Glock. He returned fire, trying to hit the driver, instead of the guy shooting at him. Another shooter emerged from the back window of the Acura and sent shots towards where Blake and Six were standing on KD's porch.

Cordale rolled down his window and aimed his .40 Desert Eagle. He waited until the Acura was right next to his truck and started dumping his clip into the window. He knew he had killed the passenger when he saw him slump forward. He then focused his next barrage of bullets on the back seat, trying to kill the other gunman. The driver of the Acura hit the gas and almost crashed, trying to turn down 84th Street, but he didn't and got away.

Cordale jumped out of his truck and ran to where Lil Ced was hiding behind a Nissan truck. He had his Glock in his hand and wore a mask of terror on his blood covered face. "You good?" Cordale asked, rushing to his side.

"Yeah, I'm straight but…" Lil Ced stopped speaking when his eyes found the woman he was talking to, stretched on the sidewalk, with her brains oozing out the hole in her forehead. He was the reason she stopped. If she hadn't been right there speaking to him, maybe she would still be alive.

"Get up, bruh, we gotta get from right here," Cordale snatched him up, snapping him out of his trance. Once he was up off the ground, Lil Ced took one last look at the woman before running off to his Jeep.

Later that night, everybody was back on the block like nothing had happened. Lil Ced was still shaken up, but he was on his third cup of Remy, and the liquor was calming his nerves. His father was preparing to light twenty-five hundred dollars' worth of fireworks and the block was full of people from old to young. A few grills were going., Some of the folks had started a dice game and the younger kids were having a dance contest.

"Pass the wood, G." KD gruffed to Lil Ced, who had drifted off in his thoughts while smoking. KD wasn't out there earlier that day when the block had got shot up and ever since he popped out, he'd been in Lil Ced's ear about retaliating.

KD loved his block, and he loved his role as a enforcer. Cordale loved KD, he reminded him of a younger version on Ed, so he made sure he kept money in KD's pocket. "What the fuck is we waiting on?" KD asked, blowing smoke in the air.

"As soon as my pops start lighting his fireworks, we gone," Lil Ced replied, before killing his cup of Remy. "Blake, you driving. Six, you not coming with us on this one," he added, causing Blake to smack his lips.

"I'm tryna get busy too," he complained.

"Ok, we gone park and walk up."

"Say less," Blake replied. They continued taking shots and rotating woods until Cordale started his firework show. He had some of the best fireworks. The ones that lit up the sky and held people's attention.

"Come on," KD told Lil Ced and Blake, leading them to a red Chevy Cobalt he'd borrowed from one of his lady friends. They had found out through *Instagram* that Meechie and a gang of others were celebrating the Fourth at Washington Park. They rode back and forth through Washington Park until they spotted Meechie's yellow Camaro. "Park right here," Lil Ced pointed to an open parking space.

Blake parked and they got out with the car still running. Washington Park was lit. It was packed with people enjoying themselves and the good weather. Nobody paid much attention to the three men who had their heads down and their caps pulled low, trying to conceal their identities. Not too far from Meechie's car, Lil Ced spotted DB, one of Meechie's homies. His hand slipped to where his Glock 9 rested on his hip. He didn't want to shoot from a distance, he wanted to make this hit count.

He was no more than ten feet away from DB when he heard shots going off. No doubt it was KD s .357 Sig Sauer. He saw DB duck, then reach for his pistol. That's when he upped his Glock and ran up on him, squeezing his trigger.

The first shot hit DB in his shoulder, twisting his body. Another shot hit him in his neck. He tried to run but tripped over a lawn chair. Lil Ced ran up and pumped two shots into the back of his head. He looked up and emptied the rest of his clip at the scattering crowd. When his clip was empty, he took off sprinting to the car, satisfied with his work.

***

"Wake up, bruh." Cordale elbowed Lil Ced in his ribs. They were sitting in service at the House of Hope Church on 114th. Ever since TayTay got murdered, Cordale made it his duty to go to church every Sunday. She left an enormous hole in his heart that only God could heal. It had been over a year, but things still hadn't gotten better. The pain still hadn't faded. He still had dreams of her beautiful smile. Sometimes, he heard her voice in his head. Sometimes, he dreamed she was still there with him, and when he woke up alone it hurt like hell.

Hearing the reverend speak always helped Cordale. He always left church feeling powerful and uplifted.

"My bad," Lil Ced mumbled, shifting in his seat. Unlike his father, he didn't really enjoy church. He always felt as if the reverend was speaking directly to him. He felt uncomfortable in church, knowing he was far from a saint, and most likely on his way to sin again as soon as he left. He was always sincere when he repented, but he felt like a hypocrite when he asked God for forgiveness and then went out and did the same shit. He prayed every night. That was a habit he got from his mother. He felt like God knew why he was doing what he was doing in the streets. He was avenging the death of his mother. Nothing more, nothing less.

He got up from his seat and went to the bathroom to take a piss. On his way out, he ran into a young lady that he went to school with. "What's the word, Alexis?" he asked. Alexis was short about five foot two, with big breasts and wide hips. Her stomach wasn't the flattest, but she was bad. Her skin tone was high yellow, and she had juicy lips and slanted hazel brown eyes.

"Hey, Lil Ced. Look at you all dressed up," Alexis giggled admiring Lil Ced's outfit. He was dressed in a black Burberry button-up, a pair of black skinny jeans and a pair of black Burberry shoes that read "Burberry" in white along the side of the shoe. He always dressed up for church.

"I must be looking good, huh?" he asked, smiling and Alexis nodded in agreement. "Thanks. I didn't know you went to church here," Lil Ced said, slowly walking back to where service was being held.

"Yeah, my granny been coming here for years. I don't make it every week, but I try to make it as much as possible," Alexis said.

The way she looked at Lil Ced let him know that if he shot his shot, he wouldn't miss, so he went for it. "Put yo number in my phone and let me take you out later on," he told her, pulling out his iPhone.

"And where you plan on taking me?" she asked, while putting her number in his phone.

"You can decide where we go. I just wanna vibe with you."

"Ok." Alexis smiled, before going to sit next to her grandmother

After church, Lil Ced made his way to the hood. He had a few jars of X and a couple pounds to sell. Not to mention, some money to collect from a few niggas that owed him. On the block, Six was sitting in Blake's car, waiting for Lil Ced.

He was tryna buy a few pounds that he already had a sale for. Lil Ced found it funny how Six would sell his drugs before he even had them. He had graduated from selling bags and only sold weight.

When Lil Ced pulled up, Six jumped out of Blake's car and casually strolled to his Jeep and jumped in. "What's good, folks?" he asked Lil Ced, shaking up with him.

"Shit, just came from church. What you on?"

"Shit, bout to dump these niggas from the heights and then I'm out here," Six said, while counting his money out.

"I just bumped a decent ass bitch at church, boy. God work in mysterious ways!" Lil Ced chuckled.

"Stop playin so much," Six laughed, crossing his chest.

"I'm bout to take her out and then hopefully take her down. You know what I'm on."

Six passed Lil Ced a wad of twenty-, fifty-, and hundred-dollar bills. "That's eleven grand," he said. Lil Ced reached in his back seat and grabbed a white plastic bag.

"That's five pounds," he told Six, who grabbed the handle to the door. As soon as he opened the door, shots erupted.

Both Lil Ced and Six ducked, trying to avoid getting shot. Whoever was shooting had to have a thirty, because he was shooting for a while. Lil Ced wanted to shoot back, but he didn't know where the shots were coming from. When he finally looked up, he saw his uncle's car sitting on the corner with the driver's door open.

Lil Ced hopped out of his car and quickly ran to where Ladale's car was, with his Glock in his hand. When he got to the corner, he saw Ladale running his way, holding his Glock 18 that had a stick in it.

"That was just Willis hoe ass! I think he was following me, tryna get up on me but I just blew his ass down," Ladale told Lil Ced, out of breath and hurrying to his car. "Get from out here until later," he told Lil Ced before climbing in his car and speeding off. Lil Ced scurried to his car and did the same thing.

***

Lil Ced's date with Alexis went well. He took her to Weber's Grill, and they had a good time getting to know each other. They found out they had a lot in common. Alexis grew up living with her grandmother, a God-fearing woman that worked her ass off to provide for her family. Alexis was cool. She made him laugh and she was very down to earth, not stuck up like one would assume a woman as pretty as her would be. As bad as he wanted to fuck her, Lil Ced didn't even try. It was something about her that made him wanna take his time with her. After their dinner, they went to the lakefront and kicked it for a while, before Lil Ced dropped her off at home. They agreed to hang out again the next day.

After a couple of months of fucking around without a label, Lil Ced officially made Alexis his girl. She was head over heels in love with him. He, on the other hand, liked Alexis, but love wasn't an option. Shana was the only woman, besides his mother, that he ever loved. He never even played with a woman's emotions by telling her he loved her, when he knew he didn't. He never even entertained the thought of loving another woman. The women he did get close to were cool, but the relationship never went beyond sex, and his feelings never went beyond close friends.

He liked kicking it with Alexis. She was mature for her age and brought the grown man out of him. It was more than sex for the both of them. They connected mentally. They had a solid bond. Most days she would be in his passenger's seat while he rode around getting money. She stayed on his ass about stacking his money and had even persuaded him to buy a safe.

One thing he didn't do was involve Alexis in his business

when it came to putting in work. He never told her about any hits and refused to speak business in front of her. That was something his pops had taught him. The less she knew about what he did in the streets, the less she could tell about. Cordale and Ed had been instilling that in his head since he was younger.

Ladale's name had become hot again. He was still up to his old tricks, scheming and running with the savages. He kept a young wild nigga around him. He wasn't doing as well as he once was, but he knew how to stay afloat. He stayed in Cordale's ear about Willis. He knew Willis had money on his head and the streets knew it too, so he made sure he stayed on point. A lot of people were surprised he'd made it this far. Fear was what got him this far. He would get high and let his paranoia take over. He used his shorties to put fear in everybody's hearts. He only really got his hands dirty when his back was against the wall, when he had the ups, or when he was tryna impress someone.

Plenty of times, Cordale contemplated reaching out to Willis but every time he brought it up, Ladale chastised him, telling him how Willis was the reason why TayTay was dead. He always said that even if they squashed it, Willis would eventually snake him. Ladale was always plotting on Willis. He wore the hate he had for him on his sleeves for everyone to see.

Willis, on the other hand, kept his hand closed when it came to how he felt. Everyone knew about Ladale killing Winky. Everyone knew about the war that was going on. And everyone knew he was the main suspect in TayTay's murder. Whenever someone mentioned his involvement in TayTay's murder, he denied it vehemently. Willis loved TayTay like a sister and claimed he would never hurt her.

He had a hard time explaining to his kids why Lil Ced couldn't come around anymore. Shana took it the hardest. She was in love with Lil Ced and he knew it. He even knew about the two of them sneaking around together. At first, he thought it was cute but after TayTay got murdered, he told Shana she had to cut all ties with Lil Ced because it was too dangerous.

To make sure she followed his orders and stayed away from

Lil Ced, he had Meechie drop her off and pick her up from school. He didn't want her getting hurt over a love he didn't feel was real. Lil Ced and Shana were still kids, the feelings they had for one another weren't true, or at least that's what Willis told himself. At first Shana wouldn't even speak to him. It took her a couple months and even then, she didn't say much.

She buried herself in schoolwork and stayed to herself. "She'll get over it," Willis told himself but as time went by, he noticed she wasn't getting better.

The happy, fun-loving daughter he knew had grown bitter, and was now withdrawn and quiet. She just wasn't the same anymore.

Willis was hearing more and more about Lil Ced as of late. His name was coming up in a lot of shootings, and even a couple murders. Willis had a few sleepless nights, laid up thinking about what he would do if Lil Ced was to ever come his way looking for trouble. He was like a nephew to him. He was there when he was born. He would hate to have to harm him in any way, but he didn't know what type of bullshit Cordale and Ladale were putting into his head. Not to mention, Lil Ced had lost his mother and the streets were blaming him for it, so he had no doubt he would be looking for get back. He prayed they never crossed paths, but if they did, then he would do whatever he had to do to ensure his survival.

Molotti

Chapter 8

January 2017

Lil Ced zipped up his army fatigue Canada Goose and threw the hood over his head. He was leaving out of the Burberry store downtown and had to walk a block over to get to his car. The frigid January air sent chills down his spine.

Alexis was with him, wearing a matching coat. They always dressed alike in the latest designer, that was their thing.

It was Lil Ced's nineteenth birthday and Alexis had just bought him a pair of eight-hundred-and-fifty-dollar Burberry boots and a Burberry outfit for him to wear to the party they had planned for the night. A black Hellcat Charger creeping past made Lil Ced reach for his Glock 20. The niggas he was beefing with had money, and they slid out of all types of cars, from buckets to luxury vehicles and foreigns.

Cordale had bought him a matte black Audi R8 for his birthday and he was in love with it already. He popped the locks and slid into the driver's seat.

As soon as the car started, a Chief Keef song started playing loudly. Lil Ced smoothly navigated through traffic. The vibrating of his phone made him turn down the volume of the radio. "What's up, gang?" he answered for Blake.

"Where you at, G?" Blake asked, smiling. They were on FaceTime.

"Leaving downtown. What's the word?"

"Shit, me and KD just caught something on 47th."

"Y'all ain't wrap his ass up doe."

"Don't disrespect our aim." Blake chuckled. He was supposed to be getting dressed for Lil Ced's party, but he was out catching bodies instead.

"Where Six at?" Lil Ced asked, flaming up a Backwood stuffed with Gelato.

"Getting dressed, you know it take him three hours, so he had to start early."

"I know he got a raw ass fit, but I think I'ma fuck him up with this Burberry fit my baby just bought for me," Lil Ced bragged, causing Alexis to blush. They had been together for two years now. Lil Ced took care of her, and she held him down. Lil Ced had gotten caught up plenty of times fucking with other women. He was young and lit and Alexis knew the price of having a man of his caliber. She had fought a few women, but after so long, the cheating slowed down and Lil Ced started to show her more respect. If he did cheat, he made sure it didn't get back to her. "Meet me at my slot," he told Blake, ending the call and turning the Chief Keef back up.

Lil Ced and Alexis had their own one-bedroom house in the Beverly area on 99th and Ashland. At first, he was reluctant to move out and leave his pops alone, but he and Alexis needed their own space. When they made it home, they left the door unlocked for Blake and went straight to the shower. They had fucked a million times in every position they could think of, but she still turned him on, like they never did it before at all.

Lil Ced got in the shower and the sight of Alexis' body covered in soap suds turned him right on. "Yo lil bad ass," he told her, stepping behind her.

She took a step back, pressing her big ass on his semi-hard dick. She reached back and grabbed his dick, softly stroking him. She had tattoos all over her back and ass. She had his real name, "Cedric" tatted from her ass, down her thigh, stopping right above her knee. It was surrounded by hearts and flowers.

Lil Ced grabbed her hair and pulled, bringing her head back before kissing her. He used his free hand to gently massage her clit. Once he was fully hard, he bent her over and entered her from behind. Water splashed off of her back as he hit her with slow, hard strokes. Her moans sounded like a love song, and he was the producer. He picked up speed and stuck his thumb in her ass, making her cum instantly.

She turned around and sat on the edge of the tub, and greedily stuffed his dick in her mouth. She was a beast with her mouth. She knew how to make him buss within minutes. He grabbed the back of her neck and held her head still while he fucked her face. She gagged and snot ran out of her nose as she deep throated him, making him moan and grunt.

When he felt like he was about to nut, he pulled out and told Alexis to stand up. He bent her over and began assaulting her pussy from behind again. She threw her ass back while looking at Lil Ced, biting her bottom lip. In five minutes, he was exploding inside of her. "How about we say fuck that party and we stay in and make a porn?" Lil Ced asked, only halfway joking.

Alexis giggled before grabbing Lil Ced's washcloth and lathering it up with his favorite Dove for Men's bodywash. When they got out of the shower, Blake was in their living room, playing Call of Duty on the big flatscreen TV that hung on their living room wall. "Hurry up and get dressed, with y'all freaky asses!" he yelled, making Alexis blush.

Alexis put on a Burberry dress that matched the Burberry polo shirt Lil Ced was wearing. Her six-inch red bottom heels made her almost as tall as Lil Ced.

After getting dressed, they both looked in the mirror and decided they looked extra good. Lil Ced put on a thick diamond Cuban link chain his father had bought him for his last birthday. His waves were on point. He looked good and was ready to party.

"Look at y'all fresh asses," Blake said to the couple when they entered the living room. He was dressed in a pair of light blue Amiri jeans, a light blue Amiri jean jacket with no shirt on under it and a pair of white, low-top Air Ones. He had his Glock 27 on his waistline, tucked in his PSD boxer briefs. "I'ma give you yo gift when we get to the club," he told Lil Ced as they prepared to leave.

Blake's Range Rover was parked behind Lil Ced's Audi. Before they pulled off, Lil Ced had a flashback of when he, Blake and Six used to ride bikes together. They had come a long way from those days. For the first time in a long time, Shana crossed his mind. Her gorgeous smile appeared in his head. The way she used to hold his hand while they kissed ran across his mind. He thought about how much he missed her. He started to wonder where she was and how she was doing. Someway, somehow, Willis' image appeared in his mind and made him angry. He honked the horn, signaling for Blake to pull out. He was ready to leave.

Lil Ced's party was at the Red Diamond strip club. When they got there, it was already bussing. Lil Ced and Blake both hit the security guard with a few hundred to get in with only a light pat-down. Six already had their section lit. He was dressed in a pair of black Balmain jeans, a black Dior shirt that said "3Dior" in light blue letters, a Dior scarf was tied around his head over his long dreads, and he wore a pair of white and blue Dior tennis shoes. He had a table covered in bottles of Remy, Dussé, Patrón, Bel Air and Ace of Spades. "Happy G-day, folks," he told Lil Ced, shaking up with him.

"Thanks, lil bro." Lil Ced smiled, looking around the club. It was packed and he was looking for familiar faces. He saw his Vice Lord homie Domo from 104th and Aberdeen. Lil Ced knew him through his older cousin Fatty Mac, who did business with his pops.

In another section was his homie Lil Kenny, one of the folks from off Jackson and California. He was there to show love. They had met in Cook County Jail when Lil Ced sat for a month for a gun case he caught. When they both were released, they linked up and built a bond.

"This bitch bussin." Lil Ced grinned, picking up a bottle of Ace of Spades. He popped the bottle and the champagne erupted like lava from a volcano.

Cordale and Ed arrived a little before midnight. Cordale told Blake to go live while he gave Lil Ced his present. "My baby boy getting old on me. Happy birthday, son. I love you," he said, passing Lil Ced a small gift bag. Inside the bag was a jewelry box. Lil Ced opened it to see an iced-out diamond Cartier wristwatch.

"Thanks, Pops, you snapped with this one," Lil Ced told his father, smiling while putting the bus-down Cartier on his wrist. The diamonds were dancing, even in the darkness of the club. Cordale was smiling proudly.

Ed stepped up next and handed Lil Ced a brick of fifty- and hundred-dollar bills. "That ain't shit but twenty-five stacks. I didn't know what to get you, so you just go buy yoself something nice," he told Lil Ced, giving him a half-hug.

Six stepped up and handed Lil Ced a Nordstrom's bag. Lil Ced reached in the bag and pulled out a white and blue Moncler bubble coat and a pair of white and blue Louis Vuitton shoes. Blake's gift came last. He passed Lil Ced a key fob. "I couldn't afford no Trackhawk, so I bought you a RT Durango," he said nonchalantly. Lil Ced felt good. His peoples had showed up and showed out for him.

Lil Ced left his section. He wanted the whole club to see his watch, so he walked around and mingled with different men and women throughout the club. The strippers were going crazy. They knew it was a lot of niggas with money in the club, so ass was shaking everywhere.

"Happy birthday to Lil Ced, 0-8-3 in the building!" the DJ said over the music. Lil Ced and his people got loud. "The wild hundreds in this bitch, 10-4. What's up?" the DJ yelled. Not only did Domo and the Travelers get loud, but another section started screaming and jumping up and down.

"That's them niggas from Risky Road," Blake told Lil Ced, who was staring at the guys trying to figure out who they were. He'd heard of Risky Road. Ed lived over there in their hood, plus KD had a cousin from over there.

Blake passed Lil Ced twenty-five hundred in singles and they went back to their sections. Future's "March Madness" came on and they started making it rain. The strippers were going crazy, all trying to get as close to Lil Ced as possible. Then Drake and Future's "Diamonds Dancing" came on and Lil Ced rapped while holding his wrist in the air. A thick, brown-skinned stripper was bent over, making her ass jump and bounce in front of him. He slammed a wad of ones on her ass.

A bottle girl tapped Lil Ced's shoulder, grabbing his attention. He turned around to see her holding a tray with thirty shots of Remy on it. She pointed to a small crowd that stood on the other side of the club. Lil Ced squinted, trying to recognize out of the crowd. His eyes stopped on Shana's cousin, Melvo. He was one of the folks from Welch World. He was damn near thirty years old. Lil Ced only knew him because he used to come over Shana's house to kick it with her father.

Lil Ced screwed his face up and smacked the tray out of the lady's hands.

He then grabbed a bottle of Ace of Spades, shaking it up as he made his way to where Melvo was posted. Once he was close enough, he aimed the bottle at Melvo and popped the top. Champagne erupted, drenching Melvo and his homies. One guy rushed Lil Ced, only to get smacked with a Dussé bottle by KD. The club went up from there. Bottles and fists were flying everywhere. Lil Ced and KD stomped one guy out, while laughing the whole time. Once the fight was over and everyone got kicked out the club, the parking lot was bussin.

A green Jeep Compass crept through the parking lot. Nobody was paying it much attention because everyone was recapping the fight. The back door of the Jeep opened and a tall guy wearing a ski mask jumped out, cradling a Draco. He squeezed the trigger, waving the rifle from side to side, trying to hit everybody. Lil Ced ducked when he heard the Draco going off. He felt somebody fall on him. He pushed the weight off of him and the person's lifeless body smacked the ground with a thud. It was his boy Lil Mike, a bullet through the heart had killed him instantly.

Lil Ced popped up with his Glock aimed in the direction of where he heard the shots coming from. He started shooting, not really aiming at anybody. People were screaming and running in every direction, trying not to get hit by a stray bullet.

"Lil Ced!" Cordale screamed from his car. He was parked not too far from where Lil Ced was standing. He quickly made it to the car and climbed in. Cordale sped off. "You good?" he asked, looking over at Lil Ced.

"Yeah, I'm good," Lil Ced replied with a chuckle.

"What the fuck you laughing at?"

"My birthday was lit!" he replied, putting a smile on his

father's face.

"I'm glad you enjoyed yourself, son."

"Thanks for the watch, I love it," Lil Ced told his father, looking at his watch. The diamonds were glistening

"You got fifty thousand on yo wrist, lil nigga. You better love it," Cordale said. The two joked and made small talk until they made it to Lil Ced's house.

Alexis was with Blake and would be pulling up at any moment. I forgot to tell you I saw Melvo in the club. That's who we was fighting," Lil Ced told his father while scrolling his text messages.

"Who the fuck is Melvo?" Cordale asked, flaming up a Newport.

"Shana nem cousin. He the one that's like from 43rd."

"And nine times outta ten, that was Meechie in the parking lot shooting," Cordale said, with a small smile on his face. He and Willis was doing that twenty years ago. One would enter the club and start a fight to draw the enemy outside, and the other would be waiting in the parking lot in a car full of guns. Willis was grooming Meechie, just like he was grooming Lil Ced to take over, when their time was up. They both were teaching their sons the things they'd learned together.

***

Lil Ced's first time counting up a hundred thousand was with his father, and it was all his father's money. The first time he counted his own hundred thousand was today. He was in his bedroom with Alexis, and they were both sitting on their California king-sized bed, counting money. They had been counting for over an hour now. Lil Ced was used to seeing this type of money, but Alexis wasn't. She grew up in a modest household and wasn't as fortunate as he was.

"Baby, you need to invest some of this money into something legit," Alexis said, wrapping ten thousand dollars' worth of twenty-dollar bills in a rubber band.

"Like what?" Lil Ced said, pausing to flame up a wood stuffed with Ice Cream Cake.

"We got enough money to buy a few foreclosed houses, renovate them and rent them out."

"That shit sound good, but don't neither one of us know shit about buying or renting out houses. If I invest my bread in something, it's gone be something I got some knowledge of."

Alexis didn't respond, she went back to counting money and putting it in rubber bands. This wasn't the first time she tried to convince Lil Ced to put his money into something legit.

"You do hair, so how about you go get yo license and we open up a salon?" Lil Ced suggested, passing her the wood.

She was surprised by his suggestion. "That could work, it's all about location doe, so we'll have to find the right spot," she said. One thing Cordale taught Lil Ced was that if he had a good woman, he should invest in her dreams. He had never involved TayTay in his affairs and as soon as he made enough money, he paid for her to go to college and helped her achieve her goal in becoming a dentist. Lil Ced felt like Alexis was a good woman and he wanted to do the same for her.

"Lil Ced, I really love you," Alexis told him.

In return, he smiled and said, "Love is more than a word, it's a behavior. So as long as you 'showing' me you love me, you don't never gotta say it," before hitting the wood and blowing a thick cloud of smoke towards the ceiling.

Alexis threw a brick of money at him. "Is it that hard for you to say, 'I love you too?'" she asked.

"It ain't hard at all. I'm just letting you know words ain't shit without a meaning. I can say anything and not mean it, but actions tell it all," Lil Ced explained Alexis understood his philosophy, but she would've felt way better if he would've said it back.

"Well, I'ma show and tell you how I feel," she said defeatedly. They went back to counting and rubber banding money in silence, both deep in their thoughts. One was thinking about getting married and running away, while the other thought of simply running it up.

After his birthday, Lil Ced had tunnel vision, he was stacking every penny.

Six, with a little help from Blake, was able to buy their mother a house in the suburbs so she was far away from the city's violence. He also gave her enough money to rent out a small storefront and open up a candy store.

Their whole team had a buzz in the streets. Six had gotten robbed before. One unlucky guy tried to rob Lil Ced, only for Blake to leave him dead on the scene. Time after time, they proved to the streets they weren't sweet. You'd die if you played with them.

Every Wednesday, Lil Ced, Blake and Six would meet up with Cordale and Ed at The Hidden Cafe, a restaurant in Matteson, IL. They would eat while discussing business, as well as whatever else was going on in their lives, a ritual that Cordale and Ed used to share with Willis and Winky. That seemed like another lifetime ago, but it still made Cordale reminisce and start to feel a certain way. Lil Ced was the last to arrive at the table.

"About time. How many times do I gotta stress the importance of being on time?" Cordale asked him, visibly irritated.

"That I should always be early, because being late is just as bad as not showing up."

"Exactly. So why the fuck did you show up and you already thirty minutes late?" Lil Ced just stared at his father for a minute before speaking.

"Yo old ass musta woke up on the wrong side of the bed."

"No, I'm just tryna teach you some discipline. You starting to remind me of yo uncle," Cordale shot back.

Lil Ced knew his father was trying to insult him by comparing him to Ladale.

"Less bickering, more business," Ed cut in, trying to deviate the conversation.

"I got a new pill connect, he got Percs straight from the pharmacy. He only selling them by the hundreds," Blake told the table.

"How much?" Six asked.

"Two thousand for a hundred M-Box Perc 30s."

The table was quiet for a second, before Ed said, "Buy three hundred and open up on 83rd." Blake nodded.

"What's up with KD?" Cordale asked.

"He still on the run," Six said over a mouth full of fries. KD and Lil Ced had run into the opps at the White Palace restaurant and a shootout left one dead. The restaurant's camera caught KD's face.

"Did y'all go holla at that lawyer?" Cordale asked.

"Yeah, I gave Jerry Bischoff fifty racks, but they still want KD to turn himself in," Lil Ced explained as a waitress placed a plate of nachos in front of him.

"Why don't he just turn his self in and y'all bond him out?" Ed asked.

"He on parole for that last gun case he caught, so he'll more than likely have a parole hold on his bond," Lil Ced said before stuffing a cheesy chip in his mouth.

After a few more minutes of small talk, Cordale and Ed left.

"It's a party on 114th and Eggleston tonight, y'all tryna slide?" Six asked Lil Ced and Blake. He had a lot of hoes and was the pretty boy type that loved to party. He always knew where the hoes would be.

"That's the Ville who having a party over there?" Lil Ced questioned. Sometimes Six partied with the wrong crowd. It wasn't intentional, he just wasn't as active in the streets as Lil Ced and his brother, so he didn't know about all the beefs they had going on.

"Edina," Six said.

"You talkin about light-skinned Edina that be with lil Lexie nem?" Blake asked.

"Yeah." Six nodded.

"Aw yeah, I'm in there. I been tryna see what's to that lil bitch," Lil Ced said with a smile.

"I'm already on her ass, gang," Blake told Lil Ced, showing him his phone. He had already jumped in her dm's.

"You a thirsty ass nigga, she don't even like redbones," Lil

Ced joked, causing everyone to laugh. "I got some shit to do, so I'll get up with y'all later on," Lil Ced said, dropping a hundred-dollar bill on the table and leaving the restaurant.

Later that night, he arrived at the addy Six had sent him. When he stepped into the kickback, all eyes were on him. He wore a fitted black and white Louis Vuitton crewneck sweater, a pair of black Amiri jeans and a pair of black patent leather Prada shoes. His .45 was tucked behind his Louie belt.

The kickback was lit. In the living room, a group of young women were rapping along to a FBG Duck song. Other young women and a few niggas were sitting on a sectional couch, vibing. Lil Ced found Blake and Six in the kitchen, shooting dice with a few other niggas. "What y'all shooting?" he asked pulling out a bankroll.

"Twenties," a big, black nigga mumbled, not even looking at him.

"He hit a dub," Lil Ced said, trying to ride with Blake who was on the dice.

Before he could get a bet, somebody came and threw an arm around his neck. He turned to see that it was Magic, one of his close friends. She was like the sister he never had. "What's the word, sis?" he asked, greeting her with a tight hug.

Magic stood five foot five, with caramel-colored skin and she had her hair dyed a vibrant red. "Hey, bro. What you doing here?" she asked.

"Six told me that this was the place to be tonight, so I had to slide through."

"You know yo boo in here, don't you?"

"Who?" Lil Ced asked, raising an eyebrow.

"Gucci," Magic said, causing him to smile.

He immediately went searching for Gucci. She was one of his ex-girlfriends that he really liked, but he couldn't stop cheating on her. She left him and never let him get back in good with her, even though he always tried.

Lil Ced found Gucci standing in the corner of the living room, smoking a thick Backwood stuffed with exotic. "What's up, baby?" he asked, approaching her with his arms spread for a hug.

"Hey, Lil Ced." She smiled, giving him a hug.

"I should be getting on yo ass." He frowned.

"Why?" Gucci asked, caught off guard by the sudden shift of his vibe.

"Cause you the only woman in the world that leave me on read every time I text you."

Gucci's lips flipped from a frown to a smile. "Aw," she said, hitting her wood. "You know I'm not fucking with you like that. I don't even know why you still try." She chuckled, being brutally honest. Lil Ced had fucked her over so many times, she vowed to never let him hurt her again.

"It's been years and you still—" Lil Ced was cut off by someone bumping into him a little too hard for him to let it slide. He turned around ready to bug, but who he saw standing there, threw him off and made him forget what he wanted to say.

The woman standing in front of him was taller than he was, she had to be about five-nine. She had the most perfect honey-colored skin he'd ever seen. Her big, light brown eyes were almost hazel. She had big breasts and a nice set of legs that complimented her big ass. She smiled, showing her pretty white teeth. Lil Ced stared at her in amazement. "Stop acting weird," she giggled.

Lil Ced couldn't believe it. He thought his eyes were playing tricks on him. His heart was beating so fast he thought it would blow up. "Say something," the woman urged, slightly frowning her pretty face up.

"What you doing here?" Lil Ced asked.

"It's a kickback. I came with my sister and a couple of our friends," she said. Lil Ced's eyes darted around the room, looking for any other familiar faces.

"It's just us," she assured him.

"You look good," he told her, grabbing her hand. Her touch was comforting yet new, like he never held her hand before

"Aye, Lil Ced, guess who here!" Blake yelled, approaching Lil Ced. He stopped once he saw who he was talking to.

"What's up, Blake?" the woman asked.

"Hey Shana, how you been?" Blake asked, giving her an awkward hug. It had been years since they'd last seen Shana, and it was quite surprising for them to be at the same party. "You cool?" he asked Lil Ced, seeing how stuck he looked.

"Yeah, I'm well," Lil Ced told him, turning back to Shana. "Let's go outside and talk," he told her. She followed him to his Audi and they got in.

Shana turned in her seat and grabbed Lil Ced's face with both hands. "I miss you so much!" she whispered, staring in his eyes.

At first, Lil Ced couldn't speak, he didn't know what to say. Here was the love of his life, who had gotten abruptly snatched from his life, sitting right in his face. The only woman he'd ever been in love with. The daughter of the man who killed his mother. After all these years, Shana was right in his reach. "I miss you too," he finally replied.

Shana's smile grew wider. "You still look the same," she said.

"I could say the same about you. You always been beautiful, but damn, you grew up." Lil Ced chuckled.

Shana grew quiet. "I be hearing all type of crazy about you. Every time I turn around, it's Lil Ced did this, or Lil Ced did that. Always in somebody's mouth."

"You believe everything you hear?" Lil Ced countered.

Shana pondered her answer before responding. "No, but I know it's not a coincidence that everybody saying the same things about you."

"What is everybody saying?" Lil Ced asked, unrolling a Backwood.

"That you're some big drug dealer and you supposed to be a killer now," Shana said and Lil Ced nodded in agreement. "Is that true?" she asked.

He smiled, not really wanting to speak on what he was doing.

"I also heard you're also a little hoe now and can't keep your dick in your pants," Shana said, punching him in his shoulder.

"You know I wasn't raised like that," Lil Ced joked, breaking down buds of pink. Shana stared at Lil Ced while he rolled up his wood.

"I still be having the nightmares I used to have about you and my daddy," she confessed. Lil Ced knew for a fact that she knew he was active in the streets, and if opportunity presented itself, he would kill Willis in an instant. He didn't know how to respond, so he said nothing.

"So many nights I had to cry myself to sleep because I couldn't see you or talk to you. I went through a deep depression," Shana admitted. The mood shifted.

"I was hurt behind that shit too and I didn't know how to express what I was feeling, so I fell deeper and deeper into the streets," Lil Ced said. He tried to pass her the wood, but she frowned and waved it off.

"I'm sorry about what happened to your mom," she said. Lil Ced tensed up. He wondered if she was sorry because her father was behind it, or whether she was genuinely sorry for his loss.

"After she died, my pops told me I couldn't see you and Blue anymore, because your pops might hurt me."

"My daddy said the same thing," Shana said. The two spoke for hours. Before they knew it, the party was over.

"Damn, it was so good to see you here. I wish this night didn't have to end," Lil Ced told Shana, watching people leave the house where the party was. Time flew while they were catching up on each other's lives. Neither of them could stop smiling. "Can I get yo number? Or would that be asking for too much?" he asked. Shana smacked her lips.

"Now why would that be a problem?" She giggled and gave him her number.

They both knew it could be a lot of problems behind them reconnecting. "Wait!" Lil Ced yelled as Shana was getting out of his car.

"What's wrong?" Shana asked.

"I want a hug," Lil Ced told her, getting out and walking around the car. Shana smiled and they hugged for what seemed like forever, neither wanted to let go. "It was nice seeing you, Shana. I missed you so much," he whispered in her ear, letting his lips brush against her ear with every word.

"I missed you too," she replied, loving the smell of his Gucci Guilty cologne. "Call me," she told him before walking off to find Millie and their friends.

Lil Ced stood there staring in awe. He was almost in a trance watching her ass as she walked off. She was perfect. She still gave him butterflies. She was the only woman he'd ever been in love with, and he felt those feelings being stirred, just off the few hours that they'd just spent together. What were the odds of them bumping heads like this? One in a million if you asked him. It had to be a part of God's plan. No matter if it was meant to be or not, Lil Ced wasn't letting Shana get away again. He didn't care who felt a way, he had to follow his heart.

Molotti

Chapter 9

"Bro, where the fuck you go last night?" Blake asked Lil Ced. They were at Blake and Six's apartment, playing Call of Duty.

"I didn't go nowhere, we was sitting in my car," he replied, not taking his eyes off the TV.

"Did y'all see how thick Millie got?" Six asked, pausing the game.

"Naw, I didn't even see her," Lil Ced chuckled.

"Bro that lil bitch got it back there!" Six dragged.

"What the fuck was you and Shana talking about for so long?" Blake asked. Just thinking of Shana made Lil Ced smile, blushing. "We wasn't on shit, just catching up." Blake knew his right-hand man well enough to know when he was fronting his shit. If he wasn't so dark, he'd probably be blushing. He shrugged nonchalantly.

"I couldn't even relax and catch a vibe in that bitch. I thought them hoes was on some back door shit," he confessed.

Lil Ced frowned before asking, "Why would you think some dumb shit like that?"

Both Blake and Six looked at him like he was crazy.

"Cause we into it with they whole fucking family!" Six stated matter of factly.

"So, y'all think Shana would oop me?"

"On folks nem grave like Chris Paul to Blake Griffin when they played for the Clippers," Blake said, making Six laugh loudly.

"Hell naw," Lil Ced gruffed, becoming angry. They didn't know Shana like he did, so he couldn't expect for them to understand. They were best friends. They were loyal to each other. Loyalty is Everything. He decided not to mention that he had plans on linking up with her later on that night. "Fuck all that doe, did y'all see Gucci bad ass in that bitch?" he asked, changing the subject.

"Yeah, I heard she treated yo goofy ass," Six laughed, making Lil Ced even angrier. He hated when the joke was on him.

"That bitch ain't treat shit. She told me she wasn't fucking with me, that's about it," Lil Ced replied, before his phone started ringing. It was Shana, FaceTiming him.

"Yoooo," he answered coolly.

"Hey, what you doing?" Shana asked, smiling into the camera. Lil Ced loved her deep dimples.

"Playing the game with G nem. What's up with you?"Lil Ced asked looking at Blake and Six who were tuned in to his conversation

"Who is that?" Six mouthed to Blake who was seated next to Lil Ced on the couch. Blake peeked over and saw Shana's face.

"That opp bitch," he whispered, shaking his head.

"So, we still on for later, right?" Shana asked Lil Ced. Blake's face lit up with a shocked expression.

"Whatttttt?" he whispered, making Six laugh even harder.

Lil Ced, mad that they were in his business, got up and went to the kitchen so he could speak in private. "Yeah, we still on but you know yo peoples can't know we're together, right?" he asked, just to be on the safe side.

"I know."

"Ok, I'll meet you at our spot at seven and when we get off the phone, I want you to listen to this song by Trey Songz called 'Song Goes Off.' I heard it earlier and couldn't help but think of you."

"Ok, I'ma check it out," Shana said, before disconnecting the call.

All eyes were on Lil Ced when he entered the living room. "What?" he asked Blake.

"Bro, you planning on linking with that bitch?" he asked, screwing his face up. He always gave Lil Ced credit for being a thinker, but at the moment, he was second guessing his boy's ability to think.

Lil Ced cringed at hearing Blake call Shana a bitch. He wanted to say something about it, but he chose not to. Instead, he said, "All we doing is going out to eat, nothing major G, so relax."

"What if she setting you up?" Six asked. He felt the same way

Blake did about the whole situation.

"I trust Shana. I know she wouldn't do me like that," Lil Ced stated confidently. It was nothing in the world that could make him believe Shana would do anything to put his life in danger.

"I don't think you should go," Blake said, shaking his head. He knew talking to Lil Ced was like talking to a brick wall. Once he had his mind set, he was unbending. He wanted to make a big deal out of it, but he didn't feel like arguing with Lil Ced. He knew how crazy he was about Shana

"Just trust me, G, I'm good."

"Just be safe, man," Blake mumbled before focusing on the game.

"On folks grave, yo ass cappin," Six chuckled but he was dead serious.

Tension was starting to build in the room. Neither Blake nor Six trusted Shana and they wouldn't pretend they did. A lot of blood had been shed between them and her family. They wanted her father and brother dead, and Lil Ced was trying to go on a date with her. Blake didn't understand how Lil Ced could be so trusting.

Love was a mufucka. It made niggas blind. It made niggas move wrong. Lil Ced was the last nigga Blake thought would be moving wrong out of love, but he didn't know how much Lil Ced loved Shana.

***

When Lil Ced entered the Giordano's in Hyde Park, the place gave him a nostalgic feeling. It was him and Shana's favorite pizza place. They used to come here to escape reality and enjoy each other's company.

Lil Ced sat at a table in the corner of the restaurant. He sat facing the window so he could watch everybody coming in and walking past the restaurant.

When Shana arrived, he was drinking a strawberry Crush, scrolling through his *IG* timeline. She had on a red mini dress that showed off her sexy legs and a pair of red Chanel pumps that added to her height. She smiled when she spotted Lil Ced.

"You looking good as hell on folks nem grave," he told her, getting up to give her a hug.

She eyed his Givenchy outfit and said, "You look good too, and you smell good."

They ordered a half-cheese, half-pepperoni pizza, both of their favorites.

"The last time we were together, I never would've thought that would be the last time, for such a long time," Shana said, breaking the silence.

Lil Ced thought about the last time they were together. It was a bittersweet memory. Bitter, because it was the day that his mother had gotten murdered, and sweet because it was the day, he took Shana's virginity. A memory he relived over and over in his head a million times. The memory of that day haunted him as much as it put him in a state of euphoria.

"They say that yo pops was behind my OG getting killed, so it had to be like that," he said as the waiter put their pizza on the table. He was trying to see how she would respond to that piece of information.

Her eyes met his and she studied his face, waiting for him to show her a sign he was joking. But when he didn't show that sign, she said, "Why would he hurt her, out of everybody?"

"Because Ladale killed Winky."

"I know that part, but our fathers were best friends. He wouldn't have did that to your mom," Shana said, shaking her head. She refused to believe her father was that much of a monster, but what she didn't know was that men would do anything to get even. It got awkwardly quiet again. The conversation was uneasy for the both of them.

"Well, until we know for sure, I'm carrying it like it was yo daddy. And I'm not a lil kid no more, I'm frontline with this shit," Lil Ced stated proudly. He wanted her to know he was a man whose name held weight in the streets. He wasn't no average ass nigga.

"So, what're you saying, Cedric?" Shana asked, before taking a bite out of a square of cheese pizza.

"I'm saying I'm fully involved in the war that's going on," Lil Ced said, calling himself putting it all on the table. They locked eyes and he saw nothing but pain in her eyes.

"So, that mean you gone hurt me?" she asked.

It was hard for Lil Ced to tell if the question was genuine or if she was being sarcastic. The Shana sitting in front of him wasn't the same little girl he'd known inside and out. Time changed people, and he didn't know what the years they spent apart did to her. He was different. He had grown and matured, so he had to assume she'd done the same. "I would never hurt you," he stated. "I just need to know I can trust you."

Shana was taken aback by his last statement. "First of all, I'm a lady. I'm not involved in nothing that's going on in the streets and not only that, I'd never, ever do anything to put you in harm's way," she said, making Lil Ced smile.

"I know it's a lot going on, but I wanna be a part of yo life again," Lil Ced told her, grabbing her hand and giving it a light squeeze. Before she could respond, his phone started ringing. He saw it was Alexis calling and rejected it. She called back and he rejected the call again. Then he got a text. He didn't even open it.

"That must be one of your little girlfriends blowing you up like that?" Shana grinned

"Something like that," Lil Ced replied truthfully.

"I knew it. I told Millie that you looked too good to be single."

"I feel the same way about you. I know it be niggas all on yo ass," Lil Ced replied. Shana shifted in her seat.

"My boyfriend is away at school."

"You got a lil college boy, huh?" Lil Ced chuckled, trying to hide the instant wave of jealousy he felt.

"He play football for Ohio State."

"What position?"

"Cornerback."

"I bet I can Moss his weak ass," Lil Ced gruffed, not hiding his jealousy anymore. He started to wonder if she 'd been giving up that pussy, he just didn't want to ask.

"I see your still the jealous type," Shana pointed out. She found it cute.

The two spoke for another hour until Cordale sent Lil Ced the 9-1-1 text. "I gotta go handle some business, when can I see you again?" Lil Ced asked.

"Whenever you're free."

"I'll always find a way to be free for you," Lil Ced shot back, standing up and spreading his arms. "Now give me a hug," he said, and Shana got up and stepped into his warm embrace. For him, it felt good to be holding the one he loved more than anything and for her, it felt good to be held by someone she knew for sure loved her. "I'll call you in a couple hours," he said, before planting a kiss on her cheek and walking off.

Lil Ced rushed to his father's house. The 9-1-1 text had his stomach in knots. He made it in less than thirty minutes and parked behind Ladale's car. He noticed that Ed and Blake's cars were there too. He walked in the house without knocking. "What's going on?" he asked Ladale, who was sitting in the living room on the couch, with his feet on the coffee table.

"Somebody ran in Lucky's crib, they killed him and took 50 racks," he replied dryly like that wasn't a big deal.

"Damn," Lil Ced said. He couldn't believe someone would kill old Lucky.

"Hit his hype ass in the head," Ladale said, showing no emotion. You wouldn't have known that Lucky was like an uncle to him.

"Where you been?" Cordale asked Lil Ced, entering the living room. His eyes were red and puffy, you could tell he'd been crying.

"Out handling some business."

"They done killed old Lucky and took the money I had put up at his crib," Cordale said, and his face twisted into an angry mug.

"And the only people that knew about that money are the niggas that's here right now!" he yelled. Everyone that wasn't in the living room, entered the living room to hear him speak. "It's a snake ass nigga amongst us!" he growled, spittle flying out of his mouth with every word

"How you figure that?" Lil Ced asked. The moment was intense. He couldn't remember when he saw his father this mad. He was the only one in the room comfortable enough to speak.

"Because I put the money there and told only the people in this room about it," Cordale said. He was a calculated thinker like that. He knew somebody on the inside had been hijacking his pick-ups and he formed the plan to set a trap.

Everybody in the room looked at each other in disbelief.

"How do you know it wasn't Lucky?" Ladale asked.

"First and foremost, get yo muthafuckin feet off my table!" Cordale snarled. "Secondly, do you think I'm dumb enough to tell Lucky I had money stashed in his crib, when I know he get high?" he added. It wasn't a secret that Lucky smoked crack. He was a functional addict though.

"So, what was fifty thousand doing there?" Ladale asked, frowning. Cordale was blowing him with all the riddles.

"It wasn't fifty thousand. I lied just to make somebody jump out there. It was really like fifteen thousand. I put some hundred-and fifty-dollar bills over a buncha ones. I planted it there to confirm my suspicions that we got a snake in our circle," Cordale said and the room fell silent. Nobody knew what to say. Cordale took his time to look every man in his eyes before speaking. "One thing I can't deal with is a disloyal ass nigga," he said calmly. He had on all-black and was giving off Nino Brown vibes.

"So, when I find out which one of you niggas been stealing from me, when I'm open arms to all you niggas!" his voice was raising again. "I'ma cut yo fucking head off!" he said in a menacing tone. "Now get the fuck out my house." Nobody needed for him to say it twice, they were all happy to leave.

"Meet me on the block," Lil Ced told Blake and Six, before jumping into his car.

When Lil Ced made it on 83rd, he saw Alexis' BMW parked in the middle of the block. He parked and walked to her car, startling her when he knocked on the window. "Where the fuck you been at?" she snapped, opening her car door and stepping out. She had on a Chanel jogging suit, a pair of low-top white Air Ones and a Chanel cap pulled over her ponytail.

"I was at my pops crib," Lil Ced replied.

"You ain't been over there, cause I went over there, just like I went to Blake crib. So, where the fuck have you been at?" Alexis screamed, stepping into his face.

"Chill the fuck out, man, you frontin yo shit," Lil Ced snapped back, not liking the way that she was talking to him. She wasn't his mother nor his wife, so she had no right to be coming at him like she was.

"I'm not frontin shit. You frontin yo shit, always thinkin you slick. You cheating, dirty-dick ass nigga!" Alexis yelled, making a scene. The whole block was tuned in.

"On folks nem, you wanna chase it in front of all these people? Get yo lame ass outta here," Lil Ced gruffed, walking off on her.

She grabbed him by the back of his designer shirt and yanked with all her might, making him fall on his ass. He quickly jumped up and grabbed her by her throat, slamming her against her car. "Bitch, is you crazy?" he growled, tightening his grip on her neck.

Alexis' face turned red as she struggled to breathe. Lil Ced felt a pair of hands grab him by his neck and snatch him off of Alexis. It was Ladale. Lil Ced was amped up and reacted without thinking. He rushed Ladale, throwing a flurry of punches. Ladale easily dodged a few but caught a hard left to his jaw that made him stumble. He swung back, hitting Lil Ced with a two-piece. He wasn't a fighter, but he figured he could beat Lil Ced because of the height advantage.

Lil Ced went in with his head down. He closed the distance between him and Ladale, then scooped him up and slammed him hard on the pavement. Ladale was stunned for a second, before regaining his composure and putting Lil Ced in a headlock.

Lil Ced twisted and turned, trying to break out of the lock but Ladale had a hold on him. It took a few of the folks to separate the two.

As soon as he was on his feet, Lil Ced was pulling his Glock out of his PSD boxer briefs. "I ah leave yo bitch ass right here!" he snarled, aiming his gun at Ladale who was trying to duck behind one of the folks named Nu Nu.

"Cedric," Cordale yelled, marching up the block with Ed beside him. "Put that muthafuckin gun up!" he yelled with veins coming out of his neck and forehead. "What the fuck is yo problem?" he asked, stepping in Lil Ced's face.

"He put his hands on me," Lil Ced told his father, putting his gun away. Once his gun was tucked, Ladale tried to rush him, but was stopped by Ed.

"I wish you would, bruh," Cordale threatened his brother before turning back to his son. "That's yo uncle, you don't supposed to bear arms against him," he said. Lil Ced waved him off.

"He shouldn't have put his hands on me," he argued, smacking his lips.

Cordale shoved Lil Ced hard, knocking him into Alexis who was standing behind him crying. "Who the fuck do you think you is, boy?" he roared, staring daggers in Lil Ced, who was slightly embarrassed. Cordale had never put his hands on him.

"Yo ass cappin on the G," Lil Ced told his father, pointing a finger in his face. That did it. Cordale tried to grab him, but he missed.

"I see I gotta show you that you not as grown as you think you is!" Cordale yelled, trying to get his hands on Lil Ced, who danced around him and ran to his car and zoomed off.

Thirty minutes later, Lil Ced was in a room at the Sleep Inn on Torrence in Lansing, IL, laying on the bed with Shana. He needed to get away from everyone else and clear his mind. He knew for sure being next to her would put his mind at ease.

"I listened to that song and now it's stuck in my head," Shana told him.

"You like it?"

"Yeah."

"It's like he made that shit just for us, right?"

"Yes, and that's why I like it so much," Shana said, before Lil Ced leaned in and kissed her.

"So, have you thought about me and you getting back together?" he asked, pulling wood out of the pack and unrolling it.

"Yes."

"And?" he asked, opening a baggie holding a seven of White Runtz.

"How we gone be together and we can't even be seen with each other? And not only that, but we both involved with someone else," Shana replied, she had been thinking about it though.

"It's ways around us not being able to be seen together. Look at us now." Lil Ced paused to roll the wood. "And as for any other woman or nigga, fuck them." He shrugged.

"It's not that simple," Shana said.

"It's not that complicated either," he shot back. He loved her and was willing to do whatever it took to be with her. He fucked with Alexis, but for Shana, he wouldn't think twice about leaving her.

"We'll figure it out, let's just take things one step at a time for now," Shana told him.

He wanted to apply pressure, but he chose not to. He didn't plan on letting her get out of his grasp again. He knew that everything he wanted with Shana he would get, so he planned on letting her have her way and taking it slow for now. He would just enjoy the time they had together.

***

After a month, Lil Ced and Shana were sneaking around every chance they got. They were best friends again and they had also fell back in love. Only this time, they were grown, and they knew exactly what they were feeling. He kept Alexis around, but that was just for show, so people wouldn't start wondering where he was, or who he was with. Now that Shana was back in the picture, he had lost all interest in Alexis. Everything she did irritated him. She could barely get his dick hard. She noticed his sudden dislike of her and tried to fix whatever it was that was broken. Love had her blind to the fact that it was because of another woman. She told herself they were better than that and she'd earned his heart.

Lil Ced didn't do much to hide that he was seeing someone else. He barely spoke to Alexis, but love was a strong drug, and she was too high to see he would be with her physically but emotionally he was a million miles away.

Blake was another story. He saw what was going on and tried like hell to snap Lil Ced out of it. He didn't trust Shana and felt like she was stringing him along to set him up. He was in Lil Ced's ear every chance he got. A few times, he wanted to bring the situation up to Cordale or Ed, but he didn't want to put his boy on blast like that.

He couldn't even imagine how Cordale would react to hearing that his son was sleeping with the enemy. It got to a point where Blake would accompany Lil Ced in sneaking to get up with Shana, just so he could watch his back. Lil Ced was too far gone and he wouldn't listen, so now all Blake could do was watch his back for him

One day, while on a date with Shana at Hollywood Park, Lil Ced ran into Ed, who was with his daughter. When Ed first saw Shana, he didn't recognize her. It took a few seconds for recognition to kick in. "Let me holla at you real quick," Ed told Lil Ced, trying to mask the fact that he was bothered by what he was seeing. He led Lil Ced near the Go Kart track where Shana was out of earshot. "What the fuck is you thinking, lil bro?" he asked, his voice an octave higher than it usually was.

Lil Ced thought before he spoke. "Shana cool. She don't got nothing to do with what we got going on," Lil Ced said, making Ed look at him like he was stupid.

"Nigga, yo OG didn't have shit to do with what we had going on, but she was still targeted, wasn't she? So what the fuck is you talkin about?" Ed asked, steaming. Lil Ced bit the inside of his jaw. He wanted to check Ed for mentioning his mother, but he held his composure.

"G, I'm tellin you she not on that typa time, shorty thorough. I trust her," he told Ed, who shook his head in contempt.

It was nothing Lil Ced could've told him to make him understand why he was on a date with the enemy. He wondered how long this had been going on. Lil Ced was playing with fire in gasoline boxers.

"You can't say shit to my pops, you know he a bug behind this," Lil Ced said, reading Ed's mind. He knew his pops would have a fit if he knew he was seeing Shana. Cordale hated her whole bloodline, and all the love he had for her was a thing of the past, no matter how much involved she was or wasn't. He'd lost the love of his life, and nothing could heal the wound that she left on his heart. Killing Willis would make him feel better, but it wouldn't heal him.

"You gotta end this shit after today. If I even feel like you still fucking with shorty, I'ma have to let yo pops know the business," Ed said, looking around, hoping that none of their opps were around waiting on them.

"Bro, I'ma grown ass man and you talking about telling my daddy on me. That's lame as hell," Lil Ced gruffed angrily.

"Because I don't want yo grown, dumb ass to get smoked cause you out here being stupid!" Ed shot back.

"You right, G," Lil Ced said calmly. They were starting to make a scene.

"Get out yo feelings and stop playin in yo ass like shit ain't real out here," Ed said sharply before storming off.

"Everything ok?" Shana asked Lil Ced when he walked back up.

His conversation with Ed had fucked up his good mood and he was visibly irritated. "Yeah, some shit happened in the hood that he needed to holla at me about," he lied. Shana already wanted to take things slow, he wasn't about to scare her more by telling her what Ed was saying.

"I got the feeling he wanted to holla at you about me," Shana said, causing Lil Ced to look at the ground.

"Fuck him," he mumbled. He was mad that Ed was in his business. He was a grown ass man, and he didn't need help with living his life.

"I don't want to cause any problems—"

"It's good," Lil Ced stated firmly, cutting her off. "Let's go get on these Go Karts and have some fun." he suggested, leading her to the karts. He already had his mind made up. He felt no danger in being with Shana, so he was gonna keep doing what he was doing. He was happy and he was starting to feel like it was the ones closest to him that didn't want to see him happy.

After Hollywood Park, Lil Ced dropped Shana off at one her friend's house and went home. Alexis was already in bed lightly snoring when he climbed in next to her. This had become a routine and she'd given up on waiting up for him to come in. She wanted to give up on their relationship, but she couldn't. They'd made it through a lot of bad times before and call her crazy, but she still had hope. Lil Ced sent a text to Shana, letting her know that he made it in safely, before he turned his phone on vibrate and went to bed.

Weeks went past and despite Ed's warning Lil Ced was still sneaking around with Shana. He was comfortable and moving loose at times. Truth was, he was deeper in love with her than he'd ever been before. She was perfect to him. He found peace in being with her. What started out as a every other day thing, had now become almost full-time. He was seeing Shana more than he was seeing Blake and Six. He tried to find time to chill with his boys but that wasn't what he was trying to do, he wanted to spend all his time with Shana.

His relationship with Alexis was totally ruined. When she ran to Cordale for help, he approached Lil Ced about who this other woman was that had him treating Alexis wrong. Lil Ced told him he just wasn't feeling her anymore.

He made it seem like it was her and not another woman. Lil Ced was always on pins and needles, thinking Ed might let his father know about Shana. He wasn't ready for that at all.

"I got something for you," Lil Ced told Shana. They were sitting in his car after a couples' massage at a downtown spa called Ancient Baths. Lil Ced went in his armrest and pulled out a jewelry box.

"What's this?" Shana asked smiling. She opened it to see a 24-karat rose gold diamond ring. Her hand flew up to her mouth. "Oh, my God! Cedric, this is beautiful," she whispered.

"I know," he replied confidently. He knew she was crazy about jewelry. She'd been that way since they were kids.

Shana slid the ring on and admired the big diamond. "I love it. Thank you." She leaned over and they kissed.

"I love you, Shana," Lil Ced told her. This was the first time since they were kids that he'd said those words to a woman. She was the only woman who could make him feel how he was feeling at the moment. Powerless and at her mercy. She could've told him that the sun was cold, and the moon was made of cheese, and he wouldn't have questioned it.

"I love you more," she said before going in for another kiss. The two kissed passionately, neither wanting the kiss to end. Shana's phone going off interrupted their kiss. "It's my daddy," she told Lil Ced, putting a finger over her lips indicating for him to be quiet. "Yeah, Daddy?" she answered nicely. She was quiet for a second while listening before saying, "Ok," and hanging up. "Somebody saw us" she told Lil Ced, whose eyes got big.

"Who?" he asked, starting his car up.

"I don't know but my daddy just called me tweaking," she said. Lil Ced navigated through traffic, his eyes darting to every one of his mirrors.

He was paranoid now. "So, what he talking about?" he asked.

"He told me to come home."

"Fuck!" Lil Ced spat, smacking the steering wheel. Once on the highway, he found what he was looking for, a white Chrysler 300 was following him. His first thought was to lead the car through his block and have Blake nem on point, but that would risk them thinking Shana had set him up. His mind raced as he tried to figure out his next move. "Somebody following us," he finally told Shana.

"Who?" she asked, turning in her seat to look out of the back windshield.

"I don't know who it is, but they in that white 300 and they been following us since we left the spa," he told her. He could tell the news frightened her but the last thing he needed her to do was start panicking.

"I'm about to call my daddy right now," Shana said, grabbing her phone.

"Naw, don't call him. They not gone do shit as long as you in the car," Lil Ced replied, pulling out his Glock and sitting it on his lap. He was trying to think of a plan.

After riding for a while, Lil Ced made his way towards Shana's home. He had a plan. It probably wasn't the best plan, but it was worth a shot. "Look, when I stop, jump out and run," he told Shana. He planned on dropping Shana off in front of her crib and then making his pursuers chase him. They would have to work for this score

If he was scared, he did a good job at hiding it. When they pulled up to where Shana lived, someone was sitting on the front porch. He couldn't tell who it was because as soon as Shana's feet touched the ground, he stomped the gas. The 300 was half a block behind him. He flew up the block and looked through his rearview mirror to see the 300 trying to close the distance between them. He ran a red light and the 300 did too, barely avoiding a collision. A red Grand Prix trying to buss a U-turn got in his way. He tried to go around it and was hit by another car, causing his Audi to spin out. That's when a barrage of about sixty shots went off in less than five seconds.

Lil Ced felt pain erupt in different parts of his body. He heard tires screeching and tried to move, but he couldn't. Part of his body felt numb, and he was dizzy from the crash. He found the strength to lift his left hand and applied pressure to his horn. He needed help. He knew he had been hit.

After what felt like an eternity, the door to his car opened and he was being pulled out. He cried out in agony from the explosion of pain he felt. He started to see stars and thought he would pass out. It was getting harder for him to breathe. Police and paramedics were everywhere.

For once in his life, he was happy to see them. He fought to stay conscious as they put him on the stretcher. "My pops," he whispered to a young paramedic, but passed out before he could finish his sentence.

Chapter 10

When Lil Ced came to and saw the look on his father's face, he wanted to pass back out. Anger exuded off Cordale and his face was twisted into a mask of anger, mixed with disgust. "Look who's woke," he said to Ed, Blake and Six, who were in Lil Ced's hospital room with him.

Lil Ced didn't speak. He knew it was nothing he could say in his defense. He was sure Ed had told his father about him and Shana, so it was no point in lying.

"You just got shot five times. Five fucking times!" Cordale yelled, unable to control his emotions. He was hurt but mad, sad but disgusted. "All because you chasin some bitch. How dumb could you be?" he asked, shaking his head in disgust.

Lil Ced shot Ed a nasty look. He wanted to say something, but he couldn't.

Instead of being worried about his well-being, his father was more concerned with who he was fucking. That hurt him. He had a lump in his throat and had to fight back tears.

"That lame ass nigga Meechie all on social media, claiming his work," Blake told Lil Ced. He was just as mad as Cordale was, but he refused to rub it in his homie's face. He was angrier at himself for not being there to watch his back. He felt as if he failed Lil Ced as his best friend. "I'm bout to go get up with KD. You know what time it is," he told Lil Ced, before getting up and leaving the room, followed by Six.

"Let me get some alone time with my son," Cordale told Ed, who left without a word. Cordale grabbed a chair and sat it next to Lil Ced's bed. "I could've lost you, son. For a minute, I was scared I was going to lose you," he said. His voice cracked more and more with each word. The anger had calmed and now he was overwhelmed with sorrow and grief. "You all I got left, son. I can't lose you," he said. Lil Ced looked over to see his father was crying. The only other time he'd ever seen his father cry was when his mother died. Tears began to well in his eyes, and the lump in his throat grew larger.

"I know yo' mom looking down, frowning at me for how I raised you. She wanted better for you. She wanted you to become a chef or an accountant or something. Anything but a street nigga. She told me that shit all the time. And by me letting you dive headfirst in the streets, I failed her," Cordale said, with tears falling freely from his eyes.

Lil Ced was also crying.

"Deep down, that's one of my only regrets. That, and not marrying your mother when I had the chance. I feel like I failed her as a man and failed *you* as a father. Do you know how weak that made me feel?" Cordale asked. He was releasing several years' worth of frustration, remorse and pain. Feelings that nobody, not even Lil Ced, knew he had been holding in. "I gotta do better," Cordale sobbed.

Lil Ced moved his arm and even though it hurt like hell, he found the strength to grab his father's hand. Guilt ate at Lil Ced's soul. He was the reason why his father was breaking down. He was moving selfishly, only thinking about his own happiness and not thinking about how his actions affected the ones close to him. He felt worse than bad. "I'm sorry," he told his father through a dry throat.

Cordale just stared at him with misery in his eyes. "No, son. I'm sorry," he said, wiping Lil Ced's tears away and kissing him on his forehead, before leaving. Lil Ced was able to leave the hospital a week later. He had spoken to Shana every night since he'd gotten shot. She blamed herself and had a big fight with Meechie. They agreed to let things cool down before spending time together again.

They both knew they'd have extra eyes on them, and it wasn't safe for them to be together. Plus, Lil Ced needed a cast on one of his legs and he had to wear a walking boot to move around.

Alexis was the one who picked Lil Ced up from the hospital. She had visited him every day since he got shot. She had even attempted to repair their relationship. Alexis picked Lil Ced up from the hospital. She was happy to feel needed. She'd visited him every day while he was in the hospital, ever since he got shot.

Lil Ced had lost weight. He was already small, but now he had lost the little size he did have. "Ugh, you skinny as hell now." Alexis frowned up her pretty face while helping Lil Ced into the passenger's seat of her car.

"Them bullets knock weight off forreal, you thought that shit was just a saying?" Lil Ced asked, trying to get comfortable in his seat. "Take me through the hood real quick," he said. Alexis cut her eyes at him. She wanted to argue with him, but she didn't, she knew how difficult he could be.

"Did you bring that weed out?" Lil Ced asked, hooking his phone up to the car's Bluetooth.

"Yes," she replied dryly.

"What's wrong?" he questioned.

"Nothing," she lied quickly. Lil Ced knew her well enough to know when it was something on her mind. He grabbed her thigh and gave it a light squeeze.

"Talk to me, big head, what's on yo mind?" Lil Ced asked.

"You fresh out the hospital and you wanna go right on the block, instead of in the house with me, where it's safe," she said in a whiny tone. It had been a long time since he'd given her his attention and she craved it desperately.

"You wanna go home and chill?" he asked, already knowing what her answer would be.

"Yup," she said, not able to contain her smile. Her cheeks were turning red.

"If we go straight home, you gotta play the game with me," Lil Ced bargained.

"Deal," Alexis beamed.

After an hour of playing zombies, Lil Ced and Alexis showered and retired to their bedroom to a watch a movie. Halfway through the movie, Lil Ced pushed Alexis' head towards his stomach. She knew that meant he wanted some head. She pulled down his Versace briefs and put his soft dick into her wet mouth. She sucked, licked and slurped until he was hard as metal. She gave him a show, spitting on his dick then using it to smack her big, juicy lips.

When Lil Ced nutted, she swallowed and kept sucking. She acted like she didn't notice his dick soften then harden back up. Once he was hard again, she gently climbed on top of him, careful not to hurt him. She planted both hands on his chest and rode him slowly. Lil Ced grabbed two handfuls of ass and guided her.

It must've felt like heaven to Alexis, because she quickly had an orgasm. Lil Ced motioned for her to get up and when she did, he got out of bed and stood at the edge of it. Alexis crawled to him and grabbed his dick with her lips. She sucked her cum off his dick before turning around. She was on her hands and knees with her back arched. She looked like a younger version of the porn star Pinky.

Lil Ced entered her and fiercely pounded her pussy, making her cry out in ecstasy. Her big ass bounced, and waves rippled through her massive cheeks. "I love you so fucking much, boy," she moaned, biting her bottom lip.

"Turn over," Lil Ced commanded.

Alexis laid on her back and threw her legs in the air. Lil Ced held her by her ankles and went to work. He watched his dick go in and out of her wet, creamy pussy. She squirted, wetting his stomach. When he nutted, he collapsed on top of her.

His body was in pain, but the nut had him in a state of bliss. Alexis' legs were still shaking. "Go get a towel," he told her after he heard his phone ding. It was a text from Shana. Just like that, his whole mood changed. He almost felt bad for fucking Alexis. He immediately got engulfed in Shana's conversation.

Alexis came back into the room and wiped him down before climbing into bed next to him. She tried to cuddle up, but he didn't want her to see who he was texting, so he got up and went to the kitchen. Alexis was crushed. She knew he was texting another woman. For a moment, she thought they were on their way to recovery. She was happy that she finally got some of his time and attention, but just as quick as it came, it was gone.

***

Lil Ced spent two weeks in the crib laying up recovering, and then he was back outside. Blake and KD had been sliding every other night since he'd gotten shot. One night, they got lucky and caught Willis' right-hand man, Sco, at the liquor store. They overkilled him hitting him six times in his face. He was Willis' muscle and losing him hurt bad.

A few weeks later, Lil Ced's cast came off and he thought it was due time for him to see Shana. She was still worried that her father and brother were keeping eyes on her. Lil Ced, on the other hand, wasn't worried. He had a Glock 21 with a stick and a switch on it and he was ready for whatever.

He convinced Shana to meet him at the Comfort Inn on Torrence. He was in the room watching videos on *YouTube* when she tapped on the door. He let her in and seeing her dressed in a leopard print catsuit and a pair of black Gucci pumps made his dick hard. He was used to seeing her dressed more casual and professional, but tonight she looked like a bad ass ratchet bitch. "Damn, look at you," Lil Ced said, wrapping Shana up in his arms, grabbing her big soft ass.

"Hey. You happy to see me, huh?" she asked, feeling his dick through his fitted designer jeans.

Lil Ced gave her a passionate kiss that led to an hour-long sex session.

Shana's pussy was the best that Lil Ced ever had. It was so wet and tight. Plus, she made the sexiest faces while they made love. "Do you know you're the only person I've ever had sex with?" she asked, lying next to him. They were both still naked.

"I swear to God, I wanted to ask you if you ever gave that pussy up to someone else," Lil Ced replied smiling. He was happy to know that no man had ever explored Shana's body. He felt special.

"My ex ate me out a few times," she told him, knocking the smile from his face.

"Do you still wanna get married one day?" he asked, running his eyes over her perfect, naked body.

"Yes. I think about it all the time. I wanted to be married by the time I turned twenty-five. I know exactly how I want my wedding." The excitement in her voice made Lil Ced smile. She had been planning her wedding since she was seven years old.

"How you want it?" he asked, even though he was sure he knew exactly how she wanted it.

"I want a traditional wedding with a slight twist. I want the colors to be black, white and red. I want doves to be released after I say I do. I want a huge chocolate cake and I want to hire a singer to sing while we walking down the aisle," Shana said, causing Lil Ced to chuckle. She always loved chocolate. "I don't want to wear a traditional wedding gown, I want mine to be more sexy, and I also want to jump the broom."

"So, you got it all figured out, huh?" Lil Ced asked, staring into Shana's eyes. "Do you see yourself marrying me?"

"In a perfect world, yes. In reality, it's hard to see because we can't even be seen together, so how can we get married?" she asked.

"To be honest, I haven't thought about marriage since you been out my life. You the only woman I've ever been in love with," Lil Ced admitted. Part of Shana felt special, but the other half of her felt sorry for him. She felt like he got robbed of his innocence, deprived of his happiness. And now at nineteen, he was cold and hardened by the streets. "It's getting late, how you getting home?" he asked, getting up to get dressed.

"I'll have Blue meet me somewhere off the highway," Shana said and Lil Ced smiled at the mention of his former friend. Blue used to be his boy. He started wondering what type of dude Blue had grown into.

"How my boy Blue been doing?" he asked, putting on his pants.

"He doing real good, he about to graduate from Mt. Carmel. He play football there and he got a few scholarships, but he hasn't decided which school he wants to go to yet. He doesn't really want to go pro he wants to become a doctor."

"That's what's up," Lil Ced said. He was proud of Blue and happy he chose a route other than the streets. He bet Blue could have any woman he wanted, no matter who her family was, or where she was from. He envied him for that. Sometimes he felt like gangstas got the short end of the stick. He knew too many kids that could've been something but fell victim to the streets.

"He always ask about you," Shana said, causing Lil Ced's face to frown up. Nobody was supposed to know about them. "I tell him everything. He's not involved in the streets, and he still has love for you," Shana said as if she could read his mind.

"It's cool and if he ain't with that shit, then it ain't no problem," Lil Ced replied with a shrug. After they both got dressed, Lil Ced dropped her off at the Wendy's on 87th and Wentworth. Curiosity got the best of him and he wanted to say, "What's up," to Blue, who was waiting on the inside of the restaurant.

Lil Ced strolled into Wendy's with his hand near his waist where his gun resided. He was on point just in case of a surprise. When Blue's eyes landed on Lil Ced, he smiled. His blue eyes stood out as they always did. He stood about five-eight and was still pudgy. He had a low cut, with waves and a light goatee.

"What's the word, gang?" Lil Ced asked, giving him a brotherly hug. "I heard you been on yo shit. I'm proud of you, bro."

"Thanks, bro. How you been?" Blue asked.

"I'm good, just tryna get rich and live to enjoy that shit," Lil Ced said, is eyes darted all over the restaurant and out the windows. Blue noticed he was uneasy, so he didn't want to hold him up any longer, even though a part of him wanted to invite him over for a game of Madden. He was sure he could beat him now.

"It was nice seeing you, bro. Stay safe and stay out the way, my nigga," Blue told him, giving him another brotherly hug.

"You too, gang," Lil Ced replied before giving Shana a hug and a kiss and leaving out.

In the parking lot, Lil Ced saw Ed's blue Dodge Charger parked next to his Durango. "You just don't listen, do you?" Ed barked.

"What, you following me now, G?" Lil Ced replied angrily.

He knew for sure that he'd been on point and was furious he'd gotten caught with Shana again.

Fortunately for him, it was one of his peoples and not one of hers.

"I'm making sure yo lil dumb ass good out here!" Ed said, with his eyes focused on the restaurant.

"I'm a grown ass man. I can make sure I'm good on my own," Lil Ced snapped, but Ed wasn't tryna hear it. He was focused on the guy exiting Wendy's behind Shana, who was dressed in an all-black Nike tech and a pair of black Air Max. He had his hood pulled over his head.

"There go that bitch brother!" he growled, pushing Lil Ced to the side, while upping his .45 at the same time.

Lil Ced's eyes scanned the parking lot looking for Meechie. When his eyes landed on Blue, who was walking a step behind Shana, he knew that was the brother he was speaking of. Before he could stop him, Ed let off a round towards Blue and Shana. "Wait!" Lil Ced yelled, but Ed kept shooting.

Before he knew what he was doing, Lil Ced upped his gun and tapped the trigger.

The switch went off, damn near taking Ed's head off his shoulders. His body hit the ground with a thud. The whole left side of his face and neck was mutilated.

Lil Ced looked over and saw Blue stretched out, with Shana crying over him, screaming for help. He took another look at Ed, whose brain matter and blood was pooling underneath his head and almost threw up. He had fucked up big time. He couldn't stop the tears that erupted from his eyes. He wanted to do something for Ed and for Blue, but what could he do? Ed was dead for sure and from the looks of it, Blue was too.

Lil Ced ran to his car, jumped in and sped off

"What the fuck was you thinking, G?" Blake asked Lil Ced, not attempting to disguise his anger. Lil Ced had explained everything that went down, and Blake was fuming. Ed was like an uncle to them and losing him hurt. He hadn't stopped crying since he got the news. What hurt the most was that it was Lil Ced who did it.

They were at Blake's apartment and Cordale was on his way over. The shooting was all over the news. Blue had gotten shot twice in the chest and was in critical condition, and Ed was pronounced dead on arrival. All because of Lil Ced. Once again, his selfishness had hurt the ones closest to him.

Lil Ced had texted Shana a million times, but she hadn't responded yet. He knew she felt just as guilty as he did. She wanted to give it more time before they started back seeing each other, but he persisted and convinced her everything would be ok. "On folks nem, the nigga was tweakin. I thought he was about to kill me," Lil Ced lied and made himself feel even worse. Ed was always good to him and even better to his father. He died trying to protect him. How ironic was it he got killed by the man he was trying to protect? Lil Ced's stomach flipped, making him nauseous.

"Yo pops ain't gone like this," Blake said, shaking his head. Lil Ced was his boy, but right was right and wrong was wrong, and Lil Ced was dead wrong. And Blake wasn't tryna hear any of his excuses. It was nothing he could say to justify him killing Ed.

The doorbell rang. Lil Ced knew it was his father. Butterflies flew around his stomach. He was starting to sweat, and his heart rate increased. Blake opened the door and Cordale entered the apartment, looking like a wreck. His eyes were red and puffy and dry tears stained his face. Seeing him like that broke Lil Ced's heart into a million pieces. It was like seeing his father broken was starting to become normal for him. What bothered him even more was that he had been the reason for why he was hurting lately.

"What the fuck happened, mane?" Cordale weeped, slumping down on Blake's Italian leather sofa.

Blake's eyes burned holes in Lil Ced. He wanted to hear his explanation. "I-I asked him to m-meet m-me at Wendy's and while we were there, Meechie rode past, and it went down," Lil Ced stammered, unable to look his father in his eyes. "It was a shootout and after Ed fell Meechie ran up on him," he added.

Cordale's head dropped into his lap, and he cried

uncontrollably. Blake was so disappointed and disgusted by Lil Ced's lies that he left the room. Lil Ced sat next to his father and rubbed his back.

"I can't fucking win for losin!" Cordale said, almost shrieking. "We gotta do better, son, we gotta do better," he kept repeating. Those words sent chills down Lil Ced's spine. He knew he had to do better for sure. Tears started to parade down his cheeks. He wasn't crying just for Ed. He was also crying for his father and for himself. The man he was becoming was starting to scare him. Loyalty is Everything, and his loyalty was questionable.

***

Ed's funeral was held a week later at Gatlin's Funeral Home on 101st and Halsted. Lil Ced arrived, wearing a black Gucci suit, a pair of black Gucci loafers and a pair of Gucci shades. Alexis was by his side, wearing a black Alexander McQueen dress and a pair of black Dior heels. The funeral was packed with Ed's family and friends. GDs, BDs, Stones and Vice Lords from all over the city were there to show love and respect. Ed was a real gangsta and was respected by everyone that knew him.

Lil Ced spotted his father sitting in the first pew next to Ed's mother. Blake and Six were sitting behind them. Lil Ced scooted in next to Blake. "What's the word, gang?" he asked quietly

Blake had on a pair of Dior shades, but they couldn't hide the stream of tears running down his face. "Shit," he responded dryly. He didn't even look at Lil Ced.

"I'm sorry, bro," Lil Ced whispered, causing Blake to shoot him a look of disbelief. Lil Ced caught his vibe and decided to leave him alone. Blake knew the truth and he couldn't blame him for feeling some type of way. Lil Ced sat back in his seat and listened to the pastor give his eulogy. His father held Ed's mother in his arms, they both cried and wept like babies. Guilt was eating Lil Ced alive, and he couldn't wait until the funeral was over.

After the funeral, he dropped Alexis off at work and decided to skip the burial. The guilt was killing him, and he needed to get away. He somehow convinced Shana to meet him at the Cheesecake Factory downtown. "How you feeling, bae?" he greeted her with a hug and a kiss.

"H-h-hey, you look nice." Shana smiled. After Blue got shot, she fell out with her father He blamed her and after a big argument, he kicked her out. She was staying with one of her friends for the moment.

Blue had survived the two chest shots after multiple surgeries and was now in the recovery process. Shana knew Lil Ced had just come from Ed's funeral, she could see the sorrow in his face, and she felt bad for him. He'd murdered someone he loved, trying to protect her and her brother. It was a sad story and she felt like the whole situation was getting too far out of control. She was scared and wanted Lil Ced to know and understand how she felt.

"We really need to talk," she told Lil Ced, taking a seat across from him.

"What's up?" Lil Ced replied, not in the mood for bad news.

"This shit y'all got going on is getting to be too much for me. I can't do all this sneaking around, constantly having to look over my shoulder, when all I want is to be happy," Shana said and her words hit Lil Ced in the stomach like a punch. She was ready to call it quits after all he'd sacrificed and been through to be with her. He wasn't willing to just let go and give up like that.

"Me too, and I know it's stressful, but I need for you to hold on and keep fighting with me. I won't let you get hurt," Lil Ced promised. He had already proved he was willing to kill for her, he didn't mind showing her that he would die to protect her.

"I'm already hurt," Shana said. "It's not just about me getting hurt though. I can't stand not knowing if you gone make it home at night. I can't stand the fact that we can't have a normal relationship. I want to go on dates and take pictures and show off my love, but I can't do that with you, and it hurts so bad. I'm not happy." She faded, her voice was cracking, and tears filled her eyes.

"I understand that and trust me, baby. I hate it too, but we can figure something out. Anything. I just don't wanna lose you."

"I been thinking about leaving Chicago," Shana said sadly.

Lil Ced sipped his strawberry banana milkshake while thinking of a response. He couldn't let Shana leave, at least not without him. "Just give me some time to run it up and put up enough money for us to leave and be decent, and then we can run away together," he said, not knowing if he was making the right decision. Here he was, thinking about only himself again, when he had his pops, Blake and Six to think about too. How could he just up and leave them? He was all his pops had. He was a part of a drug operation that made him good money. All he knew was selling drugs, what would he do in a city where he knew no one? He needed time to think this through, but time was against him.

"I'm serious, Cedric."

"Me too," he told Shana, locking eyes with her. The love they shared was true. There was nothing he wouldn't do to have her in his life. She was his happiness, his blessing, and for her he was determined to figure it out.

Chapter 11

Spring 2019

Slowly but surely, Cordale fell back more and more from being in the streets. Losing TayTay, then Ed, and almost losing his son hit him hard, and he was now turned off by the streets. He'd lost so much and was tired of losing. He now had a different outlook on life. He was still the man pulling the strings, but he let Ladale take over handling business in the streets. He was the new face of the operation.

Cordale had close to half a million dollars stacked up and he used some of it to open up a small soul food restaurant that he named Tay and Ed's. He hired ex-cons that had culinary experience, to give them a legit way to make some income upon being released.

Ladale was happy his brother decided to fall back. He was finally the man. Everybody had to move through him, and that gave him a sense of power. He made sure he brought his homies from the 8Ball into the fold immediately. He made sure they got hit before the folks from 83rd did. That would've never happened if Cordale was still in the mix. He didn't fuck with the 8Ball at all and didn't care if them niggas ate or starved.

Ladale made sure he fed the wolves, so they wouldn't try to eat him. He also put fifty thousand on Willis' head and another fifty thousand on Meechie's. He wanted them both dead. He didn't really fuck with Lil Ced, because he knew he was still fucking with Shana. For that reason, he felt like Lil Ced had chosen their side. Not to mention, he hadn't forgotten about him upping a gun on him. Lil Ced was lucky he got his weed and pills straight from his father, because if it was up to Ladale, he would be cut off. It was fuck him, if you asked Ladale.

Lil Ced spent his time hustling and putting everything up. He was saving up for a house in Texas that he and Shana were getting renovated from the ground up. He'd been making payments on it for a year now. He was working hard so they could leave Chicago and be comfortable. They were still seeing each other, but not as much as he would've liked, but he understood why. Bodies were still dropping, and Shana was still scared. It scared her more whenever she heard Lil Ced's name come up in the bullshit. Nobody knew about their plans of running away. Lil Ced wanted to tell his pops so many times, but he knew the news would crush him, and he'd already caused enough pain.

"What's the word, G?" Six nodded to Lil Ced. Six was sitting on KD's grandma's porch on 83rd and Vernon. It was the hottest day of the spring so far, and Lil Ced had been out dumping all morning.

"What's up?" he asked, shaking up with Six.

Six was doing good for himself. He was taking real estate courses and was ready to quit the drug game. He never wanted to be in the game for a long time. He only started hustling to help his mom out and once he saw how good he was at it, he made the plan to make enough money to buy a few properties and walk away from the streets. He was so close that he could see the finish line. He begged Blake and Lil Ced to put their money with his, and they were going to buy a bunch of houses, and even a building or two if they could but they didn't see the big picture like he did. "Shit, waiting on folks nem to pull up," he said and as if on cue, Blake's silver Range Rover hit the block. You could hear the MMG Rome that was playing loudly in the truck.

The doors opened and Blake and KD hopped out. KD was fresh home from the county. Last year, he'd gotten caught in a hotel room and charged with a murder. They would've bonded him right out, but he was on parole and had to go to Statesville Correctional Center to do his parole time. As soon as it was over, they bonded him out for a hundred thousand dollars. "Look at his fat ass!" Lil Ced said, excited to see his boy. He ran up and gave him a brotherly hug. KD must've been eating good, cause he'd put on a few pounds.

"What's up, gang? I see you done bussed yo neck down." KD smiled, admiring the thick diamond Cuban link Lil Ced wore around his neck. He took off the chain and handed it to KD.

"You can have the shirt off my back and the diamonds off my neck," Lil Ced told him in a joking matter but he was dead serious.

"Welcome home, G," Six told KD, passing him a brick of hundred- and fifty-dollar bills. Blake had his phone out and was on *Instagram Live*. "Y'all see how we comin. KD back, bitch! He came home to some paper. Y'all see the ice on my boy neck," he bragged with the camera on KD, who was thumbing through the money Six had given him.

"Them real VV's!" Lil Ced boasted. "What Lil Durk say? *These ain't no SI's these VVS's!*" he said, putting his diamond watch next to KD's chain. Blake and Six both put their buss down Cartier watches in the camera. They loved poppin their shit together.

"I'm bout to take my boy to the lot and buy him any wheels he want," Blake bragged. They were all flashing money and poppin their shit for *Live*, so they didn't notice the navy-blue Maserati creeping up the block. By the time they gave the car some attention, it was too late, an arm was already coming out of the passenger's window, holding a Glock 32 with a switch and a drum on it. Fifty shots went off in a matter of seconds. Blake dropped his phone, trying to get away from the barrage of bullets. Lil Ced was already behind Blake's truck. He fell to the ground, trying to avoid getting hit. Six and KD were the closest to the Maserati, they were standing on the curb before the shots went off.

Lil Ced popped up from the ground, shooting at the Maserati. His switch went off, shattering the back windshield and the car swerved before crashing into a parked car. The driver of the Maserati quickly reversed and turned on 82nd street. Lil Ced turned around to see Six lying face down in the grass. He had caught at least ten shots to his neck, back and head. KD was leaning against Blake's truck, holding his stomach. He had gotten hit multiple times on the right side of his body.

Blake was on the ground with Six, who he'd flipped over and was pressing down on his chest, trying to make his heart start beating again. He desperately tried to give his brother mouth to mouth. He was trying anything. Lil Ced was crying, but he managed to call 9-1-1. Six was dead and they all knew it. KD was crying out of the pain from losing a brother, not from his wounds, although he was feeling weak.

Blake bawled like a baby cradling his only sibling. The pain he felt was indescribable. Lil Ced was also crying his eyes out. KD's grandma was now on the porch, screaming and crying. The whole block was coming out to see what had happened. A female from the block ran up and took Lil Ced's gun out of his hands. She knew the police were on their way and the last thing they needed was for him to get locked up. Lil Ced started to feel dizzy. He sat down on the curb a few feet away from Six, before throwing up all over the street. The sight of Six's lifeless body was too much for him

Later that night, instead of being somewhere mourning for Six, Lil Ced and Blake were in front of Meechie's baby mother's house. They had a daughter together and she was pregnant with his son, so they were sure he would pop up sooner or later. They had been waiting in silence for almost two hours now and Blake had run out of patience. He was high off a white Louie V ecstasy pill and was ready to get some get-back for his brother.

"I'm bout to go in there and kill that bitch, since he don't wanna show up," Blake said grimly.

Lil Ced looked over at him and saw nothing but hate in his eyes. "He gone pull up, G, just chill," he told Blake who smacked his lips, opened his door and headed for the white house with the red porch as it was described to him. His girlfriend Jala had an older sister named Big T, and she knew Meechie's bm. She gave up the address for twenty thousand. Blake would've paid that twice to avenge his brother.

He made it up to the steps and knocked on the door. The door opened when Lil Ced made it to the top step of the porch. Blake pushed his way in, with his gun drawn. Lil Ced ran in behind him and closed the door behind himself.

"FaceTime, Meechie!" Blake yelled to a pretty redbone, who was screaming and crying her eyes out. They were both masked up, so when Meechie answered the phone, Blake snatched it and stared into the camera.

"Ain't no money there," Meechie told him. Blake flipped the camera and aimed it at his bm, then he shot her in the head at point-blank range. Meechie yelled frantically while watching Blake shoot his bm in her pregnant stomach.

"Mommy!" a young girl yelled, seeing her mother bleeding out on the floor. The little girl couldn't have been older than six or seven. She stood there in shock, staring at her mother.

"Let my daughter live, homie," Meechie pleaded. It's funny how a gangsta could turn into a gentleman when his family was in danger.

Blake turned the camera on the little girl before emptying the rest of his clip into her body. Meechie was going crazy. Lil Ced was sick to his stomach. This wasn't part of the plan at all. He stood there frozen in shock, until Blake bumped into him on his way out of the house. Lil Ced followed, and they ran to the stolen car they were in. Nobody said a word. They had awakened a blood thirsty beast inside of Blake and he wouldn't stop until its thirst was quenched.

***

Blake wasn't the same after losing Six. He turned his savage to the max. All he wanted to do was kill, kill, kill. When he was out riding, it better not be a soul on 47th Place, or they were dying. Meechie was the same way after losing his Bm and both of his kids. He made it scary to post on 83rd. He wanted Blake bad, he knew for a fact it was him who killed his family.

Shana was broken when her niece and nephew were murdered. Things were way out of control, and she knew her sneaking around with Lil Ced was only adding fuel to the fire. She was ready to call it quits. The deaths were getting closer and closer to home.

Lil Ced knew Blake felt some type of way about him dealing with Shana, so he felt they should play it safe and kept their distance for a while. It was their anniversary and they decided to go to Sky Zone to celebrate. They had so much fun for a moment, they forgot all about their problems.

After Sky Zone, Lil Ced had to drop her off to Millie, who was getting off from work at a bank in Lynwood, IL. When they parked in the parking lot, a Silver Range pulled next to them, bumping a Lil Zay Osama song. It was Blake. His eyes were big, glossy and red, due to him being high off X and Exotic weed. "What's up, G? Why you ain't been answering yo phone?" he asked when he got out his truck.

Lil Ced hurried up and got out of his car so Blake couldn't see Shana behind his tints. "My shit on do not disturb, G," he lied quickly.

"Who you in traffic with?" Blake asked, trying to see through Lil Ced's windshield, but it was also lightly tinted.

"Shana," Lil Ced replied, causing Blake to frown his face up. Before he could say anything, his attention was caught by a tall, thick, caramel-skinned woman walking their way. It was Millie.

Shana got out the car and met Lil Ced in front of Blake's truck to give him a hug and kiss goodbye. Blake was just as disgusted as he was angry. How could Lil Ced still be dealing with her, after her peoples killed Six? Blake had a gut feeling that he'd still been seeing her, so he'd been following him and now his suspicions were confirmed. Blake was fed up with Lil Ced's treachery. Without warning, he whipped out his Glock 27 and put it in Millie's face. "What the fuck is wrong with you?" Shana yelled, watching him grab a handful of Millie's hair.

Lil Ced took a step towards Blake, only for him to turn his Glock on him. "Stay right there or I'ma shoot this bitch shit off!" he snarled, dragging Millie to Lil Ced's car. He pushed her into the back seat and climbed in next to her." Get in and shut the fuck up!" he screamed, aiming his gun at Shana. When Lil Ced and Shana got in, Blake aimed his gun at Lil Ced from the back seat. "Drive," he demanded.

"What the fuck is you doing, G?" Lil Ced asked Blake, looking at him through the rearview mirror.

"Just drive and shut the fuck up," Blake snapped. He was tired of Lil Ced's fake ass he made Lil Ced drive him to where he had a hot car parked. He tied Millie up with a rope he had in his pocket and put her in the back seat of the hot car, before telling Shana, "Tell yo bitch ass brother it's either him or her. He got thirty minutes to choose." Then he ran back to the hot car.

Shana immediately called her father, letting him know what had just transpired. He put the blame on her before she could even tell him what all went down. He lost his mind, screaming and threatening her as well as everybody else. Lil Ced got her an Uber home. He told her not to call the police, because he was sure he could get Millie back safely. Shana told him he had an hour before she called the police, and he raced off to where he knew Blake would take Millie to.

Twenty minutes later, Lil Ced was pulling up in front of Blake's old house on 78th and Evans. He entered through the back door and tiptoed through the house until he heard muffled screams coming from the basement. He walked down the stairs into the dark basement to see Millie laying tied up on the dirty basement floor. Her eyes were puffy from crying, but it looked like Blake hadn't harmed her at all.

Lil Ced quickly untied her hands and feet and took the duct tape from her mouth. "T-Thank you," she cried, giving him a hug.

He put his finger to his lips, indicating for her to be quiet. "My car parked down the block, hurry up and get there. Lay down in the back seat and don't move until I get there," he told her, leading her up the stairs.

Both Lil Ced and Millie froze in their tracks in the middle of the kitchen when they heard noises coming from the backyard. "Hurry up and go out the front," Lil Ced told Millie, who bolted to the front door. He tried to make it out the back door and was only a few steps away when Blake swung the door open. Lil Ced didn't want to go out with Millie, he wanted to distract Blake, so she had enough time to make it to the car.

Blake mugged Lil Ced and ran to the basement, pushing past him along the way "Where that bitch at?" he yelled on his way back up the stairs. He was steaming as he ran past Lil Ced out the

Molotti

back door, and through the backyard to the alley, looking for Millie. He didn't see her in the alley, so he ran through the gangway to look down the block for her. Lil Ced met him on his way back through the gangway. Blake had his gun out. "Where the fuck did that bitch go?" he asked Lil Ced stepping into his face.

"I don't know when I came in, she was already gone, "Lil Ced lied, causing Blake to smack his lips.

"On the guys, you lyin. You came in and let that bitch go. Stop playin with me, boy," he said, already knowing how things transpired. Lil Ced was that transparent.

"Come on now, gang, you know that shit wasn't right in the first place," Lil Ced told Blake, who turned his head sideways and stared at him in disbelief.

"Not right? Not right?" he asked, raising his voice an octave. "Them killing yo OG wasn't right. Them killing Six wasn't right. You killing Ed for that bitch wasn't right. Matter fact, ain't shit you do right! You ain't right, nigga!" Blake yelled. He held his gun in his right hand and used his left hand to point in Lil Ced's face.

"You cappin," Lil Ced told Blake, not liking his body language, his tone or the words he was using.

"I'm not cappin shit, nigga, you moving weird as hell for that bitch. You done turned yo back on everybody, just to make that bitch happy. I know yo OG tossin and turnin in her grave," he said, pushing Lil Ced's button. He hated when people spoke on his mother.

"Keep my OG name out yo mouth," he snapped, stepping closer to Blake.

"Or what?" Blake challenged, not backing down. He was already fed up with Lil Ced, so if he wanted to take it there, then he wouldn't stop him. He'd lost his brother fighting their war and it seemed like Lil Ced didn't even know which side he was on. He was tired of ignoring his traitorous ways.

"You don't give a fuck about yo OG, all you care about is Shana," Blake growled and in an instant, he was staring down the barrel of Lil Ced's Glock.

"I ah leave yo bitch ass right here, nigga, stop playin with me!" Lil Ced snarled with his finger on the trigger. One tap and the switch would make Blake's head disappear.

Blake had his Glock aimed at Lil Ced's chest. His finger was also on the trigger. The two best friends held eye contact and let the silence linger in the air. "I believe you, you fake ass nigga. You scream all that loyalty shit but who you loyal to, bro?" Blake asked. His question stung. Lil Ced didn't understand how his right-hand man could be questioning his loyalty. Looking in Blake's eyes, all Lil Ced saw was pain and hatred.

He couldn't comprehend how he could have all that hatred towards him though. He never did anything wrong to him, or at least that's what he thought. He didn't see that it was his relationship with Shana that damaged their friendship. The closer he got to Shana, the further he pushed Blake and everybody else away.

"To be honest, I don't know if you on their side or ours," Blake said coldly before walking off, leaving Lil Ced standing there looking stupid, and feeling even dumber. What had he gotten himself into? Was he really moving that bogus? He wondered why nobody could see things his way. Nobody tried to talk to him and try to see and understand how he felt. Everybody attacked him and criticized his choices. At first, he felt bad about his plans to run away with Shana, but now he couldn't wait to leave. But the first thing he had to do was get Millie home.

When Lil Ced climbed in his car, Millie was laying on the floor in the back.

She looked funny, but it wasn't a time for laughter. "You good now," Lil Ced told her, pulling off.

Millie got up and sat on the seat. "Thank you so much, Lil Ced." She was only nineteen and had never been in a situation as scary as the one she was just in. Lil Ced passed her his phone.

"Call Shana and let her know you straight."

Millie dialed Shana's number and explained everything to her. She couldn't help but to start back crying as she told her how Lil Ced rescued her. She knew Six had gotten killed and she just knew

Blake was going to kill her. "Here, she wanna talk to you." She passed Lil Ced his phone back.

"Yeah," Lil Ced said.

"Thank you so much, Cedric. I love you so much," Shana cried. Her emotions were all over the place.

"I love you too," Lil Ced replied dryly.

"What's wrong?" Shana asked, she could sense that his vibe was off.

"Nothing. I'ma drop Millie off on the corner of y'all block, make sure it ain't nobody waiting on me," he said before hanging up. He didn't mean to sound rude, but his confrontation with Blake had him feeling some type of way. He was risking it all for the other side. He peeked at Millie through the rearview mirror. She was innocent. He shouldn't have felt bad for helping her. She never hurt anyone. He kept telling himself what he'd done was the right thing to do, but in the back of his mind, he knew he would be the only one who thought that.

***

Cordale couldn't believe the news he'd just gotten. When he got the call from Ladale, saying he needed to holla at him in person, he was hesitant. He thought he had fucked up some money or drugs. He never thought he would have Blake with him, with a story to tell.

Blake told him how Lil Ced had been sneaking around with Shana for years now. He told him how Lil Ced was the one who killed Ed, trying to protect Shana and Blue, and how he'd just let Millie go after he snatched her up.

Hearing how Lil Ced was involved in all this fuckery made Cordale feel like he was on the verge of having a heart attack. He was hurt and disappointed by his son's decisions.

Ladale was furious and blamed Lil Ced for everything that happened over the years. All the trucks that got hijacked, Lucky's death and even other things that happened in the hood that they couldn't figure out who was behind.

Cordale tried calling Lil Ced to get his side of the story, but he wouldn't answer any of his calls or respond to any of his texts. "That lil snake ass nigga probably tryna kill us all one by one," Ladale said angrily, making Cordale mad.

"Be serious!" he snapped.

"He killed Ed!" Ladale shouted, knowing the revelation touched Cordale more than anybody else. His best friend murdered by his son. That was a big pill to swallow. "He killed Ed and went to the man's funeral! That's some sick, twisted shit!" He frowned. "Not to mention, he upped a gun on me and Blake. He basically letting us know we're next if he get the chance," he added.

As much as he hated to admit it, Ladale was right. He had a point and that only added to Cordale's frustration. "He's just going through some shit right now," Cordale said weakly, defending his son. Even when Lil Ced was dead wrong, he would protect him and tell him about himself later.

"Going through something like what? A killing spree?" Ladale asked

"Come on, mane, you know Lil Ced ain't like that at all, he just made a few bad decisions."

"I don't know what he like. I thought I did but clearly, I was fooled," Ladale said, lighting up a Newport.

"Just let me handle him. I'll figure it out," Cordale said.

Both Ladale and Blake knew Cordale wouldn't really penalize his son. That was a hard task for any father, so they wouldn't understand. "Keep that nigga away from me, bruh," Ladale warned as he and Blake left Cordale's home.

"Let the streets know we got fifty-k on Lil Ced's head," Ladale told Blake once they were in the car.

"You for real?"

Blake asked. He was mad at Lil Ced to the point where he wanted to fall back from him and give him some space, but he didn't know if he wanted him dead.

"Hell yeah, I'm forreal. If he killed Ed, then what do you think he a do to us?" He paused to let Blake speak, but kept going without letting him get a word in. "He was closer to Ed than he was to either one of us and I'm his uncle. That nigga chose his side, so we gone treat him like he one of them."

Ladale's theory made sense to Blake, so he shrugged and said, "Say less." And just like that, Lil Ced was a target.

Chapter 12

Lil Ced finally answered the phone for his dad after the fiftieth call. He didn't want to talk to him, but he knew he had to. He already knew Blake ran and told his pops everything. He knew that once again he was the cause of his father's pain.

"What's up, Pops?" he answered dryly. He was riding through the burbs, looking for a lowkey hotel he could stay at.

"Where you at, mane?" Cordale asked. Lil Ced's eyes shot to his rearview mirrors, he was paranoid. He didn't know if he was being followed by one of the opps or his own guys. If Blake felt how he felt about him, he could only imagine how everybody else from the hood felt. Many lives were lost during the course of their war and Lil Ced was rocking with the other side. "I'm in traffic," he replied.

Cordale took a deep breath, before saying, "Tell me that the shit Blake saying ain't true."

Lil Ced thought about lying, but he was tired of doing that. "I don't know how to explain it," he said with a sigh.

"Fuck explaining it. I wanna know is it the truth or not?" Cordale asked and Lil Ced's silence let him know he was guilty of everything he'd been accused of. "I been instilling this loyalty shit in yo head since you was a baby, and you grew up to be a whole snake. I don't understand it, son," Cordale snapped, his words cutting Lil Ced like a sword. "I gave you everything you could ever want or need, and in return, you stab me in my back. I don't get that. How you gone kill Ed?" Cordale asked.

Lil Ced could tell he was crying. *Here we go again*, he thought. "I'm sorry, Pops. That shit happened so fast."

"You ain't sorry!" Cordale shouted, then lowered his voice. "You did that shit to protect that bitch. Then you let Millie go when that man Blake just lost his brother. How you gone get in the way of his get back?"

"Millie don't got shit to do with nothing. That shit was bogus."

"Who are you to decide that?"

"Come on, Pops, you know that shit wasn't right," Lil Ced said, and it got quiet for a minute.

"Yo mother died behind this shit that wasn't right and you fuckin with the side that killed her. That ain't right, since we speaking on what's right and what's wrong. I didn't raise you like that. You a disloyal, weak ass nigga and I don't want shit to do with you!" Cordale said, hanging up on Lil Ced.

Lil Ced was crushed, he never heard his father speak to him that way. He knew he had really fucked up. Cordale followed up with a text that read, 'you ain't no son of mines, go be with Willis nem'. Lil Ced's regret and remorse quickly faded and was replaced by raw anger. How dare his father say some shit like that to him? He found a Travelodge in Chicago Heights and spent the night there, feeling more alone than he ever felt in his life.

The next morning, Lil Ced went to his house to get some money, drugs and clothes but found it ransacked and almost empty. His heart sank to his stomach when he walked through the open front door. He ran to his bedroom, to the closet hoping that his safe was still there. "Fuck!" he roared, punching the closet's wall, cracking the drywall. His safe and all of his clothes were gone. He had a little over sixty thousand in his safe and over a thousand X pills. He went to his bathroom and looked in the back of the toilet where he had another twenty-five thousand stashed. That was gone too.

Lil Ced pulled out his cell phone and called Alexis. "What?" she answered with an attitude.

"Where you at?" he asked, walking through his home.

"Why?"

"The fuck you mean why, bitch? Somebody been in my crib, and they took everything!" Lil Ced snapped. Alexis giggled, making him even more angry.

"I'm the one that been there, and I took everything. Yo clothes, yo drugs and all yo money and I'm giving this shit to another nigga, since you wanna play me for another bitch. I hope you die with yo bitch ass!" Alexis said cruelly before hanging up in his face. Blake must've told her about Shana.

Lil Ced was furious. He wanted to go find Alexis and shoot her in her shit. All he had to his name was the twenty thousand in his bank account, the few thousand dollars he had in his pockets, and it was a few niggas in the streets that owed him for drugs. That was all he had. He left his home and went to the apartment in the hundreds where he kept his weed. It was also empty. Alexis had cleaned him out. He was in kill mode now. He hit the streets, looking for somebody to kill.

Lil Ced rode down Cottage Grove and saw a black Benz truck turning off of 47th Place, going towards 48th and Cottage Grove. He made a U-turn and was three cars behind the Benz truck. He knew if it wasn't Meechie or Willis driving the Benz, then it was somebody close to them. It didn't matter who it was, Lil Ced was about to send whoever it was to meet God. He followed the truck all the way to 65th and Maryland. The truck parked and a brown-skinned guy got out and went into a house on the middle of the block.

Lil Ced parked and waited for the guy to come back out. He had his Glock 20 ready to go. When the guy came out, Lil Ced hopped out of his car and made his way towards the Benz truck. The guy didn't pay much attention to him and that was a fatal mistake. Lil Ced was a few feet away from him when the guy made it to his truck. It was too late when he looked over and saw Lil Ced. He tried to reach for his gun but Lil Ced tapped his trigger and filled the guy up with the big .10 mm bullets. The passenger's door opened and another guy hopped out shooting a .40 at Lil Ced, who ducked and ran back to his car. He jumped in and threw the car in reverse. The guy was in front of his car throwing into the windshield. Bullets shattered the glass and whizzed past Lil Ced's head as he tried to reverse down the block without crashing. He made it down the block and whipped his car up 64th Street and sped away.

***

Ladale was finally where he wanted to be in life, at the top of the food chain. Cordale was out of the picture, Lil Ced couldn't come back to the hood, and that left Ladale in charge. He was the one with all the money and he made sure he kept the wolves fed so they were always on go for him. He put fifty-k on Lil Ced's head and now the same niggas he used to run with were now on his ass.

He didn't really expect for anybody from 83rd to collect the money but he knew niggas from other hoods that were stretching niggas for free so for them fifty thousand was like signing a record deal. Ladale had even put twenty-five thousand on Shana's head and told everybody that he had a extra twenty-five thousand if they caught them together. He didn't give a fuck about Lil Ced being his nephew. He upped a gun on him, he shoulda used it.

Ladale pulled into the parking lot of the apartment buildings on 104th and Maryland. He hated pulling up to the buildings because he knew the 4's and the Stones were deep in the buildings. He also knew that there were GD's in the buildings too. But the thing with that was the GDs wouldn't save him if something jumped off. Nobody cared about what you were now a days. It was all about where you were from or who you fucked with.

Ladale honked his horn when he spotted a brown-skinned guy, with long dreads that he had braided into two big braids that hung down his back. Ladale looked around the parking lot and saw different crowds of men and women standing around politicking. He noticed men standing on balconies looking at his truck. No doubt they were on Security. The guy with the dreads waved for him to get out the truck

Ladale got out and strolled to where the guy was standing. "What's up, lil bro?" he greeted the guy who frowned his face up.

"I'm not yo lil bro. Don't get fucked up tryna be cool," The guy checked Ladale smoothly. Power radiated off of him as well as confidence. He wore a few diamond Cuban link chains, one had a 'Double R' piece on it that was dancing in the sunlight. He had on a bussdown diamond Rolex on his wrist and was dripped in designer. He was Lil Ty, somebody like God in his hood.

"My bad," Ladale mumbled. Lil Ty was the man when it came

to bricks and keys. He was young in his mid- to late twenties and had a name for himself way beyond Chicago. He was a killer and a stick-up man that got rich off licks. He put his whole hood on and for that he was loved and respected by all.

They were meeting because Ladale wanted a new plug so he wouldn't have to keep going through Cordale's crybaby ass. Plus, Lil Ty had coke and heroin, Cordale only fucked with exotic weed and X pills, so Ladale wanted to expand the business.

"I know you ain't come here just to stare at my chains on some fan shit, so what's up?" Lil Ty asked Ladale rudely. He had no respect for him and that was obvious. "I'm taxing forty for my bricks of coke and sixty for a key of dope," he added.

"I want five," Ladale said quickly. He regretted the words as soon as they came out. He only came to buy one brick, but he wanted to impress Lil Ty and make it seem like he was on something. He was almost twenty years older than Lil Ty, but felt like a shorty in his presence.

"That's gone cost you two hundred racks and next time, don't reach out to me unless you grabbin twenty or more. I got shorties with five bricks," Lil Ty laughed, belittling Ladale. It wasn't intentional, that was just how he was. He was cocky, arrogant and lit. "Take the bread to the third balcony and give it to that old lady. She gone let you know what to do from there."

"I gotta go get the rest of the money," Ladale said.

"What?" Lil Ty snarled. "You come over here like you tryna cop and you don't even got the money on you?" he asked, upping his gun and pointing it at Ladale's face. "Take that shit off!" he demanded. Ladale took a little too long to move, so Lil Ty smacked him across the face with his gun, dropping him. "Get naked, bitch!" he barked.

Ladale quickly stripped out of his clothes. Lil Ty wanted to see if he was wearing a wire or something. He knew the feds were always nearby when you were getting money. "Get yo stupid ass from over here," he told Ladale. By now he was surrounded by different men, they all looked like they were ready to kill him. He snatched up his clothes and scurried to his truck and within seconds, he was out of the building's parking lot with no plans of ever returning. Karma was a bitch.

***

Lil Ced was living from hotel to hotel, with no real plan of what to do

He needed money in the worst ways. After Blake kidnapped Millie, Willis cut Shana off. He took the apartment he'd rented for her, the car he bought for her, and froze all of her bank accounts, so she'd been staying with Lil Ced. They were pressed for money, because they still had to make payments on the house that they were getting renovated.

Lil Ced was out of drugs, so it wasn't any money coming in just money going out. "Why you looking like that, big head? What's on your mind?" he asked Shana, who was strolling through *IG* looking gloomy. She'd been depressed lately. She tried to hide it, but he knew her too well. He could read her like a book. Her normally bright eyes were clouded with pain and frustration. Seeing her hurt fucked with his mood. He sat on the bed and grabbed one of her feet and gave her a foot rub.

"I'm still thinking about all the fucked-up shit Meechie and my daddy said to me," she told him, closing her eyes. She had told him how Meechie had put his hands on her and threatened to kill her. Lil Ced didn't say it out loud, but he vowed to kill Meechie for his disrespect. He'd never put his hands on Shana, and he'd be damned if he let another nigga get away with it, brother or not.

"It's like everybody mad at us because we're in love. That's some miserable, hating ass shit," Shana added feebly.

"Don't trip, pretty soon we'll be in Texas, walking around naked in our big ass house," Lil Ced said. That put a smile on Shana's face.

"And we can start planning and saving for our wedding," she said, as if she didn't have the whole thing planned out already.

Lil Ced switched feet and continued to rub. "I'll understand it if you wanna fall back and make things right with yo family," he said. He tried his best to make her as comfortable as possible, but it was hard getting comfortable when you were basically living on the run. He knew she was torn between being with him and running back to her family. He couldn't blame her.

"It'll never be able to be right with them, as long as I'm with you," she said. It took Lil Ced a moment to find his words.

"I know. And I'll understand if you wanna let go of what we got and make it right with them," he said, not really meaning what he was saying.

Shana was confused and caught off guard. She was going through all this because she chose to be with Lil Ced. She never thought twice about it, but it seemed like he was having second thoughts. The truth was that he was tired of being selfish. His selfishness was affecting the ones closest to him. He knew Shana was hurting and at this point, he'd do anything to make her feel better, even if that meant sacrificing his own happiness.

"Why would I walk away from my happiness, just for their acceptance? That don't even make sense. Yes, I would be living better if I went back, but I wouldn't be happier. I'm happy here with you."

"You're not happy right now. You're going through it and I'm hurting. I love you forreal. I'm in love with you and when you really love a muthafucka, you ah do anything to ensure their happiness, even if it hurts you. So, if it'll make you happier for us to just let go, then I'm willing to do that," Lil Ced offered, planting a soft kiss on the bottom of her foot. Shana was consumed by the depth of his feelings. He said losing her would be the equivalent of a bullet to his head, but he loved her enough to sacrifice his happiness for hers. Love didn't get any realer than that.

Shana was touched. It seemed like Lil Ced always found new ways to sweep her off her feet. "Loyalty is everything, Cedric. You taught me that when neither of us knew what loyalty meant for real." Shana giggled, then continued. "My loyalty belongs to you, and it always will. They say a man's loyalty is tested when he has everything, and a woman's loyalty to her man is tested when he has nothing. When you had it all, you was ready and willing to walk away from it all for me, and now look at us." She waved her hand around the hotel. "We have nothing. But I'm choosing *you*. I'ma choose you every single time."

Lil Ced smiled. Despite everything they were going through, they were together, and it was enough to make him happy. The ringing phone interrupted their conversation. It was Yatta, one of his homies that owed Lil Ced some money for a few pounds he'd fronted him. Lil Ced answered. "I got that lil pay-pay for you. Where you at, gang?" Yatta asked.

Lil Ced wasn't giving up his whereabouts. "I'm in traffic, pull up."

"I'm in the hood," Yatta replied.

Lil Ced didn't know what type of shit Blake had going on to trust meeting Yatta in the hood. "Meet me at the Shell's on 111th," he told Yatta. The gas station was right down the street from the 5th District Police Station.

"Bet," Yatta said, disconnecting the call.

Lil Ced rode alone to meet up with Yatta. He made it to the gas station in twenty minutes and waited on the side by the vacuum cleaners. A tinted-up gray G Wagon entered the lot and parked at one of the pumps. Yatta called Lil Ced. "Where you at, folks?" he asked.

"I'm over here in this black Malibu. Hop out and come holla at me," Lil Ced told him.

Instead of hopping out, Yatta pulled the Jeep next to Lil Ced's car. Lil Ced tried to see through the dark tints, but his windows were tinted too, so it was impossible. Instead of Yatta's door opening, the driver's window and the back window on the driver's side dropped. Somebody started to stick a Micro Draco out of the back window, but Lil Ced was already in motion, putting his car in drive.

The Draco went off just as Lil Ced stomped the gas. His window shattered from a 7.62 shell ripping through it.

Lil Ced chose to meet up at the gas station because it was close to the police station, and he thought it would make somebody think twice about trying to take him out, but he was wrong. The G Wagon whipped out and followed him to the highway, which was right there. A guy with a shirt tied around his face hung from the back window, blowing the Drac.

It wasn't much traffic on the highway and Lil Ced was stomping the Malibu, trying to get away, but the G Wagon stayed on him. He ducked down as 7.62 bullets flew through his back windshield. The big 7.62 shells were tearing through the Malibu like it was made out of cloth.

He whipped to the right and stomped up the shoulder of the highway and quickly swerved left in front of an 18-wheeler. He went over a lane and lightly tapped the brakes, letting the 18-wheeler get in between him and the G Wagon, which was still riding the shoulder. He watched the shadow of the G Wagon's tires under the truck and made sure he stayed with them. He rolled his window down and used his right arm to aim his Glock 20. He let the 18-wheeler past and as soon as the G Wagon was visible, he tapped his trigger. The switch emptied his clip in a second. The G Wagon swerved and flew off the road.

Lil Ced rushed back to the hotel, anxious to get out of the bullet riddled car. He had heard rumors that it was a check on his head. At first, he didn't believe it, but after seeing how Yatta nem was just tryna get at him confirmed that rumor to be true. Blake immediately came to mind. He had to be the reason why everybody was on his ass. He had told all of his secrets and exposed him for being a snake. All of a sudden it made sense to him, people he hadn't heard from in months were reaching out to him.

Some were trying to set up drug deals, others were trying to link and kick it, but Lil Ced was smarter than that. He knew when someone was playing back door games. Every time someone reached out to him, he gave them the runaround. Shana was his only friend, and she was the only one he trusted.

Being broke was a man's worst enemy and when a nigga was broke, it affected his ability to reason. Being broke clouded a nigga's judgement. It made a nigga desperate. At the moment, Lil

Ced was as desperate as ever. That's why he was trailing the Ashley's Furniture van two cars ahead of him. He knew inside the van was over a hundred pounds of different strains of exotic weed coming in from Cali.

The shipment was his father's, and he was about to intercept it. He was in a stolen Intrepid, something old and lowkey. When the truck entered a McDonald's and parked, he thanked God for making the lick so easy. He whipped in next to the truck and hopped out right behind the driver of the truck. "Yo," he said, and the guy turned around. He saw Lil Ced's gun before he actually saw his face, but when he did, he recognized him instantly.

"What you doing, Lil Ced?" the guy asked. He was one of the older folks from the hood named Fat Man.

"Just give me the keys and get the fuck on," Lil Ced told him.

Fat Man had heard about Lil Ced being the one who killed Ed, so he quickly passed him the keys. He didn't want to end up his next victim. "Yo pops ain't gone like this shit," he told Lil Ced as he climbed into the truck.

"Fuck him!" Lil Ced told him, slamming the door in his face and pulling off.

Twenty minutes later, Ladale was blowing Lil Ced's phone up. "What?" he answered, not wanting to hear whatever Ladale had to say. He had cleared the truck of the hundred and twenty-five pounds and had lucked up on two bricks of cocaine.

"Where the fuck my shit at, lil nigga?" Ladale spat angrily.

"I'm fucked up, Unc. I needed that kit," Lil Ced chuckled. "You can buy this shit back if you want to," he added.

"You got me fucked up, bruh! I can't wait till we catch yo pussy ass!" Ladale growled, hanging up the phone.

Five minutes later, Cordale called. "Yeah, Pops?" Lil Ced answered dryly. He already knew why his father was calling.

"So, all this time it's been you stealing from me?" Cordale asked dismally.

"Hell naw!" Lil Ced replied quickly. "This the first time I ever pulled some shit like this, but I'm fucked up forreal, Pops."

Cordale was quiet. A part of him felt bad and wanted to offer help, but Lil Ced was a grown man and had to lay in the bed he made for himself.

"Y'all got the hood tryna kill me and shit, but y'all call me a snake," Lil Ced scoffed.

This was news to Cordale. "The hood tryna kill you?" he asked.

"Hell yeah, the streets say y'all got fifty-k on my head, twenty-five-k on Shana and an extra twenty-five if they catch us together."

"Why the fuck would I put money on you, son? I don't want you dead, I want you to grow up. I feel like we can fix all this bullshit that's going on," Cordale said, making Lil Ced snicker. He knew things were way beyond repair.

"I'm straight, Pops. You been preparing me all this time to be on my own. I'ma figure this shit out on my own," Lil Ced said. He didn't know it, but at that moment he made Cordale a proud father.

He saw that the lessons he spent years implanting in Lil Ced's head had an effect on the man he grew to be. He was the one who taught him that loyalty is everything. At the moment, he realized Lil Ced wasn't being as disloyal as everyone portrayed him to be. In all actuality, he was being penalized for being loyal. He was loyal to Shana. Always was. Always would be. And now the whole world was against him for moving how he was taught to move. This was the first time Cordale actually took a step back and looked at things from Lil Ced's perspective.

His heart started to ache for his son's situation. "I know you will, son. I got faith in you," Cordale said, surprising Lil Ced.

"Thanks, Pops." he replied.

"I love you, mane. Be safe out there and take care of that girl."

I will, and I love you too, Pops," Lil Ced said, before hanging up. He felt good after their conversation. He didn't know what shifted his father's attitude, but he felt like his father understood him more. His next plan was to find a few trustworthy people to sell the pounds and bricks to, so he could check some paper.

Molotti

Chapter 13

One thing about Lil Ced was that he could hustle. He found a way to quickly dump a few pounds and then rented himself an apartment on the north side of the city. It was just something to hold them over until their crib in Texas was finished

The north side of the city was alien territory to him, and he felt comfortable moving around and taking Shana out, because nobody knew them. They had no enemies up north. At first it was rough for them, but they were slowly but surely adjusting to their new lives.

"Damn, that food got my stomach bubbling already," Shana complained. They were leaving out of some Indian restaurant.

"Don't tell me you gotta shit already," Lil Ced chuckled as they exited the restaurant. A familiar face knocked the smile off Lil Ced's face immediately.

KD was on his way into the restaurant with a pretty young lady Lil Ced had never seen before. Lil Ced's hand dropped near his waist. He didn't know if he should dap him or clap him. "What's that fuckin word, gang?" KD asked smiling. His smile was a friendly one and it made Lil Ced feel more comfortable. He looked as if he was happy to see him.

Lil Ced was unsure though, because he knew it was money on his head. "What's up, gang? How you comin?" Lil Ced asked, flashing a fake smile, trying to hide his nervousness. He knew KD was like that forreal, so he wasn't letting his guards down. He scanned the lot, looking for any other familiar faces.

"You good, gang. I ain't on none of that fuck shit. You know you my boy," KD assured him when he caught his vibe.

"Go sit in the car and let me holla at bro real quick," Lil Ced told Shana, passing her the key before turning back to KD. "I heard y'all got fifty on me What's to that shit?"

"That's yo uncle work and he standing on that shit. He been putting all type a dirt on yo name," KD replied. They were always close. He took Lil Ced on his first hit and sold him his first gun. They got money together and fucked bitches together. They came from the same mud and KD had nothing but love and respect for Lil Ced.

"The guys been on my ass. Lil Yatta nem chased me on the highway, dumpin a Drac at me," Lil Ced said and the two friends shared a laugh.

"That fifty-k got niggas moving like John Wick," He joked. "You been straight doe? You don't need shit, do you?" KD asked, genuinely concerned for his boy.

"Yeah, I'm straight. I wiped Ladale's nose for a load, and I been gettin that shit off. I'm saving up so we can run away and get married," Lil Ced said.

KD chuckled, even though he didn't know if Lil Ced was serious or not. "That sound like the best move for you to make. Everybody ain't as thorough as I am," he said with warning behind his words. He knew that just as he had just bumped into Lil Ced, somebody else could too and it wouldn't be any words, just action.

"I know if it was any one of the other guys, he woulda smoked me or at least tried to," Lil Ced stated and KD nodded in agreement.

"You know I'm cut different, G."

"Fasho. Stay thorough, gang," Lil Ced told him, giving him a brotherly hug. He held him tight. It felt good knowing he still had a friend out there. "I love you, bro," he added.

"Stay dangerous, gang," KD said to Lil Ced as he walked off.

On his way to his car, Lil Ced never looked over his shoulder or checked his surroundings. He knew the man behind him would still kill for him and not kill him. It was true that God did bless the gangstas every now and then.

***

When the anniversary of Winky's death came around, Shana asked Lil Ced to take her to his gravesite. It was a family tradition and she wanted to keep it going, despite the differences she was having with her family. Lil Ced felt strange being there, knowing that his uncle was the one who murdered him. He stayed for an hour without complaining

The cemetery was on 127th and when they were leaving, he noticed his tank was empty. He needed to stop at a gas station. He made it to the BP on 127th and Wentworth and pulled to a pump. He got out and jogged into the gas station. He was wearing a blue and black Nike tech with his hood pulled over his head.

Inside the store, he was grabbing some candy and chips when Shana entered, looking scared. "Bae, my daddy nem outside," she told him. She was terrified and it showed.

"Fuck!" Lil Ced gruffed. Shana was crying now. This was a day she prayed she could avoid. All she could think about was the nightmares she'd been having since she was a kid, of Lil Ced killing her father. Lil Ced looked out the door and saw Willis and Meechie climbing out of a Benz. "Fuck!" he gruffed again, startling the old man who was in front of him. "Stay right here," he told Shana, before heading towards the door.

As soon as he looked out the door, he and Meechie locked eyes. Meechie reached for his gun, but Lil Ced already had his in his hand. He shot, causing Meechie to duck and return fire. Lil Ced stood in the gas station's doorway, trading shots with Meechie. Meechie's first few shots shattered the glass to the gas station's door. Bullets ripped through chip bags and honey buns. Everybody in the gas station was hollering and trying to avoid getting shot.

Lil Ced hit Meechie in his chest, knocking him backwards. He ran up and hit him two more times. Willis, who had tripped over his own feet trying to dodge bullets, balled up and Meechie fell back on top of him. Lil Ced stood over Meechie and shot him three more times, all in his face.

Willis looked up and was staring down the barrel of Lil Ced's Glock 31. Lil Ced was ready to shoot, but was stopped by Shana screaming, "No!" He and Willis locked eyes. Lil Ced finally had his man, but for some reason he couldn't pull the trigger. This was the man who was behind his mother's death. The man who they'd been trying to kill for years. He had him and could end it all with one shot.

"Please baby, no," Shana cried. Lil Ced looked at her and saw the pain in her eyes and took off running to his car. She looked at her father and mouthed the words, "I'm sorry," before running off and jumping in the car with Lil Ced.

Willis laid in a puddle of blood and looked up at the sky. *What the fuck just happened*? he thought. Tears fell from his eyes and mixed with his son's blood. Lil Ced could've killed him, and he knew it. Part of him wished he had killed him, instead of killing Meechie. The way Shana looked at him made him feel worse.

How could she watch a man murder her brother and then run off with him? She did stop Lil Ced from killing him, so the feeling was bittersweet. Was love that powerful? Willis closed his eyes and tried to control his breathing. Meechie was his firstborn and now he was gone. Shana was still breathing, but he felt like he'd lost both of them. The pain was immeasurable.

Lil Ced parked his car a few blocks away from the gas station and got him and Shana a Lyft home. She cried the whole ride. Lil Ced held her tight and tried to comfort her, but the whole time he was beating himself up on the inside. He was the reason why she was hurting. This was a recurring theme in his life. It seemed like no matter what he did, it was always the wrong thing.

Once they made it to their apartment, Lil Ced laid Shana down then rolled himself a thick Backwood. He needed to smoke and relax his mind. His phone started to go off with text, a few DM's from different people, asking him was he good and telling him to keep his head up. He was confused and didn't know what was going on, until Blake sent him a video of a news clip. The news clip was of the shooting at the BP. You could see him and Shana clearly and they even said their names.

Lil Ced's heart sank to his stomach. They were wanted for murder. He didn't want to let Shana know because she was already going through losing her brother. This news would only scare her more and he didn't want that. Lil Ced smoked the wood while trying to figure out how he should let Shana know what was going on. He FaceTimed his father.

"How you doing, son?" Cordale asked, smiling into the

camera. His smile quickly faded when he saw the look on Lil Ced's face. "What's going on?" he asked with panic in his voice.

"I killed Meechie on camera and now the police looking for me and Shana," Lil Ced explained, speaking so fast he was stumbling over his words.

Cordale couldn't hide the anguish he suddenly felt. His one and only son was being destroyed by a war he was never supposed to be a part of. Instead of pushing him to do better, he'd led Lil Ced down this path of destruction. He made the streets look like the best option, when it really wasn't. He never told Lil Ced the chances of a nigga really making it were slim to none. He had gotten lucky, but at the same time, he felt cursed. "Let's pray, bow your head," he told Lil Ced, who did as told.

"Dear Heavenly Father, we come to you today asking for you to bless my son. Protect him and give him as well as myself, the strength, willpower and guidance needed to make it through these dark times. Lord, we come to you for salvation, for help and for better days. In your name, we pray. Amen."

"Amen," Lil Ced mumbled. He wiped the tears that fell sometime during the prayer off his face.

Cordale didn't even try to fight the tears he felt coming. He let them fall freely. "I'm bonding you out, son. I don't care how much yo bond is, I'm coming to get you immediately," he promised but Lil Ced shook his head.

"I'm not bonding out and leaving Shana in there," he said.

Cordale admired his loyalty, but this wasn't the time for that. He was facing a murder charge. He needed to put that love shit in his back pockets and think about what was best for him. "Fuck all that shit, son, you gotta think about yourself," he argued.

"Thinking about myself is what got me in this fucked-up situation. You taught me that a man is accountable for his actions, right?" Lil Ced asked, and Cordale nodded. "Ok, then," he said. The father and son sat in silence for a moment. "I love you, Pops."

"I love you too, son," Cordale said before Lil Ced hung up on him.

The apartment Lil Ced and Shana were staying in was rented

under an alias, so they were good staying there. Nobody in that area knew who they were, so they were lowkey. They had gotten rid of their phones and bought TracFones so they couldn't get traced back to them.

One day, Lil Ced decided to reach out to Blake. "Yo?" Blake answered, not recognizing the number.

"What's the word, gang?" Lil Ced asked, and Blake recognized the voice instantly.

"What's up, bro? You cool?" he asked. He knew Lil Ced was going through it and his heart ached for his old best friend.

"I'm still free so I guess I'm good."

"They been tearing the hood up lookin for you."

"Shit, they must not know I ain't even welcome over there," Lil Ced chuckled, but Blake didn't. He knew that he was part of the reason why he wasn't good. He felt like if Lil Ced wasn't cast out from the hood, he would've never been going through what he was going through.

"When I lost my lil brother, I lost myself, bro. I was moving off emotions and I put you in a fucked-up position. I'm sorry, bro," Blake apologized sincerely.

"Don't apologize to me, G, you lost yo brother. I would never know how that feels. I could only imagine," Lil Ced replied, looking at Shana who was lying next to him sleeping peacefully. She'd been a mess since he killed her brother. "I'm the one that should be sorry and I am. I wish I could go back and make some better decisions. But I can't, G, and that shit eat at my soul every day."

"I hate you going through all the shit you're going through. Shit don't supposed to be like this, but I'm here for you if you need anything, bro."

"All I need from you is for you to look after my pops if something was to ever happen to me," Lil Ced said grimly. Blake cringed at the tone of his words. It was like he knew something would happen to him sooner or later.

"Fasho," Blake said.

"Thanks, broski. I love you."

"I love you too, Bloody, be safe," Blake said before Lil Ced disconnected the call.

Life was too short for to be mad at the ones you loved the most. In a second, life could be taken away. Lil Ced knew that for a fact. He'd spent the majority of the last decade of his life hating people. Hate and revenge had consumed him. At this point, all he wanted to do was give love and feel love.

***

"So, now what?" Shana asked Lil Ced. They were laid up watching old episodes of *Martin*. He'd told her about the police looking for them and she took the news better than he thought she would. She didn't break down like he expected. She simply shrugged and asked to see the news clips. That confirmed to him that she was emotionally depleted. She was tired of crying and being hurt.

"Now we gotta decide whether we gone turn ourselves in or run," Lil Ced replied, already knowing he planned on doing the latter. It was no way in hell he was turning himself in to fight a body. "You should get right out, cause you really didn't do shit. I might have to sit doe," he added sadly.

Shana just nodded. They'd made it this far and gone through unmeasurable amounts of pain together. She wasn't willing to let Lil Ced turn himself in. Without him, she would have nothing. Even if she tried making things right with her family, she didn't know if they'd take her back with open arms. She was the reason why Blue had gotten shot. Millie had gotten kidnapped and Meechie killed. She was almost positive she wasn't welcomed back at home. This was all her fault. She knew that and guilt ate at her soul every day and night. She'd been going through a deep depression and was in desperate need of a way to ease her pain

"Turning ourselves in is out of the question. We can run and hide for the rest of our lives. As long as we're together, we'll find a way to be ok," Shana said, trying to convince herself more than Lil Ced. He leaned over and kissed her on her forehead.

"I love the fuck outta you, girl." He smiled. It took more than a hard woman to stick through the type of hard times that she stuck through with him. Most women would've folded when the money was gone, but it seemed like the harder life got for Lil Ced, the deeper Shana's love for him got. She risked her freedom, life and happiness for him without hesitation.

"We can't stay in Chicago for too much longer. That's the quickest way to end up in a cell, but before we leave, I need to collect some more bread and get us some fake ID's and driver's licenses so we can live under aliases," Lil Ced said.

"Where we gone go?" Shana asked and that was a good question. He hadn't thought things out that far.

"How about South Dakota?" he asked, and Shana frowned up.

"I was thinking more like Cali or Miami."

"Baby, we going on the run, not vacation!" Lil Ced replied and they shared a good laugh. They needed that one. Lil Ced couldn't remember the last time he'd seen her pretty smile.

"We can be living in a cardboard box under a bridge in Delaware, as long as I get to sleep in your arms, I won't complain," Shana said and she meant every word. That touched Lil Ced. He responded with a kiss. That kiss turned into a deeper, more passionate kiss.

Lil Ced pulled Shana's T shirt over her head, revealing her big breasts. He grabbed one and slowly flicked his tongue over her nipple. She let out a soft moan. Lil Ced took his time sucking, biting and licking all over each one of her breasts, before he pulled off her boy shorts, revealing her pretty, fat pussy. She had a pair of pussy lips that hung just the right way. Lil Ced spread her legs and dove in headfirst. He used his tongue to attack her clit. She gasped when he stuck his middle finger inside her pussy, while still licking her clit.

He pulled his finger out and put it in his mouth, it was creamy with her juices. He was ready to feel her. He slid out of his Ethika's and climbed on top of her. He rubbed the head of his dick up and down her opening, before slowly penetrating her. He leaned in and kissed her passionately, while slowly stroking in and out of her. He never fucked her fast. He always took his time and made love to her, just like she liked it.

He grabbed one of her legs and folded her up so her toes were damn near by her ears, then slammed his dick in her as deep as he could go, making her scream out in pleasure. Lil Ced pulled out and smacked her pussy with his dick.

She loved when he did that. She flipped over and arched her back. He grabbed her by her ponytail and began pounding her out from behind. "Fuck! Fuck! Fuck!" Shana shouted, throwing her big ass back.

Lil Ced smacked her ass with his free hand and continued to assault her pussy with deep strokes. She came multiple times, before he finally bussed a big nut inside of her. After sex, the two lovers washed each other up and cuddled naked while formulating a plan for their future.

Around 8:00 am the next morning, Lil Ced left out to make a few runs. He'd gotten a text from his father, saying he stashed fifty thousand cash in a Kia Optima that he could use to get around in. Lil Ced needed the money badly and he could use the car too. It was parked at Gately Stadium on 103rd Street.

Lil Ced made it there without a problem. From there, he went to Kay's Jewelers.

He spent five thousand dollars on a beautiful diamond engagement ring for Shana. He figured he'd surprise her with it, just to put a smile on her face. After that, he went to serve ten pounds of Wedding Cake to one of the folks from Pocket Town named Kevo. He was hungry, so he decided to stop at Taurus Hoagies. As he was pulling out of the lot, a blue and white patrol car was riding past.

He watched the blue and white make a U-turn in his rearview mirror. His heart almost stopped beating. He sped up but made sure not to go too fast. The light on 111th and Michigan was yellow, so he zoomed around the car in front of him and ran the light. The blue and whites did the same thing and hit their light. "Shit!" Lil Ced said to himself, stomping the gas. Michigan was a big main street, and he was able to weave around a lot of traffic.

He knew he could get on the highway on 99th and Michigan, so he was trying to put some distance between him and the blue and whites before he got there. The patrol car stayed with him until he ran the light on 103rd and Michigan. The blue and whites did too but was hit by a black Ford truck. That caused a bad wreck. He didn't care though, all he was worried about was getting away.

Once he made it to the highway, he felt a wave of relief which quickly became worry, when he saw two state troopers, sitting on the shoulder of the road.

When he rode past, they got behind him. He forced himself to remain cool. They didn't have their lights on so maybe he was good. He decided to get off the highway on 87th and was nervous all over again when both of the state troopers followed him off the highway. On the exit ramp, the state trooper that was right behind him, hit its lights and swerved around him. The other car did the same thing. They must've gotten a call and were needed somewhere else.

Lil Ced had to be the luckiest guy in the world at the moment. He hurried up and got back on the highway to make it back home before his luck ran out. He saw a Newport that his father must've left in the car and flamed it up. He didn't smoke cigarettes, but he needed one at the moment to calm his nerves. He drove cautiously, trying to make it home without drawing any more attention.

***

Lil Ced woke up hearing Shana singing Beyoncé and JayZ's song, "On The Run." She wasn't a good singer at all, but he loved hearing her try. "Good afternoon, sexy face," Lil Ced told her, giving her a hug from behind and planting a soft kiss on the nape of her neck. She was in a better mood than she'd been in a very long time. For some reason, she was beaming with joy and that made Lil Ced happy.

"So, I was thinking right?" she said, making him a plate. She had just made tacos, his favorite food.

"And?" Lil Ced replied, taking a seat at the kitchen table.

"How about we go to Memphis? You got family down there, right?"

"Yeah, but I don't know none of they ass at all," Lil Ced said, picking up a taco and taking a huge bite from it.

"But I'm sure they'd be willing to help us," Shana said. Lil Ced chewed his food while pondering a response.

"Or they might turn us in for whatever reward money they could get for us. Just because they're blood, don't mean they're trustworthy."

"You're right," Shana agreed. "We won't be able to run forever. Eventually we'll get caught and go to jail. We should just kill ourselves like Romeo and Juliet," she suggested.

Lil Ced stared at her, looking for some sign that she was just kidding. "Baby, I'm not shooting myself in my shit. You cappin," he chuckled. She was out of her rabbit ass mind if she thought he was going out like that.

"Maybe we can drink some poison or something," she said over a mouthful of taco.

"You serious?" Lil Ced asked, and Shana nodded. He looked down at his plate. Suddenly, he'd lost his appetite. He definitely didn't want to go to jail but killing himself didn't sound too appealing either. They said stress and depression could drive you crazy. He didn't understand how true those words were until now. Shana was talking like she'd lost her mind. The truth was, she was tired. Tired of running. Tired of hiding. Tired of being targeted. And tired of fighting. She was starting to feel like death was the easiest option.

"You always say how you'd rather be dead than in jail. How long do you really think we can run before we get caught? Yo own family got money on your head and mines. We gone get killed in the streets if the police don't catch us first. I don't know about you, but I'd rather die on my own terms," Shana said. Her expression showed every sign that she already had her mind made up. This was something she'd been thinking about for some time now.

"Give me some time to try and figure some shit out, and if we can't come up with a better plan, then we can go with yours."

"Ok," Shana said and Lil Ced shot her a weak smile. It killed him to know things had gotten this bad for them. He was now more afraid than he'd ever been in his life. Shana had ridden as long and as far as she could, now she was ready to die. But Lil Ced didn't know if he was.

The next day Lil Ced left out early to handle some business. He liked moving when it was early in the day and not much going on. He stopped at David's Bridal and bought himself a black Louis Vuitton suit, with a pair of Louie loafers. He picked out a sexy white wedding gown for Shana. It wasn't the traditional wedding gown, one that would show off her sexy frame. He complimented the dress with a pair of Dior heels.

When he made it home, Shana was watching *Love & Basketball*. "Baby, I got something I wanna ask you," he told her after giving her a kiss on the lips. He sat his prepaid iPhone down on the TV stand. Unbeknownst to her, he had it recording them.

"Yeah, bae?" Shana asked.

Lil Ced got down on one knee and pulled a ring box from his back pocket.

"You been my best friend since we were in pampers. You were my first and only love. You've always had my back and you've always been loyal to me. I love you more than anything in this world. Will you marry me?" he asked.

Shana covered her mouth with her hand. The diamond ring was so beautiful. Even at their darkest hours, Lil Ced knew how to bring light to her life. "Yes! Yes! Yes!" she cried while he slid the ring on her finger. "I love you so much, Cedric," she told him, hugging him tightly.

"I love you more, Shana," he said. The truth was, they both loved each other unconditionally and if she wanted to die in his arms, then he was gonna hold her until their last breath.

Chapter 14

March 31, 2020

Lil Ced stood in his bedroom, looking at the body-length mirror that hung on the back of his bedroom's door. He ran a brush over his freshly cut, deeply waved head and fixed the collar on the black suit jacket he wore. Behind him, Shana was sitting on their bed in her beautiful white wedding gown. "You look amazing," Lil Ced complimented her, turning to face her with a small smile on his face. His smile hid his nervousness.

"Thanks, and you look as handsome as I always imagined you would on our wedding day," Shana said, forcing a weak smile of her own.

The two had been in love since before they knew what love truly was. Lil Ced had never met a woman as perfect as Shana. And she'd never met a man that could compare to him. They were each other's first and only love. They were best friends and soulmates, with a bond that most people never got to experience.

"Girl, I'm in love with you, but this ain't the honeymoon. We're past the infatuation phase. We're right in the thick of love, at times we get sick of love, it seems like we argue every day," Lil Ced sang along with John Legend, staring deep into Shana's big, brown eyes. She smiled, showing her perfect white teeth. She knew that was one of his favorite songs. Whenever they weren't seeing eye to eye, he would put that song on repeat.

"What if we went to Idaho or Wyoming? We should be good there. I never hear about anybody getting killed in Wyoming," Shana said.

Lil Ced locked eyes with her and saw a sign of hope, a glimmer of faith, and he hated the fact that he had to be the one to ruin that. "Just because you don't hear about it don't mean it's not happening. And no matter where we go, they always gone come searching. And if they don't, the police will," he said before leaving the room.

He returned, holding a white bottle of Bel Air and two plastic cups. "Why won't they just leave us alone and let us be happy?" Shana asked sadly. That was a good question. One Lil Ced wished he had the answer to.

"Because they don't understand how deep this love is and I'm tired of tryna force them to understand. I'm tired of running too. I'm tired of all this shit," Lil Ced gruffed. He could feel himself getting angry, just thinking about everything they endured over the course of their twenty-two years on earth. Shana stood up directly in front of him

"Will you dance with me?" she asked as Ed Sheeran and Beyoncé's duet, "Perfect" started playing on the Bluetooth speaker.

"Of course. But take off those heels so we don't look so funny," Lil Ced said, like there was someone there to see them.

Shana slid out of her heels and the two lovers danced in each other's arms "Cause we were just kids when we fell in love, not knowing what it was, I will not give you up this time. Darling just kiss me slow, your heart is all I own and in your eyes you're holding mine," Lil Ced sang to Shana. She always loved how he loved to sing, even though he couldn't sing at all.

"We are still kids but we're so in love, fighting against all odds, I know we'll be alright this time. Darling just hold my hand, I'll be your girl you'll be my man, and I see my future in your eyes. Well baby, I'm dancing in the dark, with you between my arms, barefoot on the grass, while listening to our favorite song."

Shana sang Beyoncé's verse while they danced and stared deeply into each other's eyes. This was indeed Shana's favorite song and Lil Ced knew that.

"When I saw you in that dress, looking so beautiful, I don't deserve this. Darling, you look perfect, tonight," Lil Ced sang. He had tears in his eyes. "I love you," he whispered to her.

"I love you more, ugly," she replied. After their dance they sat on the soft gray carpet and poured cups of champagne." Do you remember Valentine's Day, 2012? You bought me this necklace." Shana asked, touching the gold necklace she wore.

Lil Ced took a gulp from his cup before answering, "How

could I forget? I convinced you to ditch school so we could go to the movies."

"And my daddy caught us. He chased you from 87th to 103rd. He was so mad he couldn't catch you. I never saw him run so fast!" They shared a good laugh together.

"I'm not gone lie, he had me a lil scared that day," Lil Ced admitted, laughing even louder. He dug in his pocket and pulled out a vial containing a yellowish liquid. "You ready?" he asked Shana, waving the vial at her.

"As ready as I'll ever be," she replied sadly. This was her idea, but now she was having second thoughts. It was too late for all that though. The tears she'd been fighting were now freely falling down her cheeks.

"Head up, gangsta, what I tell you about all that soft shit?" Lil Ced asked with a fake smile. He tried his best not to show her he was just as scared as she was.

"You was just crying, so shut up, punk!" Shana teased.

Lil Ced twisted the cap off the vial and split its contents between the two cups of champagne. "I love you, my beautiful wife," he told Shana, making her smile.

"And I love you more, my handsome husband," she replied. They were both crying now.

Lil Ced picked up his cup and sniffed it. They then wrapped their arms around each other and lifted their cups to each other's mouths. "Till death do us part," they said in unison before gulping down the cups.

Shana's eyes grew as big as two full moons when Lil Ced started convulsing wildly. Before she could do anything, she started to convulse in the same way. The two lovers laid wrapped together, convulsing in a sad ball of love and pain until Lil Ced stopped moving and Shana lifted up, spitting the liquid out of her mouth.

She coughed violently. The poison had burned her mouth making it numb and left a disgusting taste in her mouth. She looked at Lil Ced's dead body and smiled. Her plan worked to a T . . .

At least that's how Willis wished it went. The truth was that his daughter was gone. His princess. His second-born. She was gone and they hadn't even gotten the opportunity to talk and make amends before she left. He thought about all the bad words he'd said to her and how he pushed her away. Now he was wishing he could take it all back and do things differently.

He wished he could rewind time and support Shana, instead of shunning her. He felt like he pushed her to an early grave. He wished he could let her know how much he loved her. His daughter was gone and the only thing he had left was memories, and the videos Lil Ced recorded of them before they committed suicide. He recorded the proposal and the makeshift wedding, as well as the suicide.

The videos were bittersweet. Willis was happy to see Lil Ced get on one knee and propose to Shana. He saw the happiness in her eyes, and it made him weak. They even looked good in their suit and wedding gown. He had watched the videos a hundred times already, his heart breaking over and over again, every time they ended. For the first time in his life, he contemplated suicide. He wanted to blow his own brains out, but he couldn't. He still had Blue and Millie to live for. He vowed to be a better father to them. All the wrong decisions he made in Meechie and Shana's lives, he would make sure he didn't make them twice. He'd lost his two eldest children. He wouldn't lose the two he had left.

**

The cold metal inside his mouth made Cordale shiver. Goosebumps grew on his arms. He was drunk as hell, and this was his third time putting the Glock inside his mouth. He wanted to pull the trigger so badly, but he couldn't. He was too weak to kill himself. You had to be a special kind of strong to take your own life.

Miserable was an understatement of how he felt. He'd been fighting depression and battling for his sanity ever since he watched the video of Lil Ced's suicide.

Out of all the things that could've been Lil Ced's downfall, it was the lessons he taught him that did it. Loyalty is everything. That's what he taught him. Loyalty was a characteristic that was admirable. How could a trait so honorable be a man's downfall? Lil Ced was penalized for being unconditionally loyal to the woman he was in love with. A woman who never hurt him and loved him the same way. He was made out to be a bad guy for being an actual stand-up man for his woman. He was in a lose-lose situation. He was a victim of being too loyal. That in itself was a sad story.

A knock at the front door startled Cordale. He wasn't expecting any visitors. He put his gun on his waist and sluggishly walked to the door. He looked through the peephole and saw it was Detective Pendarves. "How can I help you, Detective?" he asked after swinging the door open. He hadn't seen the detective since TayTay had gotten murdered. It seemed like when he saw the detective, it only was under the worst circumstances. It had been years since they last time they saw each other, but the detective still looked the same. Bald head, salt and pepper goatee, with dark eyes that watched everything

"May I step in?" he asked.

Cordale wasn't in the mood for questioning, but he stepped aside and let him in.

"I heard about your son, I'm sorry for your loss," Detective Pendarves said, and Cordale nodded. "I've been working on your wife's murder for eight years now and after I heard about your son's suicide, I was determined to find some breakthrough to give you some type of closure—"

"And?" Cordale cut him off. He didn't mean to be rude. he just wasn't in the mood for small talk.

"We got video from a camera in the backyard of a daycare that was located on the next block."

"And what it show?" Cordale asked eagerly.

"I came to show you the video and maybe you can see more than I did," Detective Pendarves said, pulling out his iPhone and going to a video before passing the phone to Cordale, who watched the grainy video. You couldn't see nothing but half of the front of their home and even that was from a distance.

"What am I looking for?" he snapped. All he saw were different cars riding past.

Detective Pendarves grabbed the phone, rewound the video and paused it. "That car right there." He pointed to the screen, "Parked and was there for about thirty minutes before leaving. The problem is we can't see who got in or out of the car. I was hoping maybe the car looked familiar. Maybe it was somebody you knew," he said. You could only see a portion of the back of the car. If you knew cars, you could easily identify the make and model of the car. Cordale did recognize the car, but he didn't tell the detective that.

"Forensics determined that she got murdered some time after the car pulled up. So, once we can determine the driver of that car, we'll have a lead on a main suspect," Detective Pendarves said.

Tears threatened to pour from Cordale's eyes. His heart was heavy at the moment. "I don't recognize the car, but I appreciate you devoting so much time to solving the case," he told Detective Pendarves, offering him his hand which he shook firmly.

"Stay strong, brother. I'll keep you in my prayers," Detective Pendarves replied, opening the door to leave.

"Thank you, I appreciate that," Cordale told him sincerely.

As soon as the door closed, Cordale broke down. He finally had closure. He finally knew for sure who murdered TayTay. He cried for hours. After he got himself together, he made a few calls to get a number that he needed. It took him another hour to gather his composure and build up enough courage to actually dial the number. "Hello?" a familiar voice answered. A voice he hadn't heard in years.

Cordale hesitated before speaking. "I'm sorry, bruh," he apologized.

The phone went silent. He had to check and make sure the call was still connected. "Who is this?" the guy on the other end asked. He recognized the voice, but he still thought his ears were playing tricks on him.

"Cordale." Again, it got silent, awkwardly silent. "All these years I blamed you for killing TayTay and it wasn't even you. A lot of shit could've been different, a lot of shit could've been prevented. I know sorry ain't enough, but it's all I got, bruh," Cordale said. He was talking to Willis, the man he'd spent the last decade hating.

"If the shoe was on the other foot, I would've reacted the same way. I'm part of the blame too. I blamed you for your brother's actions. I wish we would've handled shit better as men, as brothers. We was never supposed to let things spiral this far out of control. At the end of the day, nobody lost more than what we lost. We paid a price that any normal man couldn't afford to pay," Willis said, and it got quiet again.

"I found out who killed TayTay," Cordale said somberly.

"Who was it?"

"Ladale." Cordale said his name like it was cursed.

This whole time, Ladale had been manipulating Cordale to think Willis was against him. He killed his wife and instigated a war that ended up forcing his son to commit suicide.

"I know that's yo blood, but I been telling you that nigga wasn't right. It been him since the beginning. My spot getting hit. Yo loads getting jacked. It was all him," Willis said.

"You was right, bruh. You was right the whole time. I'm man enough to admit that," Cordale told his former best friend. "I'm sorry, bruh," he added sincerely.

The two spoke for hours catching up and venting. Cordale lost his wife and only child. Willis lost his two oldest children. They both knew pain too well.

More apologizing came at the end of the conversation. They both needed somebody, and never in a million years did they think they would be helping each other again. They never expected to speak again. But it felt good to both of them. Both men felt like the weight of the world was lifted from their shoulders.

***

Cordale and Willis held a big, beautiful joint funeral for Lil Ced and Shana. They laid them to rest in a huge mahogany casket, side by side, dressed as husband and wife. The funeral was the saddest one ever. They played the video of Ced's proposal, as well as the video of them dancing together minutes before they committed suicide. Everyone cried their eyes out. The rapper Molotti, who was from the city, went to school with Shana and made a song for her and Lil Ced. He performed the song along with a choir. It was a beautiful, touching song.

Cordale noticed that Ladale didn't show up, so he FaceTimed him. "You couldn't make it to your own nephew's funeral huh?" he asked when Ladale answered. He was high as hell somewhere

"Man... bruh, you got Willis there. I don't know what type of soft ass shit you on, but I'm not on that type of time," Ladale snapped with a mug on his face.

"This day ain't about Willis, or you, or myself. It's for us to say our last goodbyes to Lil Ced."

"I said goodbye to him when he upped on me," Ladale said with a small smirk on his face. Cordale fought to hold his composure. "I know TayTay flippin in her grave right now seeing you next to Willis bitch ass," he added.

"Naw, she tossing and turning because I didn't see through yo fake ass a long time ago. I know it was you who killed TayTay. You gone get yours, bruh, I promise you that much," Cordale said calmly, hanging up on his brother.

Ladale sent a text saying, "Fuck you, TayTay, and Lil Ced." Cordale's blood started to boil. He quickly checked himself doe Ladale would get his soon enough.

After the funeral, Cordale found Blake and KD in the parking lot smoking a Wood. Blake had beat himself up bad when he found out Ladale had been manipulating him and everyone else since the beginning. He let Ladale manipulate him into believing that Lil Ced was a snake. He was too blinded by his own emotions to see Ladale was the real snake.

"I don't want him dead. I got two hundred thousand for anybody that can bring Ladale to me alive," Cordale told the two savages. They were the closest things he had to sons.

"I got you, Unc, but you know yo money ain't no good with me," Blake told him. Getting up with Ladale was personal on his behalf. He lost two brothers because of him. KD, on the other hand, didn't know if he had enough willpower and self-control to see Ladale and not kill him on sight.

"Thanks, man. Both of y'all were good friends to Lil Ced. More like brothers. He loved both of y'all," Cordale said.

"He was my ace. We did it all together. I miss the fuck outta him already. I wish I woulda saw this shit comin," Blake said. Tears started to fall from his eyes.

"We most definitely gone keep broski name alive and stay lit in his memory," KD said.

"Thank y'all," Cordale said before Willis walked up with worry all in his expression.

"Y'all dirty?" he asked. Blake and KD nodded. They didn't go anywhere without their Glocks, but Cordale shook his head.

"Why? What's up?"Cordale asked.

"The feds in the front," Willis said, making everybody's heart drop. If it wasn't one thing, it was another.

To Be Continued...
Loyalty is Everything 2
Coming Soon

Lock Down Publications and Ca$h Presents assisted
publishing packages.

BASIC PACKAGE $499
Editing
Cover Design
Formatting

UPGRADED PACKAGE $800
Typing
Editing
Cover Design
Formatting

ADVANCE PACKAGE $1,200
Typing
Editing
Cover Design
Formatting
Copyright registration
Proofreading
Upload book to Amazon

LDP SUPREME PACKAGE $1,500
Typing
Editing
Cover Design
Formatting
Copyright registration
Proofreading
Set up Amazon account
Upload book to Amazon

Loyalty is Everything

Advertise on LDP Amazon and Facebook page

***Other services available upon request. Additional charges may apply
Lock Down Publications
P.O. Box 944
Stockbridge, GA 30281-9998
Phone # 470 303-9761

Submission Guideline

Submit the first three chapters of your completed manuscript to ldpsubmissions@gmail.com, subject line: Your book's title. The manuscript must be in a .doc file and sent as an attachment. Document should be in Times New Roman, double spaced and in size 12 font. Also, provide your synopsis and full contact information. If sending multiple submissions, they must each be in a separate email.

Have a story but no way to send it electronically? You can still submit to LDP/Ca$h Presents. Send in the first three chapters, written or typed, of your completed manuscript to:

LDP: Submissions Dept
Po Box 944
Stockbridge, Ga 30281

DO NOT send original manuscript. Must be a duplicate.

Provide your synopsis and a cover letter containing your full contact information.

Thanks for considering LDP and Ca$h Presents.

NEW RELEASES

THE COCAINE PRINCESS 5 by KING RIO
FOR THE LOVE OF BLOOD 2 by JAMEL MITCHELL
RICH $AVAGE 3 by MARTELL "TROUBLESOME"
BOLDEN
CRIME BOSS by PLAYA RAY
LOYALTY IS EVERYTHING by MOLOTTI

BLOOD OF A BOSS **VI**

SHADOWS OF THE GAME II

TRAP BASTARD II

By **Askari**

LOYAL TO THE GAME **IV**

By **T.J. & Jelissa**

TRUE SAVAGE **VIII**

MIDNIGHT CARTEL IV

DOPE BOY MAGIC IV

CITY OF KINGZ III

NIGHTMARE ON SILENT AVE II

THE PLUG OF LIL MEXICO II

CLASSIC CITY II

By **Chris Green**

BLAST FOR ME **III**

A SAVAGE DOPEBOY III

CUTTHROAT MAFIA III

DUFFLE BAG CARTEL VII

HEARTLESS GOON VI

By **Ghost**

A HUSTLER'S DECEIT III

KILL ZONE II

BAE BELONGS TO ME III

TIL DEATH II

By **Aryanna**

KING OF THE TRAP III

By **T.J. Edwards**

GORILLAZ IN THE BAY V

3X KRAZY III

Loyalty is Everything

STRAIGHT BEAST MODE III

De'Kari

KINGPIN KILLAZ IV

STREET KINGS III

PAID IN BLOOD III

CARTEL KILLAZ IV

DOPE GODS III

Hood Rich

SINS OF A HUSTLA II

ASAD

YAYO V

Bred In The Game 2

S. Allen

THE STREETS WILL TALK II

By Yolanda Moore

SON OF A DOPE FIEND III

HEAVEN GOT A GHETTO II

SKI MASK MONEY II

By Renta

LOYALTY AIN'T PROMISED III

By Keith Williams

I'M NOTHING WITHOUT HIS LOVE II

SINS OF A THUG II

TO THE THUG I LOVED BEFORE II

IN A HUSTLER I TRUST II

By Monet Dragun

QUIET MONEY IV

EXTENDED CLIP III

THUG LIFE IV

By **Trai'Quan**

195

THE STREETS MADE ME IV

By **Larry D. Wright**

IF YOU CROSS ME ONCE II

ANGEL V

By **Anthony Fields**

THE STREETS WILL NEVER CLOSE IV

By K'ajji

HARD AND RUTHLESS III

KILLA KOUNTY IV

By Khufu

MONEY GAME III

By Smoove Dolla

JACK BOYS VS DOPE BOYS IV

A GANGSTA'S QUR'AN V

COKE GIRLZ II

COKE BOYS II

LIFE OF A SAVAGE V

CHI'RAQ GANGSTAS V

By Romell Tukes

MURDA WAS THE CASE III

Elijah R. Freeman

THE STREETS NEVER LET GO III

By Robert Baptiste

AN UNFORESEEN LOVE IV

BABY, I'M WINTERTIME COLD II

By **Meesha**

MONEY MAFIA II

By **Jibril Williams**

QUEEN OF THE ZOO III

Loyalty is Everything

By **Black Migo**
VICIOUS LOYALTY III

By **Kingpen**
A GANGSTA'S PAIN III

By **J-Blunt**
CONFESSIONS OF A JACKBOY III

By **Nicholas Lock**
GRIMEY WAYS III

By **Ray Vinci**
KING KILLA II

By **Vincent "Vitto" Holloway**
BETRAYAL OF A THUG III

By **Fre$h**
THE MURDER QUEENS III

By **Michael Gallon**
THE BIRTH OF A GANGSTER III

By **Delmont Player**
TREAL LOVE II

By **Le'Monica Jackson**
FOR THE LOVE OF BLOOD III

By **Jamel Mitchell**
RAN OFF ON DA PLUG II

By **Paper Boi Rari**
HOOD CONSIGLIERE III

By **Keese**
PRETTY GIRLS DO NASTY THINGS II

By **Nicole Goosby**
PROTÉGÉ OF A LEGEND II

By **Corey Robinson**
IT'S JUST ME AND YOU II

Molotti

By Ah'Million
BORN IN THE GRAVE II
By Self Made Tay
FOREVER GANGSTA III
By Adrian Dulan
GORILLAZ IN THE TRENCHES II
By SayNoMore
THE COCAINE PRINCESS VI
By King Rio
CRIME BOSS II
Playa Ray
LOYALTY IS EVERYTHING II
Molotti

Available Now

RESTRAINING ORDER **I & II**
By **CA$H & Coffee**
LOVE KNOWS NO BOUNDARIES **I II & III**
By **Coffee**
RAISED AS A GOON I, II, III & IV
BRED BY THE SLUMS I, II, III
BLAST FOR ME I & II
ROTTEN TO THE CORE I II III
A BRONX TALE I, II, III
DUFFLE BAG CARTEL I II III IV V VI
HEARTLESS GOON I II III IV V

Loyalty is Everything

A SAVAGE DOPEBOY I II

DRUG LORDS I II III

CUTTHROAT MAFIA I II

KING OF THE TRENCHES

By **Ghost**

LAY IT DOWN **I & II**

LAST OF A DYING BREED I II

BLOOD STAINS OF A SHOTTA I & II III

By **Jamaica**

LOYAL TO THE GAME I II III

LIFE OF SIN I, II III

By **TJ & Jelissa**

BLOODY COMMAS I & II

SKI MASK CARTEL I II & III

KING OF NEW YORK I II,III IV V

RISE TO POWER I II III

COKE KINGS I II III IV V

BORN HEARTLESS I II III IV

KING OF THE TRAP I II

By **T.J. Edwards**

IF LOVING HIM IS WRONG…I & II

LOVE ME EVEN WHEN IT HURTS I II III

By **Jelissa**

WHEN THE STREETS CLAP BACK I & II III

THE HEART OF A SAVAGE I II III IV

MONEY MAFIA

LOYAL TO THE SOIL I II III

By **Jibril Williams**

A DISTINGUISHED THUG STOLE MY HEART I II & III

LOVE SHOULDN'T HURT I II III IV

RENEGADE BOYS I II III IV

PAID IN KARMA I II III

SAVAGE STORMS I II III

AN UNFORESEEN LOVE I II III

BABY, I'M WINTERTIME COLD

By **Meesha**

A GANGSTER'S CODE I &, II III

A GANGSTER'S SYN I II III

THE SAVAGE LIFE I II III

CHAINED TO THE STREETS I II III

BLOOD ON THE MONEY I II III

A GANGSTA'S PAIN I II

By J-Blunt

PUSH IT TO THE LIMIT

By **Bre' Hayes**

BLOOD OF A BOSS **I, II, III, IV, V**

SHADOWS OF THE GAME

TRAP BASTARD

By **Askari**

THE STREETS BLEED MURDER **I, II & III**

THE HEART OF A GANGSTA I II& III

By **Jerry Jackson**

CUM FOR ME I II III IV V VI VII VIII

An **LDP Erotica Collaboration**

BRIDE OF A HUSTLA **I II & II**

THE FETTI GIRLS **I, II& III**

CORRUPTED BY A GANGSTA I, II III, IV

BLINDED BY HIS LOVE

THE PRICE YOU PAY FOR LOVE I, II ,III

DOPE GIRL MAGIC I II III

Loyalty is Everything

By **Destiny Skai**
WHEN A GOOD GIRL GOES BAD
By **Adrienne**
THE COST OF LOYALTY I II III
By Kweli
A GANGSTER'S REVENGE **I II III & IV**
THE BOSS MAN'S DAUGHTERS I II III IV V
A SAVAGE LOVE **I & II**
BAE BELONGS TO ME I II
A HUSTLER'S DECEIT I, II, III
WHAT BAD BITCHES DO I, II, III
SOUL OF A MONSTER I II III
KILL ZONE
A DOPE BOY'S QUEEN I II III
TIL DEATH
By **Aryanna**
A KINGPIN'S AMBITON
A KINGPIN'S AMBITION **II**
I MURDER FOR THE DOUGH
By **Ambitious**
TRUE SAVAGE I II III IV V VI VII
DOPE BOY MAGIC I, II, III
MIDNIGHT CARTEL I II III
CITY OF KINGZ I II
NIGHTMARE ON SILENT AVE
THE PLUG OF LIL MEXICO II
CLASSIC CITY
By **Chris Green**
A DOPEBOY'S PRAYER
By **Eddie "Wolf" Lee**

Molotti

THE KING CARTEL **I, II & III**
By **Frank Gresham**
THESE NIGGAS AIN'T LOYAL **I, II & III**
By **Nikki Tee**
GANGSTA SHYT **I II &III**
By **CATO**
THE ULTIMATE BETRAYAL
By **Phoenix**
BOSS'N UP **I , II & III**
By **Royal Nicole**
I LOVE YOU TO DEATH
By **Destiny J**
I RIDE FOR MY HITTA
I STILL RIDE FOR MY HITTA
By **Misty Holt**
LOVE & CHASIN' PAPER
By **Qay Crockett**
TO DIE IN VAIN
SINS OF A HUSTLA
By **ASAD**
BROOKLYN HUSTLAZ
By **Boogsy Morina**
BROOKLYN ON LOCK I & II
By **Sonovia**
GANGSTA CITY
By **Teddy Duke**
A DRUG KING AND HIS DIAMOND I & II III
A DOPEMAN'S RICHES
HER MAN, MINE'S TOO I, II
CASH MONEY HO'S

Loyalty is Everything

THE WIFEY I USED TO BE I II
PRETTY GIRLS DO NASTY THINGS
By Nicole Goosby
TRAPHOUSE KING **I II & III**
KINGPIN KILLAZ I II III
STREET KINGS I II
PAID IN BLOOD **I II**
CARTEL KILLAZ I II III
DOPE GODS I II
By **Hood Rich**
LIPSTICK KILLAH **I, II, III**
CRIME OF PASSION I II & III
FRIEND OR FOE I II III
By **Mimi**
STEADY MOBBN' **I, II, III**
THE STREETS STAINED MY SOUL I II III
By **Marcellus Allen**
WHO SHOT YA **I, II, III**
SON OF A DOPE FIEND I II
HEAVEN GOT A GHETTO
SKI MASK MONEY
Renta
GORILLAZ IN THE BAY **I II III IV**
TEARS OF A GANGSTA I II
3X KRAZY I II
STRAIGHT BEAST MODE I II
DE'KARI
TRIGGADALE I II III
MURDAROBER WAS THE CASE I II
Elijah R. Freeman

Molotti

GOD BLESS THE TRAPPERS I, II, III
THESE SCANDALOUS STREETS I, II, III
FEAR MY GANGSTA I, II, III IV, V
THESE STREETS DON'T LOVE NOBODY I, II
BURY ME A G I, II, III, IV, V
A GANGSTA'S EMPIRE I, II, III, IV
THE DOPEMAN'S BODYGAURD I II
THE REALEST KILLAZ I II III
THE LAST OF THE OGS I II III
Tranay Adams
THE STREETS ARE CALLING
Duquie Wilson
MARRIED TO A BOSS I II III
By Destiny Skai & Chris Green
KINGZ OF THE GAME I II III IV V VI
CRIME BOSS
Playa Ray
SLAUGHTER GANG I II III
RUTHLESS HEART I II III
By Willie Slaughter
FUK SHYT
By Blakk Diamond
DON'T F#CK WITH MY HEART I II
By Linnea
ADDICTED TO THE DRAMA I II III
IN THE ARM OF HIS BOSS II
By Jamila
YAYO I II III IV
A SHOOTER'S AMBITION I II
BRED IN THE GAME

Loyalty is Everything

By S. Allen
TRAP GOD I II III
RICH $AVAGE I II III
MONEY IN THE GRAVE I II III
By Martell Troublesome Bolden
FOREVER GANGSTA I II
GLOCKS ON SATIN SHEETS I II
By Adrian Dulan
TOE TAGZ I II III IV
LEVELS TO THIS SHYT I II
IT'S JUST ME AND YOU
By Ah'Million
KINGPIN DREAMS I II III
RAN OFF ON DA PLUG
By Paper Boi Rari
CONFESSIONS OF A GANGSTA I II III IV
CONFESSIONS OF A JACKBOY I II
By Nicholas Lock
I'M NOTHING WITHOUT HIS LOVE
SINS OF A THUG
TO THE THUG I LOVED BEFORE
A GANGSTA SAVED XMAS
IN A HUSTLER I TRUST
By Monet Dragun
CAUGHT UP IN THE LIFE I II III
THE STREETS NEVER LET GO I II
By Robert Baptiste
NEW TO THE GAME I II III
MONEY, MURDER & MEMORIES I II III
By **Malik D. Rice**

Molotti

LIFE OF A SAVAGE I II III IV
A GANGSTA'S QUR'AN I II III IV
MURDA SEASON I II III
GANGLAND CARTEL I II III
CHI'RAQ GANGSTAS I II III IV
KILLERS ON ELM STREET I II III
JACK BOYZ N DA BRONX I II III
A DOPEBOY'S DREAM I II III
JACK BOYS VS DOPE BOYS I II III
COKE GIRLZ
COKE BOYS
By Romell Tukes
LOYALTY AIN'T PROMISED I II
By Keith Williams
QUIET MONEY I II III
THUG LIFE I II III
EXTENDED CLIP I II
A GANGSTA'S PARADISE
By **Trai'Quan**
THE STREETS MADE ME I II III
By **Larry D. Wright**
THE ULTIMATE SACRIFICE I, II, III, IV, V, VI
KHADIFI
IF YOU CROSS ME ONCE
ANGEL I II III IV
IN THE BLINK OF AN EYE
By **Anthony Fields**
THE LIFE OF A HOOD STAR
By Ca$h & Rashia Wilson
THE STREETS WILL NEVER CLOSE I II III

Loyalty is Everything

By K'ajji
CREAM I II III
THE STREETS WILL TALK
By Yolanda Moore
NIGHTMARES OF A HUSTLA I II III
By King Dream
CONCRETE KILLA I II III
VICIOUS LOYALTY I II
By Kingpen
HARD AND RUTHLESS I II
MOB TOWN 251
THE BILLIONAIRE BENTLEYS I II III
By Von Diesel
GHOST MOB
Stilloan Robinson
MOB TIES I II III IV V VI
SOUL OF A HUSTLER, HEART OF A KILLER
GORILLAZ IN THE TRENCHES
By SayNoMore
BODYMORE MURDERLAND I II III
THE BIRTH OF A GANGSTER I II
By Delmont Player
FOR THE LOVE OF A BOSS
By C. D. Blue
MOBBED UP I II III IV
THE BRICK MAN I II III IV
THE COCAINE PRINCESS I II III IV V
By King Rio
KILLA KOUNTY I II III IV
By Khufu

207

MONEY GAME I II
By Smoove Dolla
A GANGSTA'S KARMA I II
By FLAME
KING OF THE TRENCHES I II III
by **GHOST & TRANAY ADAMS**
QUEEN OF THE ZOO I II
By **Black Migo**
GRIMEY WAYS I II
By Ray Vinci
XMAS WITH AN ATL SHOOTER
By Ca$h & Destiny Skai
KING KILLA
By Vincent "Vitto" Holloway
BETRAYAL OF A THUG I II
By Fre$h
THE MURDER QUEENS I II
By Michael Gallon
TREAL LOVE
By Le'Monica Jackson
FOR THE LOVE OF BLOOD I II
By Jamel Mitchell
HOOD CONSIGLIERE I II
By Keese
PROTÉGÉ OF A LEGEND
By Corey Robinson
BORN IN THE GRAVE
By Self Made Tay
MOAN IN MY MOUTH
By XTASY

TORN BETWEEN A GANGSTER AND A GENTLEMAN

By J-BLUNT & Miss Kim

LOYALTY IS EVERYTHING

Molotti

BOOKS BY LDP'S CEO, CA$H

TRUST IN NO MAN

TRUST IN NO MAN 2

TRUST IN NO MAN 3

BONDED BY BLOOD

SHORTY GOT A THUG

THUGS CRY

THUGS CRY 2

THUGS CRY 3

TRUST NO BITCH

TRUST NO BITCH 2

TRUST NO BITCH 3

TIL MY CASKET DROPS

RESTRAINING ORDER

RESTRAINING ORDER 2

IN LOVE WITH A CONVICT

LIFE OF A HOOD STAR

XMAS WITH AN ATL SHOOTER

Loyalty is Everything

.

CPSIA information can be obtained
at www.ICGtesting.com
Printed in the USA
LVHW041740240223
740360LV00004B/602